Myfanwy

Book One of Myfanwy's People

By

Joseph H.J. Líaigh

DEDICATION

To my family: my wife, Mandy, and my sons, Timothy, James and John, who have graciously and generously put up with my writing; and to Isabella, for encouragement and generous criticism.

Published in Australia by Leach Publications.
PO Box 2123, Parkdale, Vic. 3195, Australia.
Email: leachpublications@gmail.com

First published in Australia 2015
Copyright © Leach Publications 2015
Cover design: KimG-Design.com
Editor: Isabella Kružas

ISBN: 978-0-9943481-0-4

The moral rights of the author are asserted.

Liaigh, Joseph H.J.
Myfanwy: The First Book of the Myfanwy's People Series

This is a work of fiction. Any resemblance to actual people, living or dead, is entirely coincidental.

Acknowledgments:

This book would not have been written without the encouragement and support of my family. I would also like to thank Isabella Kružas, the chief editor for the Myfanwy's People series, for her encouragement and advice.

My thanks also go to the staff and students of St. Joseph's Primary School in Chelsea, Victoria, who acted as my test readers. Their enthusiasm, encouragement and comments were all greatly appreciated.

PROLOGUE

I remember an evening in a snow covered field when men in uniform moved like shadows and men in dark robes threatened the world. Now, all these years later, after all that has happened, I am writing to fix these memories on paper. It is my hope that they might go unnoticed and so survive in some forgotten and cobwebbed corner of the world. This may well be a vain hope for I have come to understand that both memories and written words can be made to change their form like clouds blown in the wind. Only that which is hidden and forgotten is safe. If they don't know something exists, they can't change its existence.

CHAPTER 1.
A Strange and Tragic Happening

I had been surfing in the morning before we left for England and that morning is still crystal clear in my memory. I remember the bright heat of the sun, the blue waves curling over the white sand. I remember the power of the Southern Ocean and the wide, open sky. At the end of that day I climbed into a metal tube with wings, together with a few hundred other people, and sat in an uncomfortable seat for 24 hours, staring at movies I didn't want to watch and eating food I didn't want to eat. I emerged into a place that seemed to me to be grey and cramped, a world full of small, colourless people. Of course, this was the simple prejudice of a teenage boy brought up to take the bright sun for granted and by the time the English summer came around I would have a very different view. However, at this time, the dark of a London winter was a shock.

My Mum had just got a job as a photographer with a big fashion magazine and so she came to live in London and I came with her. I wasn't really given much say in the matter. Dad stayed behind. I don't think he had much say in the matter either. They were at pains to assure me that was not the beginnings of a divorce. It was not a trial separation or anything like that. It was just work. It was just the need for Mum to follow her career. Even so, Mum and I were in London and Dad was off to a job on an oil rig in the South China Sea.

These circumstances may have coloured my first impressions but it seemed to me that I had come to a place where a grey sky normally hung low over grey and crowded streets. When the sun did shine it seemed to give a watery light that struggled to illuminate row upon row of barren streets and small, ugly houses. London has always appeared to me as a place of crowds and noise, even now all these years later. Hyde Park and the area around Buckingham palace are beautiful but the rest has always seemed to me to be a tangle of twisting streets crowded with traffic and people. Almost as soon as I had stepped off the plane I missed the bright Australian sun, the wide Australian sky and the light – Australian light which is so pervasive that everything, the rocks, the trees, the people are saturated in that light. In the dark of an English winter, I was not happy.

It was in this sullen mood that I walked across Westminster Bridge, dodging between the tourists and commuters who even in winter crowded the footpath. We had moved into a house in the London suburbs. It was a single fronted house in a row of houses all joined together. It had steps leading up to an ornate front door and it faced a park in a type of square. Mum kept telling me how expensive it was and how we had never lived in anything as upmarket as this in Australia. However, it was smaller and older than our Australian house and the plumbing made some funny noises. Mum was busy setting up her studio and I had a few days before I started school, so I set off to explore London. This is how I came to be on Westminster Bridge at precisely the wrong time.

The bridge was heavy with traffic when it happened. It happened suddenly and it was over quickly. A black robed figure just appeared in the middle of the road. One moment everything was normal and the next he was there, standing in the left hand lane. Everyone around me just froze, starring at this impossible thing. It was like something out of a fantasy movie. He just appeared out of thin air. Of course, all the traffic couldn't just freeze and it looked certain that he would be run down, but that didn't happen. It was as if there was some sort of invisible wall around him and all the cars, trucks and buses just seemed to crash into it. Then he raised his arms and there was a wave of energy extending out from him; piling up the cars, buses and vans like surf on a beach. The tourists either side of me started to run. The figure just pointed and they were thrown off the bridge and into the river. I didn't run and I was left alone. I was frozen in place not so much by fear as by astonishment at what was happening. I thought it must be a dream but I knew it wasn't. I tried to make some sense of what had happened but there was no sense to be found. I tried to think but my mind couldn't cope with what my eyes were telling me.

The figure in the robe turned to face me. I could see his face clearly. He was young with pale skin and eyes that were so green they were startling. His expression was one of rage, anguish and despair. He seemed furious that I was still standing there and he pointed his finger at my chest - but nothing happened. I just stood there. He pointed both hands at me with an angry intensity and behind me I heard the rock of the bridge crack. I still just stood where I was.

You may think that I should have done something but it all happened so fast and it was so weird that I just couldn't think. I couldn't take in what was happening. As I stood there his expression changed from anger to shocked surprise. He looked at me intently and then he was gone. He just vanished and I was left starring at the empty space where he had been standing. Around me the world seemed to explode in noise with sirens and screams. I started shaking and could not stop.

Eventually some sort of order was established. Police and ambulances arrived and the seriously injured and the dead were taken away. For a long time I was left standing where I was. I didn't move, I couldn't. I was desperately trying to process what I had just seen and my mind was fully occupied trying to make sense of the experience. I know the term for this now. They call it "cognitive dissonance", where what you experience can't be reconciled with your understanding of reality. It's not something I suffer from much anymore. Anyway, I just stayed standing where I was, staring at the spot where the figure in the black robe had disappeared, until an ambulance officer came and checked me out. She clearly decided that there was not much wrong with me and she led me to where other survivors sat waiting for the police to take detailed statements. Like the others, a blanket was put on my shoulders and I was given a salty sports drink to counter the effects of shock, something I was certainly suffering from.

While the police were taking the time to get systematic, detailed statements, a TV news crew was moving along the line taking quick vox pops. I heard the old guy next to me explain, "There was this geeza see, in a black robe thing and 'e was waving 'is arms around and cars and buses were crashing about 'im like nine pins. Then it was just "poof!" and 'e was gone."

They came to me next and I told them what I had seen, still not understanding or believing it myself. The crew looked edgy and nervous. They clearly were not coping with the stories they were being told. I couldn't blame them. When I had finished the reporter said, "You're Australian. Right?" When I nodded she turned to the camera man and said, "Put that one out quickly. It should get picked up by the Australian media."

She then moved on to the woman who was sobbing quietly on my left. It was about then that I noticed a middle aged man walking calmly across the bridge, through the middle of the chaos. He was dressed very formally in a dark business suit and bowler hat. He was smiling and waving as he went but no one seemed to notice him or pay any attention to him. As he passed you could sense a certain edge to the tension being released. Everyone seemed to relax - just a little bit.

I heard the woman next to me telling the television reporter, "It was terrible. That bus just swerved and then jackknifed and all these cars crashed into it. The driver must have been going too fast but it's those jointed buses – they just aren't safe." I looked at her in surprise. That was not what had happened! As I listened to the talk around me, however, it seemed that this was the story everyone now believed. I realized that this was why the tension level was now a bit lower. This had just become another, normal accident. Certainly it was tragic but it was explainable and even, to some extent, to be expected. The emergency crews just got on with their jobs.

I looked around for the guy in the old fashioned suit and bowler hat and I spotted him walking off past the houses of parliament. He was still occasionally waving at people. I didn't know how, and I didn't know why I was unaffected, but I knew that somehow he was responsible for covering up what the guy in the black robe had done. This made me determined to tell the actual truth, since I was apparently the only one who remembered it. When the police finally got to me I began to tell what had happened, just as I had to the TV reporter, but the policeman stopped me about half way through and looked quizzically at the ambulance paramedic.

"Shock," the paramedic said, "and probably concussion. He may never remember the actual incident properly."

The policeman nodded sympathetically, "That's OK son," he said, "We've got enough to know what happened." He made a note in his book which probably said something like "knocked on the head, can't remember anything properly." I wanted to say that I was the only one who did remember properly but I didn't. My determination to tell the truth evaporated as I could see that way leading to a mental institution and a lot of very tiresome conversations about my mother. I had already had too many tiresome conversations about my mother - mostly with her. Still, I was angry. I was angry about the pain and the loss and about the strange deception but I was also angry at a deeper level. This should not have happened. This should not have been possible. And yet, this ridiculous thing had happened and people had died. The trouble was I didn't know who to be angry with because I still didn't understand what was going on.

Eventually my mother took time off from setting up her studio to come and collect me. She took me home and fussed over me and gave me hot chocolate and headache tablets. Then she called my dad in Australia and he insisted on talking to me. I told him I was okay and that the accident had happened near me but that I hadn't been hurt. I spent the rest of the day lying on a couch in the living room watching TV. In newsflashes all through the afternoon and on the news that night the same story was told. A jointed bus had been going too fast, had braked suddenly and jack-knifed in heavy traffic. They even had eyewitness interviews with people who had been on the bridge with me and all told the same story. My interview was never shown. Six people had died, including the bus driver, and forty two had been injured. There was going to be a formal inquiry but all the commentators agreed that it was a clear case of driver error and questioned the safety of the large jointed buses in heavy London traffic. They were at pains to point out that there was no indication of terrorist action and that this was simply a tragic accident. That was how it should have been. That was how it would have been if the world had made sense, if it was the safe and predictable place I had always imagined it to be. It was not, however, how it was and my sleep that night was filled with nightmares of black robed figures and people dying.

CHAPTER 2
Meeting Myfanwy

It was a few days later that I had to start school, so that morning I put on the white shirt, the dark red blazer, the matching tie and the grey slacks that formed the school uniform. As school uniforms go it wasn't too bad. I had seen far worse in Australia. Mum had booked me into St Agatha's, a private school on the outer fringe of London. It normally took me a while to get there traveling on the tube and a bus but Mum drove me on the first day and took me to my interview with the headmaster. The school years between Australia and Britain are six months out of phase and they had to decide whether I would be put forward six months or backwards. The headmaster decided to put me back the six months. This really annoyed me. I had always been good at school and was confident that I could've coped. Now I would be six months behind my friends in Australia.

The school itself had started life as a large, private house – a mansion I guess you'd call it. It was in an elaborate neo-classical style, all Corinthian columns with plaster gods and goddesses dancing around under the eaves. The school now lay at the end of a leafy street which had once been its driveway: a street of solid red brick houses dressed with lace curtains. My school in Australia was a collection of nondescript modern buildings, cream brick and plate glass, but it was surrounded by acres of playing fields and even had its own small forest where we did environmental science. By comparison, this English school, despite the mansion at its core, seemed small and cramped.

It did, however, have all the things my mum had been promised in the brochure; modern science labs, modern computer labs, modern language labs and the kids in the classes we passed on our tour all seemed reasonably happy. I was not. A lot of feelings were all jumbled up in me and I couldn't really appreciate any of this. I was mostly aware that I missed my old school, I missed my dad and I missed the wide sky and the piercing light of the Australian sun.

In due course the tour was over, mum left and I was introduced to my homeroom class. It was not something that I looked forward to but I had changed schools before and I knew the drill. I was the new boy – an outsider and an unknown quantity. I would be examined, tested and either fitted into the existing social structure or ignored. In my case the risk of becoming an outcast was very high. I was from the other side of the planet. I spoke differently and I didn't know their football teams. I didn't share their background understanding of the world.

My homeroom teacher was a Mrs. Brown. She was a small woman who had an air of having been defeated by the world. She was kind and well meaning and she really wanted the best for her students. She was, however, almost completely ineffectual as a teacher.

When I came in, she made me stand out the front while she introduced me to the class; "Attention class! This is Thomas O'Malley from Australia and he will be joining us for the rest of this year. I'm sure you will all make him welcome. Why don't you tell us something about yourself Thomas so that we can get to know you?"

I looked at her in horror. This was the sort of thing you did in primary school! I had been hoping to slink off to my desk and size up the situation and now I was being asked to give an impromptu presentation! I could not think of a worse way for an outsider new boy to start. Mrs. Brown showed no sign of understanding my reluctance. I was stuck so I decided to make it as short as possible.

"Hi everyone,' I said, "I'm Tom and I'm from Angle Creek, which is a small town on the South East Coast of Australia. My dad works on an oil rig and my mum's a fashion photographer. We're living in London while she does some work for a magazine." I looked around at my new classmates. Most were paying no attention at all. The girls of the "in" group were sitting at the back of the class and had clearly already decided, by some process known only to them, that I was not of interest. Up the front, one girl on the right, with dark and very curly hair, was studiously looking out the window. On the left there was a group of four boys all seated in the same row. They were looking at me intently. Damn! I thought. There's always a group like that and they always seem to find me. I looked at them and I knew them. The fat one in the second seat would be the leader, the two either side of him would be the henchmen while the smaller guy at the back would be the cheer squad. I was going to have trouble. I needed to finish off my talk quickly.

"I really like surfing but I don't think I'll get much of a chance while I'm here." I said.

Mrs. Brown smiled at me and then turned to the class and asked, "Would anyone like to ask Thomas a question?" I groaned inwardly. This was going to be bad. For a moment there was silence and I looked around hoping that they would show mercy and let me get to my seat. It was then that I noticed the curly haired girl again. She was still looking out the window but now there was a small bird sitting on the window ledge and singing its heart out. It was looking directly at her and it was impossible to escape the impression that it was singing for her. I was so distracted by this that I almost didn't hear the question. It was asked by an earnest looking boy in the middle of the class.

"What football team do you support?" he asked. This was my worst case scenario – a question which would point out how different from them I really was. I knew I couldn't give the real answer. My Australian Rules football team would mean nothing to them.

"I don't really have one. I don't know much about soccer," I said, "We don't play it much where I come from."

In a loud voice the fat guy on the left said, "In this country it's called football, mate." The rest of the class laughed and then started to call out names of soccer teams that I should support.

"That's enough class!" said Mrs. Brown. "Thomas, the empty desk on the right hand side is yours. You may go to it now." As I walked down to the desk she indicated I passed the curly haired girl and took the seat behind her. She looked up with mild interest. The bird had gone.

"Now class," Mrs. Brown continued, "One of your classmates has just achieved a most remarkable success. Wilson Smyth won a national essay competition. I would now like to ask Wilson to come out the front and read us his prize winning essay. Thank you Wilson." The only black student in the class, and one of the few in the school, stood up. He was almost too stereotypically nerdy to be real. He was of average height but very slightly built. He had neat clothes, glasses and a very bad haircut. I could see that Wilson, as he walked out to the front of the class, was nervous. He also clearly anticipated a very negative reaction but he wasn't going to be put off. I remember thinking, this guy has guts. Wilson got to the front and faced the class.

"My essay is entitled 'How to bend space and time'" he began.

"Well, you'd know about things that are bent." the fat one said. His friends apparently found this hilarious and there were giggles from the "in" girls at the back.

"Quiet!" said Mrs. Brown, "Go on Wilson."

"Space, matter, energy and time are all interconnected..." he began. I was expecting another interjection but just then the girl with the curly hair pointed her finger in the direction of the fat one and all four of the group suddenly went still and quiet and then slowly fell asleep. Wilson continued with his essay, it was actually a very good summary the theory of special relativity, it even included some of the equations which Wilson wrote up on the white board, but I wasn't really listening. I know all about accidental coincidence but the curly haired girl had pointed her finger and those guys had fallen asleep. Somehow, she had done it. Memories of what had happened on the bridge came flooding back and I began to feel afraid.

When Wilson had finished, the four seemed to wake from their sleep. When the fat one realized that Wilson had read his essay unhindered, he clearly decided that he needed to do something to reassert his dominance. His solution was to screw up a sheet of paper and throw it at Wilson's head. The curly haired girl pointed at it as it flew and it turned sharply in flight, missed Wilson's head and landed on Mrs. Brown's desk. I sat with my mouth open, amazed, but the rest of the class didn't react at all. I seemed to be the only one who had noticed the piece of paper's bizarre, mid-flight manoeuvre.

"Who threw that!" Mrs. Brown demanded. The class went silent. After surveying the class for a while she reached down and flattened out the crumpled piece of paper. She smiled a slight, watery sort of smile.

"Horace Trimble," she said to the fat one, "You have a detention with the headmaster after school on Friday for disruptive behaviour in class." He had thrown a piece of paper with his name on it. The fat one might be loud and confident but he was not very bright.

I can't remember what happened in the rest of the class. I kept staring at the back of the curly haired girl's head. I tried to tell myself that I was imaging things, that there was some simple explanation or strange set of coincidences that could account for what I saw, but deep down I knew that wasn't true. A bird had come to sing for her, she had pointed her finger and those boys had gone to sleep, the paper had changed course in mid-flight. It wasn't that these things were bad but that in a proper, rational world, such things could not happen. Visions of what had happened on

Westminster Bridge kept playing over and over in my mind. What was this place that I had come to?

At lunchtime I lined up to get the usual canteen rubbish and then went to sit on my own in the dining room. The dining room was really rather impressive. It had been a ball room or something similar in the original house and it had large French windows which opened onto a small colonnaded porch and looked out into one of the remaining areas of garden. It was filled with wooden tables, plastic chairs, children and noise. I chose an empty table over near the windows and sat down on my own. A hand was thrust into my vision.

"Hello," a voice said, "I'm Wilson Smyth. Welcome to the school."

"Hi Wilson," I said as I shook his hand, "Tom O'Malley from Australia. Would you like to join me?" I waved my hand to indicate the empty chairs around the table.

"Thank you." he said as he sat down. He was very polite, very formal and very precise in his movements. He's being defensive, I thought. He doesn't know me and doesn't know whether I will greet him or ridicule him.

"I really liked your essay," I said. "I particularly liked the fact that you mentioned the work O'Leary did in the development of the time dilation equations." He looked at me surprised. Then his face broke into a broad smile. It was a smile that revealed the enthusiastic energy held tight behind his defensive posture.

"Yes," he said happily, "Sometimes people think that old Albert did it all by himself." He had started to unwrap the sandwiches that he had brought from home when a shadow fell across our table. It was Horace and his three friends.

"Hey Skippy," he said. "You should be careful who you associate with. You might just be taken for another loser. You're already suspect, being descended from convicts and having an Irish name and all." From long habit, Wilson started to back his chair away towards the wall. I looked at Horace with a quizzical expression on my face but what I thought was, "Trouble, Trouble with a capital T!" I decided that it might as well start now and that it would start on my terms.

"Well Horace,..." I said. I didn't get to say anymore. He exploded. He lunged over to where I was sitting and grabbed the front of my jacket.

"You do not call me that!" he yelled. "You call me Ace or Sir or I will teach you manners!" This was the reaction I had been expecting. I stood up slowly, my face inches from his. I was a little shorter than he was and he must have been almost twice my weight.

"Horace," I said, "Do you know you have hair growing out of your left nostril?" He gripped my jacket tighter, trying to decide how best to hurt me. I don't know what would have happened next but at that point his friends started to grab him by the shoulders.

"Ace, come on. It's her." they said. I looked across in the direction they were indicating. The curly haired girl was coming towards our table with a lunch tray. Horace also saw her coming.

'This isn't over" he hissed, Then he let me go and the four of them walked away, I fixed my jacket and sat down. Wilson had a very serious expression on his face.

"Tom," he said, "You really shouldn't provoke them. Just try to avoid them. Those four are bad news, very bad." The curly haired girl came up to our table and sat down without any ceremony. She was short and lightly built, almost elfin in appearance. Her manner was formal and reserved although her long hair hung about her in a wild cascade.

"Wilson is right." she said. "You should listen to him." She spoke with a soft, musical Welsh voice. "My name is Myfanwy," she said as she held out her hand, "Myfanwy Ferchwyn. I know who you are. You are Thomas (she pronounced my name toe-mass) the surfer from Australia." I shook her hand warily.

"Hi Myfanwy," I said, "Why did those guys leave when they saw you coming?"

"Oh that!" she answered. "They think I'm a witch." She smiled broadly. "I may once have given them the impression that I could curse them with a variety of unpleasant skin complaints." She shrugged, "It's not my fault if they were silly enough to believe me." The bright smile completely changed her face. I wasn't thinking about that, however. I was thinking about why three large bullies could be scared of one very slight girl. The reason, I thought, is that birds come to sing to you when you get bored in class. It's because you can point your finger and put people to sleep.

She looked directly at me, still smiling. She had the same brilliant green eyes as the guy in black robes. I didn't wonder that Horace and his mates were scared and I didn't think it was silly at all.

The trouble with fear is that it's what drives bullies to be bullies. The more afraid they are the worse they become. That afternoon, Horace and his friends caught up with me as I was walking down the street to catch the bus home. Horace stood in front of me and the henchmen stood behind me.

"The witch girl isn't here to save you now Skippy." he said. "Think of this as your first lesson in proper behaviour." One of the henchmen grabbed me from behind and Horace raised his fist and took a step towards me. I quickly stepped forward and dropped to one knee, sending the henchman holding me flying over my shoulder. He landed flat out on the pavement between Horace and me and he let out a loud "oof!" as the air left his body. I turned around and stepped inside the wild swing that henchman two was aiming at my head. I struck him just below the sternum with the heel of my palm. He also went down winded. I will say this for Horace, he was persistent. He stepped around henchman one, who was still struggling to get up, and he swung a well aimed punch at my head. I stepped outside this one, grabbed his arm and used an elbow lock to drag him to the pavement. The cheer squad guy at the back did nothing. I stepped up and away and turned to face all four of them.

"Listen guys," I said reasonably. "Today I have been nice to you, I didn't really hurt any of you, but I didn't get my black belt by learning how to be nice to people. So I suggest that you just leave me alone or this all could get very unpleasant, Okay?" With that I turned and continued to walk towards the bus. They called out a lot of stuff behind me but I wasn't really listening to anything they said. I was listening to hear if they were going to come after me. I was also concentrating hard on making myself walk and not run. That time things had gone better than I had expected. Now I had to make sure there was no next time because the next time would not go as well. I had lied to them. I didn't have a black belt. The martial art I had studied was Tai Chi Chuan, a form of Kung Fu, and they don't give them out. I was competent and I was getting better, but I wouldn't call myself an expert.

The next day and in the following weeks I had to endure lots of "skippy" insults, convict references and shoving on the stairs and in the corridor but none of this was serious and none of it bothered me. A small group of us began to gather for lunch. I guess we were all social misfits for one reason or another and chatting together gave us a kind of belonging. There was Wilson, who was safer in a group than alone. There was Phil Trenton, the very earnest football supporter who had asked about my football team. Phil's conversation tended to be very monothematic. He was a fanatic Tottenham Hotspurs fan and was genuinely shocked to learn that soccer was a relatively minor sport in Australia and that our main football code was Australian Rules, a game he knew nothing about. Sometimes Gabriella Porter, a pleasant but somewhat plump girl, would join us – mostly when she needed Wilson's help with her mathematics' homework. Another member of our small group was a wannabe goth by the name of Rachael Harris. She couldn't be a real goth because the school dress regulations, and her parents, wouldn't let her. However, she tried hard to push the boundaries with dark makeup and stuff like that. Then there was always Myfanwy. Myfanwy, whose sudden smile would light up her normally solemn face. Myfanwy, who would talk of poetry and medieval romances. Myfanwy, who had a power that scared me silly.

Each Monday morning, school would start with a formal assembly. We would sing a hymn and the headmaster would address us. Then we would all say the Lord's Prayer and go to a shortened home room class. To say that it was not a very profound religious experience is to master the art of understatement. It was so bland and boring that only the most rabid atheist could be offended. Mrs. Harris, the piano teacher, played the hymns on a small, electric organ.

Each of us sang differently. Horace and co would try and sing what they considered to be witty parodies while the 'in' girls would just stand there and be offended that anyone could ask them to do something so embarrassingly uncool. Gabriella was a competent alto soprano while Phil shouted every hymn as if it were a soccer anthem. Wilson was completely tone deaf. He had no ear at all and his singing was painful to all concerned. Most of the time people just kept nudging him to keep quiet. Myfanwy, on the other hand, sang with a voice as clear and pure as a mountain stream.

It was during one of the headmaster's more particularly boring Monday addresses, always about doing your duty by studying hard, that I noticed Myfanwy looking down at her feet and smiling. I leaned forward to see what she was looking at and I will swear that there were two mice standing on their hind legs and doing a waltz! As soon as I leaned forward, however, Myfanwy looked at me in surprise and the two mice scuttled away. I tried to explain it away as a trick of the light or an accident of perspective, but this became progressively harder as incidents like this were happening all the time and I was the only one who seemed to notice.

The next assembly, I looked across to Myfanwy's seat and she just wasn't there. She had been there a minute ago when we were singing and now she was gone. It reminded me of the way the guy on the bridge just appeared and disappeared, but I couldn't be sure. I didn't see her leave. I stared at her empty chair for a while but I looked away as we stood up for the final dismissal. When I turned around, she was back. No one else seemed to have noticed she was ever missing.

One morning each week the boys and girls were split up and we would change our blazers and slacks (or skirts for the girls) for baggy shorts and tee shirts and have some kind of physical education class. On this day we were arranged in circles and throwing heavy medicine balls to each other. Horace waited till Wilson was looking away and then decided to throw the ball directly at Wilson's head. The ball flew in the expected curve for about half a second and then it veered at right angles in mid air and flew about ten meters to the astonished instructor, who caught it on reflex. Everyone else stared at the ball in disbelief but I looked straight away to Myfanwy's group. Sure enough, there was Myfanwy watching what was happening with her hand raised. There was a kind of astonished silence but it passed when Myfanwy waved exactly the same kind of wave that the man in the bowler hat had done on Westminster Bridge. From that point on, it was clear that everyone had forgotten about the ball's impossible flight and thought that

Horace had simply thrown it straight at the instructor – everyone but me.

"Hey, cut that out son!" yelled the instructor, who was ex-army and could yell very loudly. "Throw it to your class mates not to me. I don't want the thing!" Most of the class laughed but I didn't. For the rest of the class my reflexes were slow and I dropped the ball a lot: my head was full of the memory of dead and wounded bodies lying on Westminster Bridge.

Chapter 3
The Division for the Investigation of Anomalous Phenomena

That lunchtime I went over and sat with Myfanwy before the rest could join us. "Myfanwy," I said, "I need to talk to you."

"Really?" She said casually, "What about?" She suddenly looked up at the canteen queue on the other side of the dining room and said "Oh, no." I looked and saw Phil walking towards us with a bowl of soup on his lunch tray. Horace was just in the act of knocking the tray so as to spill the hot soup all over Phil. Myfanwy made a funny gesture with her fingers and everything just stopped. The silence was eerie. Everything had just frozen in place. Not only were none of the kids moving but even the soup half sloshed out of Phil's bowl was frozen in mid slosh. She then made a further gesture and the soup went back into the bowl and the tray became level again. I jumped to my feet, knocking my chair over.

"No!" I yelled. This was too much. This wasn't some trick of the light. I couldn't explain it away and I wanted it to stop. This couldn't happen. This was impossible! Myfanwy turned towards me, suddenly realizing that I wasn't frozen like the others. The expression on her face was exactly the expression of shock and disbelief that I had seen on the black robed guy when he had pointed at me and nothing much had happened.

"You …How can you…That's not possible…" she said. In her confusion and shock, she seemed oblivious to the irony of that last statement. She recovered quickly, however.

"Sit down," she said, "or they will notice. I can't keep doing this for long." I retrieved my chair and sat down. Then time started to flow again. It seemed to everybody else that Horace had only bumped Phil's tray. Nothing was spilt.

"Hey! Watch it!" yelled Phil. The two henchmen thought this was very funny and burst into laughter. Horace was apparently satisfied with his work and turned back to receive his friend's congratulations. I leaned across the table to Myfanwy.

"What the hell just happened? How the hell can you stop time?" I asked in a fierce whisper. "This is what I need to talk to you about. I have seen you do crazy things, impossible things. Well, I was on Westminster Bridge a while ago and a guy who had the same green eyes as you also did ridiculous, impossible things. Only then people died and no one remembers it properly but me. I need to know how all this is possible. I need to understand what is going on!" I looked at her intently and I could see that she was still upset and confused. Apparently, the fact that I did not freeze with everybody else upset her as much as the fact that she could freeze time upset me. She pointed a finger directly at my forehead.

"Forget!" she said. I looked at her in exasperation. She obviously expected her command to work and that I would just finish my lunch and talk about how bad Mrs. Brown was at teaching English. It made me angry to think that she thought she could treat me like some kind of puppet.

"How can you expect me to forget stuff like that," I whispered angrily. "People died in front of me! Somehow you can make everyone else forget, you can make everyone else freeze. Well, it doesn't work on me! It didn't work on the bridge and it doesn't work here." Myfanwy had turned as white as a sheet. I could see that she was fighting panic and tears were welling up in her eyes. I think that she had hoped that if I had forgotten on command then the world would have returned to whatever she called normal. However, for some reason this was not to be.

"You…"she started. Then she paused, clearly unsure of what to say and fighting the same existential panic that I had felt on the bridge. "I don't understand…," she said at last in a desperate and panicky voice. "How can it not work?" With this she got up and ran past Phil and out of the dining room, leaving her lunch half eaten. The other students turned and watched her go. Horace turned back to look at me with a big grin on his face. He made a couple of phony Kung Fu moves with his hands.

"Impressive Grasshopper," he said in what he imagined to be a Chinese accent. "You have scared away witch girl." The table of "in" girls clearly thought this was hilarious and they burst into laughter and loud chatter, no doubt trying to guess what I had said to her. I doubt that any of their guesses were very accurate. I glumly finished eating my lunch. Scaring her away was not what I had intended. At the same time, there was some connection between her and the guy on the bridge. I needed to know what it was.

Myfanwy did not look at me at all the next morning. All through the home room period she sat stiffly upright in the desk in front of me and I stared into the back of her head. Mrs. Brown was up to her normal standard of class control, which meant that the room was a barely suppressed riot. Horace and co. had decided to see how many times they could hit Wilson with paper planes. Wilson got hit many times, Myfanwy did nothing. Towards the end of home room I was called to the headmaster's office. When I got there, there were two guys in paramedic uniforms and the headmaster was reading an official looking letter.

"Young master O'Malley," said the headmaster. "It seems that you were unfortunate enough to be involved in that most regrettable accident on Westminster Bridge recently. As part of the follow up to the accident, these gentlemen have come to take you to the hospital for some precautionary brain scans. It seems that there was some concern at the time that you may have suffered a concussion." It was the headmaster at his pompous best. He was giving the impression that he was in control when it was clear that all these decisions had been made somewhere else. "We have cleared it with your mother. You will be at hospital doing tests for the rest of the day. You may go now." One of the paramedics smiled and winked at me as we left the office.

The other muttered under his breath, "Pompous old windbag. Why do they inflict these people on young kids?" There was a car painted a bit like an ambulance at the front door of the school. It had "Patient Transport Vehicle" printed on it. I got into the back seat while the two paramedics got into the front. As we were driving out the school gates, something occurred to me.

"How come they sent a car to pick me up from school?" I asked. "Couldn't they've just sent a letter and asked me to make an appointment? After all, I'm only going for some precautionary tests." Another thought occurred to me, "And why are there two of you?"

"All part of the service, young master O'Malley," said the driver in a very reasonable impression of the headmaster's voice. They both laughed but I was nervous and very unsure as we drove away from the school. I didn't know my way around London and I was soon lost in the maze of minor streets and main roads that they took. In the end, however, it was clear that I was not being driven to a hospital. Instead, we drove up to the gate of an army base.

"Hey!" I said. "This isn't a hospital! Where are you guys taking me?" A darker and scarier thought occurred to me. "Who are you guys?" The one in the passenger side seat turned around.

"Mr. O'Malley," he said. "You are quite safe and no harm will come to you. Later this afternoon you will be returned to your home as promised. I know you have many questions and you are quite right to ask them. However, I am not authorized to discuss any of the relevant matters with you. All will be explained to you shortly." This seemed to be a bit of a conversation killer so I sat back and kept quiet as the gate guard came over and checked the ID that the driver showed. A heavy steel gate was then raised and we were let through.

There was a large barracks building at the end of a long drive and I could see groups of soldiers doing some kind of obstacle course on the lawn. We did not go near these, however. We turned off the main drive onto a rough garden track and stopped outside an old timber building which seemed to be in the middle of a garden maintenance depot. The two fake paramedics got out and one of them came and opened the door for me. I briefly wondered what would happen if I made a run for it but I quickly decided against it. I didn't think the outcome would be good. I was escorted through the front door into a very normal looking reception area. There was a receptionist behind a desk, chairs lined the walls, there was a large door with "Director" painted on it in the back wall and there were some old magazines lying on a small table.

"Mr. O'Malley to see Director Smith," said one of my escorts. The receptionist nodded and spoke into a machine on her desk.

"Mr. O'Malley to see you sir," she said. I could just hear the reply from the machine,

"Good, send him in and call Dr. Jones," it said. She smiled at me and said, "You can go in now." As I went through the door I could see the two fake paramedics sit down and start leafing through the old magazines. They were evidently intending to wait until I was finished. I couldn't help wondering why I was so important all of a sudden.

The office I entered was large but it was mainly remarkable for its ordinariness. Behind a large but battered wooden desk sat a thin, middle aged man with distinguished looking grey hair. He was wearing an old tweed suit and had thick rimmed glasses sitting on a rather large nose. He indicated a chair in front of the desk. As I sat down, another man entered the room.

He was large with a thick mat of black hair and he was wearing a white lab coat.

"Mr. O'Malley," the man behind the desk said. "I'm sure you are wondering why you have been brought here, why the hospital deception was used and, indeed, where here is. All of these questions will be answered in due course. As you may have guessed, you are currently in a government facility. I am Director Smith and this," he said, indicating the other man, "is Dr. Jones."

I looked at them disbelievingly. "Really?" I said, my voice thick with sarcasm. "Really? Smith and Jones! That was the best you could come up with? You couldn't even try to make it believable?" The director looked at me with a calm, deadpan expression.

"Mr. O'Malley," he said evenly. "Those happen to be our names." He picked up a piece of paper from his desk and started to read it. "Mr. O'Malley," he said. "You were present on Westminster Bridge when a serious accident occurred recently. We would like to review those events with you. Could you watch these please." He pointed to a TV screen built into the opposite wall and pressed a button on his desk. A whole series of news reports about the accident then played on the screen. These were the reports that I had seen before. They were wrong, that was not the way it had happened. When they had stopped playing Dr. Jones leaned forward eagerly.

"Well," he said. "Do you have any comment?" I shook my head. I had decided that it was safer to keep quiet about the whole incident. Dr. Jones sat back in his chair and looked at the Director.

"Perhaps you will after this." The Director said. He again pushed a button on his desk and another newsreel played. This time it was the interview they did with me, the one that told the true story with the guy in the black robe appearing and disappearing, throwing cars and people around like toys. It only took a few seconds and when it was finished the Director looked at me over the top of his glasses.

"It seems," he said, "that we have two versions of the events on the bridge that day. Mr. O'Malley, would you care to give us your opinion as to which of the two is the more accurate?" I straightened up in my chair and looked at them both. The director was still looking at me calmly from over the top of his glasses. He reminded me of a teacher looking at an unruly student. Dr. Jones was eagerly leaning forward in his seat. He clearly had a big interest in my reply. I decided to tell the truth and let the consequences play out as they may.

"I told the truth that day," I said, "I don't know how it can be true and I don't know what happened to other people's memories but the way I told it is the way it actually happened." Dr. Jones clapped hands.

"Yes!" he yelled. "I told you director. There had to be one somewhere. Out of all the millions of people on this planet, there had to be at least one." The Director waved him to silence. Then he started to address me, giving a little speech.

"Mr. O'Malley, we are from DIAP, the Division for the Investigation of Anomalous Phenomena. We are tasked by the government to try and keep track of the activities of a small community of people who seem to have the power to do what most people would call – magic. We are tasked to investigate these people and to try and bring them under the control of British law and justice. Our task is made nearly impossible by the fact that, as you have undoubtedly observed, they can change memories. They can change official records and they can change digital recordings. Our only weapons are knowledge and secrecy and their only weakness is a certain lack of understanding about how our complex, modern society works. They can't alter what they don't know exists. There were many recordings that told the same story as yours and we managed to capture many of them secretly before they were altered. If we showed them to the people who made them now they would be shocked and disbelieving. They would deny that they had ever said any of that and insist that the bus accident story was the true one. You, however, are different. You came to our attention because of a partial police statement which we managed to get hold of. It was telling the same story as you told on that tape but it was made after everyone else had been made to believe something completely different. You seem to have an immunity to their magic." I sat quietly for a while. This would explain why I didn't freeze like everyone else when Myfanwy stopped time but it still didn't answer the crucial question.

"But how can magic affect anyone?" I asked. "How can magic be real?"

"Ah! I think I can answer that," said Dr. Jones enthusiastically. "The laws of Physics are not, of course, laws in the normal sense. They are simply human descriptions of how the universe normally behaves. In the understanding of Quantum Mechanics they are, at root, the result of the probabilistic behaviour of billions of essentially random events. Highly improbable events, such as an elephant appearing in this room for example, are not forbidden in any sense, they are just practically impossible because of the energy barriers against them occurring. We have postulated that there are some individuals who are able to will the improbable to occur. To use the director's colourful phrase, they can do magic. A while ago I postulated that, if this were so, then it should also work in reverse. There should be people whose instinctive awareness of their own quantum path would lead to a kind of stability. Their own understanding of themselves would not permit the will of the others to change them. They would be immune to magic. You are the first demonstration that my hypothesis is correct! This is very exciting." I looked back at the director.

"What do you want from me?" I asked. "I'm not some anti-magic agent. I'm not even British. I'm just an Australian schoolboy who would rather be surfing back home." The Director held up his hand.

"No, no," he said. "We don't want to interfere with your life. We want only two things from you. One: we really do want to do a complete CAT scan of your brain – to aid in Dr. Jones' research. Two: we would like you to watch for any anomalous events, as we call them, any occurrence of magic. You could be an extra sensor for us that they cannot corrupt." His face grew very grave and his voice dropped.

"Our work has recently become even more important. We know these people have been living alongside us for a long time and for the most part they seem to have been peaceful and to have minded their own business. Lately this has begun to change. There have been attacks like the one on Westminster Bridge and there have been other incidents, less deadly but in their own way even more unpleasant. The incident on the Westminster Bridge could also have been far more serious. If it had happened five minutes later, it would have disrupted a top secret shipment of high level radioactive waste and we would have had a major nuclear disaster in the middle of London. It was only prevented because heavy traffic on the M1 meant that the shipment was behind schedule.

Something is going on in that community and it is threatening all of us. We need to know about it." It occurred to me that these were almost exactly the same sentiments as those I had put to Myfanwy. "So it is imperative that you inform us as soon as you see something that is strange, especially if other people seem to forget it. Have you seen anything like that?"

As I thought of Myfanwy and the bird singing to her outside her window, I realized that there was no way I was going to tell these people about Myfanwy and her abilities. I don't know why, perhaps it was the way her face lit up when she smiled or the clear beauty of her singing, but somehow, I trusted her more than I trusted them.

'No," I said, "I've nothing to tell you."

"Well then, you can go back to your life now," the Director continued, "with one small proviso. Nothing that has been discussed here today must ever be mentioned to anybody. The fact of this visit must never be mentioned to anybody. If you do, not only will nobody believe you, but the full force of this agency will be deployed to keep you silent and that could well involve imprisonment. Our very survival depends on secrecy. I trust you understand." I nodded. As I left the office, the receptionist gave me a card. It looked like the card of someone who would type essays for you.

"In case you need to contact us." She said. The two DIAP agents dressed as paramedics then drove me to a real hospital where real doctors did a real and extensive scan of my brain before I was driven home. My mum even received a letter, supposedly from the Health Department, a few days later. It said:

"Your son recently received a complete series of brain scans because of a suspected concussion as a result of the Westminster Bridge accident. We are pleased to inform you that no anomalies or injuries were found and your son is free to resume his normal life."

Of course the message was really from DIAP. Mum was pleased at the standard of health care in Britain, while I was left wondering whether my life would ever be normal again.

That night the news was full of a serious nuclear accident that had happened in the north of the country. The damage had been contained without loss of life – but only just. It was a strange accident and something about the news reports made me suspicious: they were too uniform, too well prepared. I had a nagging worry that this was another 'anomalous event' and the nightmares of black robed figures and people dying started again.

CHAPTER 4
War and Peace

At school things really did start to become normal. I was accepted as a bit of an outsider but this was put down to the fact that I was Australian. Most of the kids were friendly even if they weren't going to accept me as a bosom buddy. Phil kept trying to convince me of the glories of what he called 'the beautiful game': soccer. He would come in on a Monday morning and say,

"Tom. Did you see that great game on Saturday?"

"It was a nil all draw." I would point out politely.

"Yes," he would reply. "That's why it was so good. Their attack was great but they just couldn't get through our defence and then there was that missed penalty in stoppage time…. The excitement was almost unbearable."

"No Phil," I would reply, less politely. "A nil all draw is boring and pointless." It was very clear from early on that neither of us was going to be converted to the other's sporting culture but that didn't stop Phil from trying. I think that he considered it his duty to try and educate the poor colonial.

Horace and his cronies kept trying to target Wilson. There were a number of reasons for this: he was black, he was the smartest kid in the class, he was no match for them physically, and he would not give in to them. As I said before, he had guts. Whenever we could, Myfanwy and I ran interference for him. This was made much harder by the fact that all through January and most of early February Myfanwy and I hardly spoke to each other, each of us trying to come to terms with the other's existence. It was a matter of trying to quietly observe the other's actions and filling in the gaps. I don't know what Myfanwy had done to Horace and his crew but they were terrified of her. Whenever she came to sit at Wilson's table they would quickly walk away. The same thing would happen if she stood near him while he was waiting for his mother to pick him up and, to a lesser extent, if she was in the same class. All this meant that she didn't actually have to do much magic. The fear that she might was enough.

They were wary rather than terrified of me. I had demonstrated that bothering me was going to be more trouble than it was worth so they tended to avoid me if I was on my own. If I was with Wilson they would moderate their behaviour, limiting themselves to verbal attack. They should have realized that witty repartee was not an area they excelled in. Only once in January did I have to demonstrate to Craig Trenton, henchman number one, that it didn't matter how powerful a punch is if the intended victim is no longer standing where you thought he was and also how painful a simple wrist lock can be. I didn't know it at the time, but they considered me to be a problem for which they were working out a solution.

Wilson, of course, was too smart not to notice our silent tag team protection. He confronted me with it one day over lunch. I was sitting with him because that day Myfanwy had a French class that ran over lunch time.

"Look, I know what you two are doing," he said. "But it's not necessary. I can look after myself."

"No you can't Wilson," I said. "They would beat you to a pulp. Being smart and having right on your side doesn't actually help much in a fist fight." This was so obviously true that he didn't bother to dispute it.

"Well can you and Myfanwy at least do it together?" He asked. "This constant swapping around is making my life very confusing." I shook my head but he continued, "Look, I know you both. You are both intelligent and pleasant people. Why can't you just get on?" I said nothing. "I would prefer it if my two closest friends and body guards would at least talk to each other." When I still said nothing he leaned across the table and whispered, "That day when she ran out of the dining room, what did you say to her? Can't you just apologize?" Again, I shook my head.

"I don't want to talk about this. I won't talk about this," I said. "But I've said nothing to her that I need to apologize for." As I said this it occurred to me that this might not be true. When we last spoke I had compared her to a black robed mass murderer and it was just possible that she might consider this to be unfair. I buried this thought deep down. Fear breeds anger and Myfanwy's powers scared me so I was angry with her and I was determined to stay angry.

The next day Wilson was chatting to Myfanwy as I arrived in the home room class. I took no notice and sat down at my desk. I was just sorting out my books when I heard Myfanwy yell, "No ! No! No!" She then stormed over to her desk and glared at me before sitting down. I took it from this that Wilson's peacemaking efforts hadn't gone any better with Myfanwy than they had with me.

I was leaving for home later that week, through a depressing drizzle as usual, when a long, grey limousine pulled up in front of me. A chauffer in a neat grey uniform got out and came over to shake my hand. I recognized him as one of the DIAP agents who had previously dressed as paramedics.

"Congratulations Mr. O'Malley," he said. "You have won third prize in the Hampstead Club raffle. This afternoon you have a free limousine ride, with in car catering, to the destination of your choice." I had no idea what the Hampstead Club was and I don't think anyone else had either. DIAP really had to work on their cover stories.

"Oh" I said and then added rather lamely, "Great!" Inside the limousine I found cans of soft drink, trays of chocolates and Dr. Jones. As I sat back in the soft leather seat the voice of the fake chauffer came over the intercom,

"Where to Sir?" he asked, staying perfectly in character.

"Take me home Jeeves!" I said, beginning to enjoy myself. I opened a can of drink as the limo drove off and I took a chocolate before looking at Dr. Jones. He was looking at me rather disapprovingly.

"Mr. O'Malley," he said. "You do realize that you have not actually won a raffle, don't you?"

"Sure," I replied. "But it is going to be way too complicated for a top secret government agency to charge me with stealing a few chocolates." I took another chocolate and then asked, "What do you want?"

"At least use a glass," He said, handing me one from a rack. "We thought you might like to know the results of your scans. Your brain is perfectly healthy but you do have a thickening of the cortex in areas involved in attention and sensory processing, such as the prefrontal cortex and the right anterior insula. This is similar to developments seen in people who meditate for prolonged periods. Our research into your background has shown us that you study a martial art called …" He paused and looked at some notes he had on his lap. "Tai Chi Chuan. This involves training in concentration and awareness?" I nodded. "This is very good news. It implies that some form of mental training may help in resisting the powers of these people." He paused and looked thoughtful, even wistful. "If only I could get a brain scan of one of them!"

"Hmm…I don't think it's likely that they would let you do that." I said.

"No," he said, becoming all brisk and business like. "I don't believe they would. We have some other things to tell you. The first is that there has been another anomalous event. The recent accident at the nuclear power plant up north… "

"It wasn't really an accident, was it?" I asked.

"No," he responded, shaking his head. "The power plant was modern and safe. It could not have been destroyed in the way it was by any natural engineering failure. Someone tried to cause that power plant to explode and breach its containment. That would have caused catastrophic loss of life and would have rendered a large part of the north of England uninhabitable. Fortunately they didn't succeed. Surface cracks did appear in the concrete containment vessel but they didn't penetrate the carbon steel lining of the structure."

"So," I said. "Our friend from Westminster Bridge is growing more ambitious."

"Not necessarily," Dr. Jones replied. "What you don't know is that, if it had not been for an unforeseeable traffic holdup in Hampstead, there would have been a top secret transport van carrying weapons grade plutonium crossing Westminster Bridge at the time of the first incident. If that shipment's containment had been breached in the middle of London, the results would have been catastrophic. He is clearly intent on doing major damage, so if you know anything at all, it is imperative that you tell us immediately." He paused for a moment and then continued. "What the incident up north tells us is that there are limits to his power. Limits like nearly three meters of steel and concrete." He paused again, then turned to look directly at me when he continued.

"We also think you should know that someone has been accessing the recorded material from the Westminster Bridge incident and not in any conventional way. Our secret traces are showing that the material has been accessed but there is no record of any web connection. Mr. O'Malley, we think someone is looking for you and they are using magic to do it."

I sat back and finished my drink in silence. The brain stuff I didn't care about and the power plant accident really had nothing to do with me. It was the fact that I was being hunted that bothered me. If someone magical was trying to find me in secret it couldn't be Myfanwy or anyone connected with her. They would already know where I was. This meant that it had to be the guy in the black robes. The idea that I was being hunted by a crazed mass murderer with magical powers didn't act to improve my mood. I didn't feel like another chocolate and I didn't make a lot of conversation for the rest of the journey.

It was dark by the time I was dropped off at home and I was trying to think of some explanation for being driven home in a limousine. It turned out that no explanations were necessary. As usual, Mum was in her studio doing something and didn't notice that I had returned.

The thought of being hunted weighed on my mind. I didn't sleep well. I couldn't remember any of my dreams on waking but I could remember that they were full of terror. A grey, drizzly day seemed only appropriate as I went to school. I barely spoke that morning and dragged myself from class to class like a zombie. My mind was far away, in a dark place where I was being hunted by a lunatic. At lunch time Phil again tried to convince me of how good last night's game between two European teams I had never heard of was.

I didn't have any heart for discussion so all I said was, "I didn't see it Phil, but I'm sure in was a good game." Phil looked at me is surprise. Then he looked worried.

"Are you okay?" he asked.

"Sure," I said, "I'm just a little tired. That's all." I went into English after lunch in a depressed mood. My mind kept running over the same ideas time and again. What would he do to the other students if he found me at school? What would he do to my mother if he found me at home? Had he found a way to make magic hurt me? Was that why he was hunting me? If he could destroy a nuclear power station, what might he do to me and those around me?

I could see Wilson and Phil both talking to Myfanwy before the start of the class. Eventually she got cross at whatever they were saying to her.

"I have not spoken to him," she said rather loudly. "Why would you think it has anything to do with me?" She came over to her desk but gave me a worried look before she sat down. I turned my attention out the window. The grey drizzle of the day had turned into real rain which ran down the window pane in tiny, twisting rivers. Then suddenly, against all expectation, the sun came out and the portion of the old garden beneath my window turned from grey into a bright, luminous green. The bare tree branches, which had previously just been dreary, now stood stark and dramatic against a sky of white and gold and the rivulets of rain on my window shone like liquid silver. It was only for a moment, then the clouds closed again and the rain returned. I turned around to find Myfanwy looking at me with a concerned expression. I knew that she had done it. It seemed that she was worried about me and had tried to cheer me up. Again I got a panicky feel in my stomach but I had given up trying to explain away the things that happened around Myfanwy, this was magic - it was crazy and should be impossible. However, it was not the act of an evil person, of a person who would want to hurt me. She gave a tentative half smile. I smiled back.

"Thank you," I said.

CHAPTER 5
Apophis Returns

As I got off the bus and headed up towards school the next morning, I was feeling better about the whole situation. The guy in the black robe had not found me yet. He might never find me. I doubted that there was any magical equivalent of facial recognition software. This mood evaporated as I discovered that Horace and Co. had come up with an answer to one of their problems – me. They were standing in the street, about half way between the bus and school. Standing with them was a guy about 24 years old with a shaven head. He was dressed in jeans and boots, with a leather vest over a sleeveless tee shirt, and he had barbwire tattoos around both biceps.

"Hi Skippy," said Horace. "I'd like you to meet Jason from my soccer club. He doesn't like foreigners and he thinks colonials need to be taught their manners." The guy dropped into a fighting stance and performed a stylized series of blocks and punches. He was almost impossibly fast and there was real power behind those blows. I knew immediately that I was outmatched.

"Oh yes," Horace said, "Jason has a black belt too." I dropped my school bag but noticed that it started to fall impossibly slowly. I looked up towards the school gate and there was Myfanwy, standing and looking at our little group. Jason attacked with a round house kick to my head. It was perfectly executed but apparently done very slowly. Everything was moving as if time had slowed down. Only I, as usual, was unaffected. I easily stepped inside the kick, locked his knee with my hands and then turned in the direction of the kick so that Jason's own momentum sent him falling onto his back. He fell with the same impossible slowness. Henchmen one and two grabbed my arms and Horace's arm started to slowly come over my shoulder to come across my throat.

Jason called out but his voice sounded deep and slow, like the voice of someone in a slow motion movie,

"Leave 'im! He's mine." I pushed forward slightly and felt the henchmen react by trying to hold me back. I then stepped back quickly and dropped to one knee. This caught them by surprise and sent them sprawling, in a strange slow motion sprawl. I was now kneeling directly in front of Horace with my back to him. His arm was above me, still slowly reaching to where my throat used to be. As I stood up, I grabbed his arm and threw him over my shoulder. He bounced once, almost ballet-like in slow motion, as he hit the ground. Jason jumped over Horace to attack once again. Even in his slow motion state he was still pretty fast. He was also very well balanced and clever. This time his attack was very conservative and much harder to counter. I dodged his first kick and stepped away from the punch that followed it. I blocked the second punch and was surprised to find that it held the same power as it would have if it had been delivered at full speed. It was his second kick that caught me in the stomach. I went down, winded and struggling to breath. Jason aimed a kick at my head, still in slow motion, which I managed to block. I spun around and did a side kick to the back of his supporting knee, knocking him to the ground. He rolled back to his feet, but he was limping.

Kids now came running to see what was going on. The cry went up, "Fight! Fight!" I realized that they were running at normal speed and that their cries had their normal pitch. I dropped into fighting stance, prepared for the next attack. Jason looked at the gathering crowd and at me in my fighting stance.

"Stuff it," he said. "There's something creepy 'ere. You're not normal, you're too bloody fast." He turned away and limped off back towards the buses. I retrieved my bag walked slowly and painfully over to the school gate where Myfanwy was standing. Horace and his henchmen were now chasing after Jason and arguing at him. The words "useless, weak and pathetic" seemed to be used a lot. When it happened it was very quick, Jason really was very fast. When it was over, Horace and his friends lay on the ground and Jason walked off. As I have noted before, Horace was not very bright.

As I walked with Myfanwy up to the front door of the school, I said, "I take it that was you with the slow motion thing."

She nodded and said, "It was my thought that you would take the opportunity to run away."

"That was my first thought too," I said with a wry smile.

"No, that I don't believe," she said. "I don't think you are the kind of person for whom running away is ever the first option." She looked directly at me. "That's not always a good thing." She looked around at all the students coming into the school. "You were right before, we do need to talk, but not here. We need some privacy." She took my hand and suddenly we were on the top of a hill somewhere in the country, somewhere a long way from the school.

"Aarrg!" I yelled. "No! What happened?"

"I know this sort of thing bothers you," she said, "but I needed to talk to you privately." I stared around me with my mouth open in shock, almost crying with fear. "You must realize that you bother me too," she continued. "You must understand. I am a stranger there. I come from a very different sort of place and the only protection I have from all that press of people is my magic. Then you come along and it is as if my magic has gone away. It's not even as if you are fighting or resisting it. With you, it's as if I have no magic at all and I have to trust you that you will not hurt me or ridicule me. What if you were to join Horace and his thugs against me? I have no protection against you and that leaves me feeling very vulnerable." When she finished I stopped gaping at my new surroundings and looked back at her. I realized that I was still holding her hand and I dropped it immediately. I was shaking with fear.

"Where are we? Where's the school? How did we get here?" I was yelling and on the edge of panic. I was trying hard to calm down but it was very difficult.

"The school's where it always was of course," Myfanwy said in dismissive voice. "We are on a hill in Sussex. As I said, I needed to talk to you privately."

"But how can we be here?" I asked. "People can't just suddenly be in another place."

Myfanwy frowned. "You only say that because you think of yourself as solid and the world around you as fixed and unchanging," she said. "In reality, you are just energy and the world is an entwined tangle of possibilities. In all that tangle of possibilities there was a very small probability that we were both on a hill in Sussex. I just chose that possibility." She looked at me intently. "You have no magic at all, do you? You are immune to my power but you have no magic ability or perception of your own."

I shook my head. "Until I came to London, I thought magic was just impossible, the stuff of fantasy," I said.

"Then I'm sorry," she said. "I wasn't sure about you but I can see now that coming here like that must have really bothered you."

"Myfanwy," I said, "The power you have doesn't just bother me. It terrifies me. It's not that what you do with your power is wrong. I really admire the way you protect Wilson from Horace and his mates. I would really like a bird to come and sing to me when Mrs. Brown's class gets boring but I can't make it happen. No one can - except you. You have this weird power. Do you wonder that I am afraid? All I can do is trust that you will not use your power the same way that the guy in the black robe… "

"Apophis," she interrupted. "He calls himself Apophis – the Egyptian god of chaos. That is really unfair. What he did is against everything I believe in. How can you believe that I had anything to do with that? He is vile, cruel and arrogant. He hurt and he killed people! How can you believe that I would do things like that?" I could see tears in her eyes. The connection between her and this self-styled Apophis obviously hurt her deeply. Looking at her standing on that hill, with her dark hair falling in a cascade of curls around her anxious face, and with her brilliant green eyes fighting hard not to cry, I found that I was not angry with her anymore and that, even though her power still creeped me out, I was not afraid of her anymore.

"I don't really believe any of that," I said, "and I was wrong to suggest that you were like him in any way that mattered. I was afraid and the fear made me angry and the anger made me stupid. Please forgive me." I drew a deep breath and then said something that I knew was true only as I uttered it. "I do trust you."

"Apology accepted." She said. "I trust you also Thomas from Australia, even though I have never met anyone like you before and I don't understand you at all." She said paused. "That's a strange lot of trust between school classmates but perhaps not so much between… friends?" She gave the same tentative half smile and held out her hand. I nodded and took her hand.

Suddenly we were back at the front door of the school with kids running in to class. Wilson was coming up the steps and saw us shaking hands.

"At last!" He said. "Thank goodness for that. My life was getting just too complicated." When he had gone past, I said to Myfanwy, slowly and with great determination, "Do not do that again. It freaks me out."

"I'm sorry," she said, "but I had to get us back in time for class. Otherwise it would have taken all day for us to get back from that hill." While her logic was inescapable, I was still shaken. One thing was clear, Myfanwy was going to be an interesting person to have as a friend.

As we were going to home room class something else occurred to me and I whispered to Myfanwy, "How come no one noticed us popping in and out like that?"

"Oh, I cast an inattention spell. I do that quite often." She whispered back. That afternoon, as Mrs. Brown was droning on about the metaphysical poets, a small brown bird flew up to the sill of my window, looked me in the eye and started to sing. I don't know what sort of bird it was but it had a beautiful song.

The second anomalous event I was involved in happened later that week. Each day I would walk down the street to catch the bus home. At the end of the school's street there was a busy road which had a major bus stop with many buses heading to a whole lot of destinations. As I was waiting for my bus, Myfanwy came up to me and said,

"Don't catch the bus home tonight. My uncle is coming to meet me and I think you really need to meet my uncle. He will be able to answer a lot of your questions." I was about to say okay when Horace came up behind us and said,

"What? Kung Fu Warrior and Witch Girl planning a little date together. Ugh!" He shuddered in pretend horror.

Just as I turned to tell him to shut up, I heard the sound of screeching brakes and the clash of metal that could only be a traffic accident. I turned around and there was the black robed guy, this Apophis, standing in the middle of the road. There were smashed up cars around him but there was no doubt where his attention was. He was looking at me. I doubt that he was even aware of anyone else. He was staring at me with a look of intense hatred, a hatred focused to the heat of white hot anger. He pointed his finger at me and two of the buses parked on the other side of the road leaped into the air and came flying at me like missiles. Everything was happening too fast. I had no time to react. Then everything just stopped. All the kids around me froze in panicked flight, the two buses hung in midair and even Apophis was frozen in his pointing gesture.

"Run Tom! Run!" cried Myfanwy. "There's too much energy tied up in those buses. I can't hold them like this for long." Myfanwy was already running out of the way. I turned to join her but then I remembered Horace. He was still standing frozen, directly in the path of the flying buses. I thought, "He's a pig but he doesn't deserve to die." So I turned around and grabbed his frozen form.

"Quickly Tom, I can't hold them much longer." Myfanwy called. I tried to drag him as fast as I could but he was heavy. He was very heavy. I could see that Myfanwy's concentration was slipping and the buses were starting to move. I desperately heaved Horace out of the way and then Myfanwy's strength gave out and the two buses came crashing down, missing Horace and me by only inches. One slammed into a Chestnut tree in the street behind me while the other skidded down the street a short way. Horace struggled to his feet with a look of panic on his face. The Apophis character looked a bit confused for a moment but then his anger returned and he went to point his finger again.

"No Apophis you can't!" Myfanwy called and she held up her hands in a kind of warding motion. Apophis looked at her and, I think, noticed her for the first time. He smiled but it was not a pleasant smile. It was a smile to give you nightmares.

"My dear Myfanwy," he said in a deep Welsh voice. "You are such a long way from home." His face took on a look of mock sadness. "I'm afraid the time you always dreaded has come Myfanwy." He raised both his arms as if he were about to throw something at her. I started to run towards him, my only thought to stop him. Then it was taken from my hands.

"Stop," cried another voice. "This has gone far enough Arawn. It must stop now!" This voice was strong and confident and I turned to see a man dressed in a dark, conservative business suit and wearing a bowler hat. He was holding up his hands in a warding action similar to Myfanwy's. Apophis looked at him with an expression that changed from anger, to frustration and to despair. He gave a yell, a yell of such primal rage that it was hard to believe it came from a human throat. Then he just wasn't there anymore and all the world was filled with yells and screams as people tried to come to terms with what had happened.

I knew what would come next. The man in the bowler hat paused in thought for a moment and then started to smile and wave his hand at people. I knew that memories were being altered and that by the time the police and ambulances arrived everyone would remember this as a normal accident and no one would remember that Apophis had been here at all. I also knew that the man in the bowler hat was Myfanwy's uncle.

Horace was sitting on the ground a little way away. He got up and came over to me. "I remember you dragging me out of the way," he said. "I don't know if

I would have done that for you but I'm glad you did. Thanks." He put out his hand and I shook it. I knew it would mean little in a few days' time but at that point we were at peace.

"No worries Ace," I said. "No worries at all."

CHAPTER 6
Aelred Abbey

The police came, the ambulances came, the fire trucks came and slowly order emerged from the chaos. Fortunately both buses had been nearly empty and no one had been killed although a number of people, including both bus drivers and some kids from the school, had been seriously injured. All the time that the ambulance paramedics were doing triage on the injured and the police were taking statements from witnesses, Myfanwy and her uncle sat off to one side, under one of the old chestnut trees in the street, and no one took any notice of them. Occasionally her uncle would wave and smile. It became clear that everyone now remembered one bus colliding with another and both skidding out of control across the street, crashing into cars as they went. Towards the end of the collection of witness statements a policewoman came over to me,

"We have heard that you pulled one of your classmates out of the path of one of those buses," she said.

"Yes," I said, surprised that this story had survived the memory changes "He sort of froze, from shock I guess, so I just pulled him out of the way." The policewoman nodded,

"That was a good job," she said as she put her notebook away. "A very good job."

I walked over to where Myfanwy and her uncle were sitting and sat down beside her. She introduced her uncle to me as Cadfan Ap Rhys. He shook my hand and then studied me intently as a scientist might study a specimen of a new species.

"I saw you on Westminster Bridge," I said. "You changed people's memories then so that they remember something which is untrue. They forgot that this Apophis character was ever there. You have done the same thing here today." I felt the old anger building up inside me. "What gives you the right to do this?" I asked rather loudly. "These are people, not puppets! They have a right to their lives, to their real memories. If they are being threatened, they have a right to know the nature of the threat so that they can face it. They are people with freedom and dignity! They have a right to the truth! They are not things to be manipulated by you at will!" As I finished I realized that I had been yelling. I took a deep breath and tried to calm down.

"I am sorry for yelling," I said, "but I still think it's wrong." All through this he kept looking at me with the same calm, studious expression. My outburst didn't faze him in the least.

"As it happens, in principle I agree with you Thomas." He said. "However, here I am in the position of needing to choose the lesser evil. You will notice that I not only preserved but spread the memory of you saving your classmate. A good deed deserves to be remembered, I think. We do need to discuss these things but we also need more time and more convivial surroundings. I think you should come and have dinner with us tonight and I believe that is your mother calling you." A fraction of a second later my mobile phone started to ring. It was, indeed, my mother. She had heard of the accident on the news and was checking up on me. I told her that I was alright;

and yes it was strange that big bus accidents seemed to happen near me; and yes it was lucky that I was never at the centre of the damage. She then went on talking, wondering how I was going to get home since the buses were, obviously, all fouled up, the traffic was awful and that night you couldn't get a taxi in London for a king's ransom.

"Could I speak to her for a moment Thomas?" asked Myfanwy's uncle. I gave him the phone.

"Hello Mrs. O'Malley," I heard him say. "This is Professor Rhys. My niece is a school friend of your Thomas. Yes, they are both okay but my niece is a bit shaken. I wonder if Thomas could stay and have dinner with us tonight. I would drive him home afterwards…" As he was speaking I looked at Myfanwy. She did seem upset. She was very pale and when she raised her hand to brush something from her eye, it was shaking. I rather awkwardly put one arm around her shoulder as if to say "It's okay, it's over". As soon as I did, she threw her arms around my neck and started sobbing into my shoulder. I didn't know what to do. I just sat there like a lump of wood and awkwardly tried to pat her back – as if she were a dog.

"…yes, yes I'll have him home by ten." Myfanwy's uncle was saying, "Nice to talk to you too. Bye." As he finished talking, Myfanwy pulled back and brushed the tears from her eyes.

"I'm sorry Thomas…"she said. I could see that she was embarrassed but I interrupted her,

"Hey! There is absolutely nothing to be sorry about. Friends, remember?" She smiled and nodded. "Anyway, what happened here," I looked across at her uncle, "what really happened here, was bad enough to give anyone the shakes."

Her uncle gave a small smile. "And yet you seem to have none." He said as he handed back my phone. "What happened here is worse than you know young Thomas but we can discuss that over dinner. Come on. There is a gate to my house in the next street."

I did wonder why he said 'a gate to my house' and not just 'my house'. I got more anxious when we got to the gate. It didn't seem to have a house behind it. It was an old wooden gate with a sort of archway above it. It looked perfectly normal except that it didn't lead anywhere. Behind the gate there was about three feet of grass and then the wall of an old church. Nonetheless, Professor Rhys opened the gate and invited me to walk through. As soon as I stepped through I found myself on a path through a small wood, surrounded by barren, winter birch trees. I was expecting something strange but I was still a bit stunned. I looked behind me and there was the gate, with Myfanwy and her uncle coming through it, but now it seemed to open onto a country lane. Professor Rhys walked past me.

"Come on," he said. "The house is up here." I was still standing there looking around me when Myfanwy came past.

"You are in a place that belongs to my people now Thomas," she said smiling. "Magic may not happen to you but I can promise that magic will happen around you." When I just sort of stayed standing there trying to sort things out, she grabbed my hand and almost dragged me down the path. "Come on," she said eagerly.

After a very short walk we came out of the birch wood and looked out across a coastal marsh. It was just before sunset that time, when I first saw the house, and the red light of the setting sun made it contrast sharply against the dark background of sea and evening sky. It was on a small rise in the middle of the marsh. A broad, elevated causeway connected it to the mainland where we stood. The house itself was dominated by a tall, square Norman tower with some low buildings and what looked like a church off on the right hand side. Professor Rhys made a broad sweeping gesture with his hand,

"Welcome to Aelred Abbey," he said with an obvious pride. He then set off walking down the causeway, talking as he went.

"The oldest buildings in the abbey itself have foundations that date back to the ninth century, although there could well have been a small monastic settlement here even before that. However, most of the abbey buildings are much younger. The tower was built in the 1357, during the Hundred Years' War, and garrisoned by the king's soldiers. It was to protect the coastline from raids by pirates, slavers and so on. The last time it was used as a military stronghold was during the English Civil War. A group of royalists made a stand here before they were dispossessed, rather brutally if I may say so, by Cromwell's forces. After that it was given to one of Cromwell's captains as a reward and has been in private hands ever since. The normal changes were made to the tower to change it from a fortress to a house: windows, doors, that sort of thing. The abbey buildings were converted to stables." Following along after him, I was still trying to cope with the rapid change in location.

I muttered, "Toto, I don't think we're in London anymore." I muttered it under my breath but Myfanwy heard me.

"Of course not silly, you're in Norfolk." She said. "How could you fit a great castle like that into any place in London?"

The front doors of the tower house were huge double affairs of polished wood. They swung open silently as we approached and closed after us. As we entered, the lights came on in the castle. I was half expecting to see flaming torches or floating candles but all the lights seemed to be standard electrical fittings. The entrance hall was not that huge but it did have a large wooden staircase which wound around the side and back wall, leading to the upper floors. There was a small, plain door in the back wall, under the staircase. I guessed that led to the kitchen. There were also large, polished doors to the right and left. Myfanwy's uncle turned to the right and those doors also swung open silently. This led to a large formal dining room with a long table of dark, highly polished wood in the centre. There were bright tapestries of medieval scenes hanging to cover the stone walls. Three candelabras were spaced out along the length of the table and these came alight as Myfanwy's uncle waved at them. Almost the whole back wall was taken up with a stone arch over a huge fire place. Myfanwy's uncle pointed at this and a blazing log fire appeared.

"Sit down, sit down," he said. "Dinner will be ready in a minute." We all sat down at the end of the table closest to the fire, with Myfanwy's uncle at the head and Myfanwy and I next to him and facing across from each other. This left most of the table vacant. It was like we were expecting guests who hadn't arrived yet. I smiled to myself. Three people sitting up in a place this size was faintly ridiculous.

Shortly after we sat down a tray appeared in front of us. On it there were three plates with what appeared to be frozen, microwave dinners – the kind you buy at a supermarket. There were also glasses of what turned out to be coke. I must have looked a little surprised because Myfanwy laughed,

"What were you expecting?" She asked. "A huge medieval feast with roast boar, venison and tankards of mead?"

I smiled ruefully. "Something a bit like that I guess." I said as I reached for my plate. "This seems a bit too normal to fit in with a magic castle."

As he cut into his Chicken Kiev and peas, Myfanwy's uncle explained. "Thomas, there are limits to our power. Everything you do takes energy, whether you do it by magic or physically, it takes about the same amount of energy. That's why the lights in this house are electric and take their power from the power grid just like in any other house. It's easier that way. These meals are easy to heat and serve and that's true whether you use magic or a microwave oven. The more spectacular the magic you attempt the more energy is required. If you tried to live entirely by magic, summoning your food for example, you could soon be exhausted." I thought about this for a moment and I could see an immediate problem.

"Throwing two buses into the air would take a huge amount of energy," I said. "Far more than one human could have. How can this Apophis character do it?" Myfanwy's uncle nodded.

"A good point," he said. "Talent and skill come into it. If you have the talent you can use the energy around you to do things that you could not do on your own. You might call it ambient or environmental energy. The more skilled you are the less you rely on your own energy.

Each of us has areas of magic that we are particularly good at, just as some people might have a talent for music or football. Arawn, the one who calls himself Apophis, is particularly good at telekinetics: moving material things around. Myfanwy seems to have a unique relationship with other living things. My skill on the other hand is in knowing the human mind. When I look at a person I can see the whole structure of their mind; the ordered surface thoughts, the hopes and fears of their subconscious and even down to the primal urges that drive them. Yes, I can also change them if I need to. Something I do rarely, only in great need and only with the greatest care." He paused and looked at me thoughtfully.

"Yet, when I look at you Thomas I see nothing." He continued. "No, it's more than that. When I look at you it's as if I have no magic at all, as if magic doesn't exist. You are a great surprise to us. When Myfanwy first came to me in great distress and told me of what had happened, I found it hard to believe her. In all our history we know of only one other who was anything like you. Even then, he was not quite the same. You would know him as Sir Percival or Parsifal but we remember him by his true name: Peretur."

I looked up in surprise. "You mean the knight?" I asked in disbelief. "From the Arthur legend?"

He nodded. "The same," he said. "It is extremely interesting to us that you should turn up just as Arawn Ap Cadell starts his campaign." Then he clapped his hands together and smiled broadly.

"Now, what shall we have for dessert?" he asked. "I think some chocolate pudding and ice cream is in order." With that the used plates vanished and the pudding appeared.

CHAPTER 7
Family History

After we had finished the dessert, we moved across to the room on the other side of the hall. This was a sort of combination lounge room and library. Instead of tapestries, the walls here were lined with bookshelves and there were armchairs and small tables scattered through the room. I looked at the titles of some of the books but they were perfectly ordinary, although a lot of them were in Welsh or Latin. There were no books like "Spells for Fun and Profit" or "Magic for Dummies" or anything like that. There was a fire place at one end of the room which was a mirror image of the one in the dining room. This also had a blazing log fire. We sat around this in large, leather armchairs and three mugs of hot chocolate appeared on a small table in front of us. As I sat back in my chair and sipped my hot chocolate, Myfanwy's uncle began to tell the sad tale of how Apophis came to be as he was. Professor Rhys was not a great storyteller and coming from him the story sounded a bit like a lecture on the dullest of constitutional law. During the telling, Myfanwy sat and gazed into the fire, its light reflecting off her pale skin. Her expression was hard to read. It was certainly sad and as the explanation went on it just got sadder.

"I have decided, in consultation with my community that you need to know about the person who calls himself Apophis. You need to know for two reasons. Firstly, if Apophis is hunting you, and we believe he is, then you need to know why. Secondly, we don't believe your coming at this time is accidental. There is a purpose behind this and I believe that you are destined to play a key role in this drama."

"Professor," I interrupted. "Could I ask two questions first? I am no threat to Apophis, so why is he hunting me? And why do you call him Arawn when he calls himself Apophis?"

"Both good questions to start with," he replied. "You may be no physical threat to Arawn but you do threaten his whole idea of reality. You are an abomination to him, something that shouldn't exist. It is disconcerting for Myfanwy and myself to look at you and see a blank where magic should be – for him this would be deepest horror. His whole self-image is based around the idea that his magic makes him a superior being. Your very existence suggests that perhaps he is human after all. It was a shock for him when he found he couldn't kill you by magic but he has worked out that if he hurls something large and heavy at you, like a bus, then the impact will kill you by quite natural means."

"On the bridge?" I asked. "He was trying to kill me by pointing his finger?"

"Yes Thomas," Myfanwy said. "He was trying to explode your heart. He has done it before on poor folk who did not have your unique protection." She paused. "He tried to do it to me this afternoon. He would have if uncle Cadfan hadn't intervened. He is too strong for me." I looked at her still staring into the fire, with her dark curls and her pale skin turned red in the fire's light.

"No," I said. "I would not have let him." Even if he threw the whole of the London public transit system at me, I thought, I would have not let him hurt you. Of course, I couldn't say that out loud.

Myfanwy looked up at me and smiled as she said, "Thomas the warrior!" Then she paused and said softly and seriously, "I know for certain that you would have tried your very hardest."

Her uncle gave a small cough. "Um…yes, well, as to the second question, his real name, the name he grew up with is Arawn, Arawn ap Cadell. Since his teen years he has insisted on everyone calling him Apophis. His given name means wildness while the second comes from Egyptian mythology. It is the snake of chaos which threatens to destroy the world. I prefer to call him by his given name because there is a certain, limited good in wildness: a certain freedom and joy. In chaos there is only destruction. I fear, however, that he has long ago moved from Arawn to Apophis.

This has to do with the crisis that is facing our community. A crisis as great as the one we faced 1600 years ago, when Rome withdrew from Britain. Indeed, in many ways our current crisis has its origins in those ancient, chaotic days. At that time our community was fully integrated into the general run of humanity and when Roman Britain failed, we became involved in the political process. One of our great families proposed to use magic to rule all of Britain, to establish a great Witch-queen who would hold all political and religious power. She gathered a great army from the pagan tribes to support her. Another of our great families strongly opposed this approach. They believed that magic should be used to serve and guide, not to rule. They sponsored a group of young, Romano-British officers from the local Roman militia. These were led by a young prince whom the legions voted as Dux Bellorum – war leader. Under his leadership, and with the guidance of a mentor from our people, they managed to hold together the local militia and tried to preserve order and the rule of Roman law. They succeeded for a while and this became a rare period of peace which has passed into legend. Eventually, these opposing approaches led to conflict and disaster. In that clash, there was so much death and bloodshed that our people withdrew from common contact with most of humanity in horror, the two great families retreating together into exile. We have remained in isolation ever since."

"Hang on," I interrupted, "You're talking about the Arthur legend!"

"Yes and no," he replied. "The Arthur legend in its origins, not in the form that you know it. The legend you know is heavily embroidered by French concepts of romantic, courtly love. Yet there is true memory there. The Witch-queen you will know as Morgana while the one you know as Merlin was the mentor to the young Dux Bellorum – King Arthur.

The important point here is that we went into isolation and as a result have been slowly dying ever since. You see Thomas, our people are blessed with very long life but the cost is that we have very few children, too few children. This means that each child is precious to us in a way that doesn't seem common in your world.

The two great families, however, persisted and their opposition remained as great as ever. One March, many years ago now, there was a boy, an eldest son, born to each of these families. The two boys were more talented in magic than any before them. One was Owyn who was born to Merlin's house. Owyn was like the sun. He would take joy in everything." He smiled. "I remember he once had great fun mucking out Bronwyn ap William's pigsty, by hand mind you. No magic. When the farmer Bronwyn thanked him, he simply laughed and produced a most beautiful and fragrant red rose. To cover the smell, he said. It was a spectacular and wondrous piece of magic done as casually as waving your hand. He was my brother and I loved him dearly.

Cadell was the son born to Morgana's tribe. If Owyn was the sun then Cadell was darkness. He would do nothing that he didn't have to and would use magic to perform even the smallest of tasks. He seemed to take no pleasure in anything but the exercise of his talent and he was a manipulative bully from his earliest days in the crib. The boys despised each other from the beginning.

Because we knew our world was slowly dying, we have for a long time now sent our children to be educated in normal secondary schools, so that they understand the wider world. This house," here he spread his arms wide and looked about him, "was established to be their home while at school in Britain. In their time, Owyn and Cadell were both sent to different schools. Each proved to be brilliant academically. Owyn went on the university while Cadell, on the death of his father, retreated to his family house where he lived alone with his books. He then returned to Britain and we lost track of him for about two years. When he returned he brought with him a son, almost a year old. We don't know anything about the mother nor the details of his conception and birth but Cadell set about to raise him on his own. Arawn he called him and wild he always was.

Now, at about this time I knew that Owyn was seeing someone, someone not of our community. However, it was a shock to the rest of the community when he finally brought Helen home over one university holiday. She was the first non-magical person to visit us for a long, long, long time. She is also such a loving and cheerful person that no one was surprised that my brother loved her and the community readily accepted her. Two years later they were married and I was proud to serve as best man. A mere ten months after that Myfanwy was born. It may seem ironic to you but the rapidity of her conception and the ease of her birth seemed miraculous. She was a blessing to us." He looked at Myfanwy with great affection and Myfanwy smiled back at him.

"All seemed to be well for a while. The raising of Arawn seemed to soften Cadell to some extent and, to our great joy, Helen gave birth to a boy, Carwyn, a mere three years after Myfanwy."

I turned to Myfanwy. "You have a brother?" I queried. "You have never mentioned a brother."

"There was no need." Myfanwy said. "If you must know I have both a brother and a sister and Carwyn is mostly a little pest. Anyway, he's at school in Ireland and he is not at all important."

"Be that as it may," interrupted her uncle. "About a year later Cadell returned to Britain, we think to get another child so as to match Owyn's family. This time we kept a trace on him but the visit was an absolute disaster anyway. I won't go into the details because they are most unpleasant." He paused. "No, that's not right. They are evil and cruel. Anyway, at least five poor women died and Cadell returned to our land.

Owyn was filled with disgust and anger. His fury blazed in him like a torch and he went to confront Cadell. They were both powerful and skilled and the battle between them was epic. It tore apart the forest, it tore down the sides of mountains, it left Cadell's family house, the house that had stood for over a thousand years, in ruins. Owyn was powerful and Cadell was left crippled and almost blind." He paused and took a deep breath before continuing.

"In final desperation, Cadell used a terrible spell and it left Owyn, my beloved brother, dead. It was only six months later that Myfanwy's sister, Gwyneth, was born, never to know her father." I looked quickly across at Myfanwy and tears were flowing silently and freely down her cheeks. I knew now what her expression was. It was not sorrow, it was grief. I had lost two of my grandparents in a car accident three years ago so I knew something of the bitterness of that pain. I knew that those people who speak of 'closure' have no idea what they are talking about. When Myfanwy looked up at me I silently mouthed 'sorry'. She nodded and did not bother to wipe away her tears. It was a long time before Myfanwy's uncle continued but when he did he did so quite briskly,

"So this is how Arawn was raised: alone, by his crippled father, a father who was driven mad by hate and frustrated ambition, glorying only in the exercise of his magical talent and in the ruins of his family house. What chance did he have? He was educated in his father's favorite philosophy, the philosophy of a

German by the name of Nietzsche. Nietzsche famously believed that God, whom he considered to be a cultural product, was dead but that evolution would supply a replacement – the overman or superman. This superman would have the ability and the 'will to power' to overcome all difficulties. It would be his strength of will which would ensure that the superman triumphed in the chaos that would end the rule of man and establish the rule of the superman. It was about this time that Arawn started calling himself Apophis.

Perhaps Arawn misunderstood this philosophy, perhaps not, but he came to see himself as the superman who had the necessary 'will to power'. He left our land for the wider world. He set out to create the magic empowered kingdom of his long dead ancestor, to make himself a Witch-king whose service would give meaning to the lives of those he considered little better than apes. That 'meaning' would have been a cruel servitude indeed. Fortunately, he found he couldn't do it. In a highly technical and complicated world of six billion people, his magic could do little to sway events of any significance. Even more, he found that the natural powers he so despised were still very powerful and that normal people had a strength of spirit to overmatch his own, even though they didn't have his power. All his plans, his very understanding of reality, failed.

From this point on we can only speculate about what happened because he simply disappeared from our view for several years. Until, that is, some very nasty things started to happen and people started to die in odd and cruel ways. I was sent to try and keep track of him, to capture him if possible and to preserve, as far as possible, the normal order of people's lives." Here Myfanwy's uncle paused again. When he spoke again it was slowly and thoughtfully.

"I think he is now truly mad. He seems to have become filled with a kind of mad despair. He has decided that there is no point in living a life that is meaningless to him. Unfortunately he has also decided that no one else should live either, especially not Myfanwy and her siblings who represent the hope of our people. So he has truly become Apophis, bent on destruction and chaos." There was silence for a long time after he had finished. I put my empty mug down on the table.

"So," I said, "What we are faced with is a psychotic mass murderer who has the magical power to change reality and who is bent on murder/suicide where the murder part includes the attempted destruction of the world." Professor Rhys gave a wry smile.

"Fortunately not," he said, "There is no way he could develop the power to destroy the world but he can cause a lot of damage and he can kill a lot of people." The first half of this statement proved to be simply wrong. We didn't know it at the time but Professor Rhys had overlooked something vital.

CHAPTER 8
A Holiday Proposal

"Good gracious," Professor Rhys said looking at his watch. "Is that the time? I promised to have you home by ten and we are still in Norfolk. What's your home address?" I told him and he said, "Good. I have a gate just in the next street. Come on, we will need to hurry." As the three of us crossed the causeway, as sphere of light surrounded us. Where we walked was bright as day while everywhere else it was a dark night. When we got to the gate on the other side of the wood I could see the night covered fields beyond it. Yet, when Professor Rhys invited me to go through, I ended up in a London street just around the corner from my house. Myfanwy and her uncle followed and we walked over to my house.

Mum opened the door and there were the usual introductions and mum said thank you for having me to tea and the Professor said it was no trouble and that I was a great help to Myfanwy: all the usual stuff that people go on with. The professor then held out his hand,

"Goodbye Thomas," he said. "I'm sure I will see you again very soon." I shook his hand and then turned to Myfanwy.

"Goodnight Thomas," she said. "I'll see you at school tomorrow." With that she up and kissed me on the cheek! I could feel my face burning hot. As they were walking away down the street, she looked over her shoulder with a kind of annoying, satisfied smile. When mum closed the door she had a very strange look on her face – a look like she had found out a secret.

"Why didn't you tell me about your girlfriend, young man?" she asked.

"She's not my girlfriend mum." I said, "She's just a friend." Mum raised her eyebrows quizzically.

"You must have noticed that she's gorgeous and her accent is pure music." she said. I shrugged. There are some things you don't want to discuss with your mother, no matter how much she may want you to.

The next day at school we had a special assembly where the headmaster gave an update on the students who had been injured. They were all recovering well. He then spoke at length of the trauma we had all suffered and assured us that counselling would be available for any student that needed it. Towards the end of the talk he reminded us all that next week was the start of the mid-term break and that we should all use the time to rest and recuperate from the traumatic events of the yesterday. In the stress of all that had happened, I had forgotten all about the mid-term break. I had two weeks with nothing to do but wander around London - that hadn't turned out well last time.

At lunch time Myfanwy sat down at the table while Wilson was in the process of trying explain differential calculus to Gabriella. She waved her hand and everything froze.

"We need to talk privately." She said. "Meet me in the corridor in five minutes." Then time started to flow again and Wilson was trying to contain his frustration at Gabriella's continued confusion.

"It's really very simple." He said. "I don't know why you are having this trouble." Myfanwy made an excuse and left and I finished my glass of reconstituted orange juice and followed her a few minutes later. She was waiting for me in the corridor.

"Come on," She said and took my hand. All of a sudden we were on a narrow path across the top of some cliffs overlooking the sea, a long way from London. Even though it had happened before and I guess I knew it might happen again, the shock of it was still hard to cope with. I felt a light headed at the change. Fortunately there was an old wooden seat nearby and I was glad to sit down.

"Please, I asked you not to do that! It really freaks me out," I said shakily.

"Sorry Thomas, but this is urgent," Myfanwy said. "You are in real danger and not just you but all those around you as well. Uncle Cadfan set some alarms in your street last night so that he would know if Apophis turned up. This morning they were all tripped. Thomas, he is actively hunting you and he is determined to kill you. He now knows where you live and he is figuring out how best to get at you. You and your mother need to get out of that house!"

I spread my hands in frustration. "I know that!" I said. "But how am I going to do it? Mum has her work based in London. What am I going to say to her? 'Mum, we need to go because a psychotic wizard is trying to kill us?' Somehow I don't think that would work. I'd just end up spending a lot of time chatting to those counsellors the headmaster is so fond of."

"Look, we have a plan." She said. "Uncle Cadfan can arrange for your mum to get a really great assignment covering a fashion show in Milan. Apophis has such an obsessed focus on you that I think he will ignore her once she is out of the country. You we need to get to a place where we can protect you. At this short notice Uncle Cadfan thinks that Aelred Abbey would be the best place. It would be very hard for Apophis to attack you there. The plan is this: your mother gets a job assignment she really wants to take in Milan, she doesn't know what to do with you, you then get invited to spend the mid-term break with us, she sees it as the answer to her problems and accepts. She is out of the country and you are in a protected place. After that, we can see what we can do to arrange long term protection." She paused for a while. Then she looked at me directly with her emerald green eyes.

"Thomas, this is the best plan that we can come up with but I don't want you pushed into anything. I need to know that you agree to this, that you think it is a good idea." I nodded and said,

"Sure, it sounds like a plan," I said. In fact, I was trying to keep my eagerness in check. If it were not for the psychotic wizard trying to kill me, this would be perfect. "But my Mum will never go for it."

"Good." She said. "Uncle Cadfan will talk to your mother. He has attached some inattention and confusion spells to your house. They should keep you safe for a few days, at least until the plan goes into action. Umm…they might also mean that you don't get any mail delivered for a while. Come on now, we have to get back to class."

"Wait a minute," I said. "What was all that with kissing me goodbye last night. You have raised all my mother's inquisitive instincts and that is going to cause me no end of trouble and embarrassing questions."

She looked at me with a mischievous grin. "That was the idea," she said and with that we were back in the school corridor. I found that the sudden transition didn't bother me as much this time. It is always a bit disconcerting but you do get used to it after a while.

That night mum was both excited and anxious at the same time. She was very chatty over dinner but it wasn't until dessert that she came to the point.

"Tom," she said. "I have just been given a really great opportunity. I have been asked to cover an exclusive fashion show in Milan for one of London's top society magazines. As a fashion photographer, it doesn't really get any better than that. The trouble is, if I take this job I'll be away for the two weeks of your mid-term break and I'm not sure if I can take you and I don't think I should leave you alone." This genuinely exasperated me and, in spite of what I knew of the plan, my response was quite heartfelt.

"Look mum, I'm sixteen. I'm a big boy now and I can look after myself. Mum, I want you to make the most of this chance. You came to London to progress your career, so go! Progress it!" She hesitated and started to say something. "No!" I said. "It's only for two weeks for Pete's sake. I'll be Okay." At that point the doorbell rang. It was Myfanwy's uncle, standing there holding his bowler hat in his hands and looking very apologetic.

"I am very sorry to disturb you Mrs. O'Malley. I hope you remember me, I am Professor Rhys the uncle of Myfanwy, one of Tom's school friends. I was just passing and thought I would take the opportunity to call in and offer my invitation in person." Given that she had only met him yesterday, mum did of course remember him and she invited him in for a cup of tea. As he was sitting sipping his tea, he made his pitch.

"Mrs. O'Malley, my family owns a large and historic house, well it's a sort of castle really, on the Norfolk coast. Myfanwy was planning to spend the mid-term break there by herself, with just myself and my housekeeper for company. I was wondering if Tom would like to come and stay with us for part, or indeed all of the break. We have plenty of room and it would be good for Myfanwy to have some company her own age. It would also let Tom see something of Britain other than the London crowds." Mum looked a bit doubtful but the Professor held up his hands in a reassuring gesture. "I assure you I insist on the very highest standards of behaviour and they would at all times be under the adult supervision of either myself or my housekeeper." Mum looked very doubtful and I thought she was about to say no when she suddenly smiled,

"Tom was just telling me that he was all grown up now and didn't need any adult supervision." She said. The professor rolled his eyes.

"I may be old fashioned," he said. "But I doubt that that is entirely true." My mum, of course, entirely agreed. The conversation went on for a while and mum found out that Professor Rhys held a research chair at a prestigious London university where he studied people's emotional motivations – something his particular talents would have made him very good at. I, however, was suspicious and getting angry. At last mum excused herself and asked me to help her in the kitchen. I said I would be there in a minute and that I just wanted to ask the professor a question.

When she had gone I turned to the Professor and challenged him, "You just did something to my mother's mind! She wouldn't normally agree to this."

"Now Tom, you know the plan," the professor said. "Your mother was seriously considering the options and I just gave her a small nudge to go in a direction she might not otherwise have chosen."

"But she is my mother," I whispered fiercely, "and you have manipulated her like some kind of puppet!"

The Professor looked at me sadly, "Yes Tom, I manipulated her," he said. "I manipulated her by getting her the job in Milan and I interfered with her decision making tonight. I am deeply sorry but this is the only way I can think of to keep her alive. I know for certain that even as we speak, Arawn is working out how to kill you and all those around you." I was silent for a while, caught between indignation and fear. Finally I nodded: it was better that my Mum be safe.

When I went out to the kitchen she asked, "Well young man, would you like to go and spend two weeks with your girlfriend?"

"Friend, mum," I said firmly. "Friend, not girlfriend! Do I want to have a holiday in an ancient castle by the seaside or do I want to kick around here for two weeks? I would rather take the castle thanks."

Mum nodded and when we went back we accepted the professor's offer. Mum explained that she had business in Milan and that it would help her if I could stay the whole of the break.

The professor smiled broadly, "Splendid!" he said as he shook my hand. "Tom, I look forward to getting to know you better. How about I pick you up at about noon on Saturday?" As he was leaving I looked across and for a moment thought I saw a dark shadow moving through the park. We had to get out of this house!

That Saturday, Professor Rhys drove up in a classic 1960s Rolls Royce, precisely at noon. I had my bags already packed, including a large number of thick jumpers and my warmest coat, and was ready to go. It was the need to reassure my mum that meant we had to use the car rather than just walk through the gate in the next street but it also meant I didn't have to carry my bags across the causeway.

Myfanwy was standing by the car when I dragged my travel bag down the steps. I sort of stopped where I was when I saw her. It was the first time I had seen her out of school uniform. She was just wearing jeans, joggers and a jumper, pretty much standard gear, but they fitted her in precisely the way that Mrs. Brown's clothes didn't fit her. I found myself feeling strangely shy.

"You look nice." I said quietly.

She gave a mock curtsey and answered in a highly theatrical southern American accent, "Why thank you kind sir." I could feel myself blushing so I concentrated on putting my bag in the car boot. I waved goodbye to mum and climbed into the back seat with Myfanwy. Professor Rhys said a few final words to my mother and then we drove off.

"Thomas" the professor said as we drove through the crowded London streets. "I would like to assure you that you will be completely safe at Aelred Abbey. So please, just relax and enjoy the break."

"Thank you sir," I said. "I will be glad to get out of London. It's very crowded and I don't really like crowds."

"Really?" Myfanwy said with fake disapproval, "Samuel Johnston said that the man who was sick of London was sick of life."

"Clearly," I replied, "Samuel Johnston never surfed." Myfanwy laughed and for the first time I was struck by how much I liked to hear her laugh. I quickly turned my attention out the window. This was how I noticed what a dream run we were having through London. All of the streets we drove down seemed to have little traffic, all of the traffic lights were green and we were driving very fast. Yet no one seemed to notice our passage: not the pedestrians, not the police and, I am certain, not the speed cameras. The ability to do magic clearly had a lot of advantages. It didn't take us long to get through London and on to the motorway. In fact, it didn't take long at all until the Rolls Royce was driving slowly over the gravel causeway and taking me back to the imposing bulk of Aelred Abbey.

CHAPTER 9
Brother Theophane

When we got out of the car, there was a short, rotund woman waiting to meet us at the front doors. It was hard to pick her age, although her hair was a mass of close cropped, grey curls. She was dressed in a bright floral dress with a white apron. I thought she must be the housekeeper but when Myfanwy saw her she ran up the steps, through her arms around her and said,

"Nain, Nain. It's so good to see you!" I stood there looking a little confused until Professor Rhys came up and introduced me.

"Thomas, this is Mother Perpetua. Nain, this is Thomas O'Malley from Australia. He is the boy we have been discussing." At this Myfanwy was abandoned and I found myself being embraced in a powerful hug.

"Welcome Thomas!" the grey haired woman said. "You must call me Nain. All my friends do and you are going to be one of my best friends. Now let me see." She then stared at me intently with the same emerald green eyes as the others. She stared at me for several seconds and after a while I started to get an itch between my eyes.

As I moved to scratch it she drew back and said, "Oh he's the genuine article alright. Couldn't get a grip anywhere." She burst into a huge delighted smile. "Come on, let's go to your room." She then put her hand on my shoulder and promptly disappeared. She reappeared, frowning at me, about a second later.

"Myfanwy," she said. "Could you take Thomas to the east room on the top floor please? Don't bother using all those stairs." Myfanwy looked as puzzled as I felt but she took my hand and then we were in a comfortable bedroom with three long, narrow windows overlooking the sea. I took a deep breath. It was getting easier but it was till upsetting. Nain appeared about a second later, looking very thoughtful.

"Now why is it young man that you will travel with Myfanwy but not with me?" she asked. "That you would not travel with me I can understand. It is part of your peculiar immunity to the power. But why is it then that Myfanwy can take you where she wills? There is something here I do not understand." That's okay, I thought. I don't understand any of this and I would just as soon not travel that way with anyone. Just then my luggage appeared about a foot above the bed and promptly fell, bounced and rolled off. Nain once again broke into her broad smile.

"Come on Myfanwy," she said. "Let our guest get unpacked."

As they were leaving Myfanwy turned and said, "I'll see you in the library when you're ready."

My room turned out to be really comfortable. The three windows looked east out across a small gravel beach to the sea. I was on the fourth floor so the view was pretty good. It would have been better if the windows weren't so narrow and deep. I was pleased to see that I had a normal electric light, with a light switch, and a perfectly standard reading lamp by the bed. In the west wall there were two large doors, like the doors to an enormous wardrobe. Behind one of these was indeed a kind of walk in wardrobe while behind the other was a modern en suite bathroom. All in all it was like a room in a modern hotel, except that there was no television and no clock.

When I had finished packing my stuff away, I went down to the library to find Myfanwy. This involved walking down a large wooden staircase that went in a kind of square spiral down the outside wall, stopping at each floor and then starting again on the opposite wall. When I got to the entrance hall the doors of the library were open. In the library there were three large, mullioned windows which looked back, across the marsh, towards the land. Looking through them I could see a patchwork of small woods, hedgerows and fields. This was an alien land to me. It was small and well ordered. Australia, on the other hand, was large, untidy and untamed.

Myfanwy was in the library, sprawled sideways across a large leather chair and reading a book. When I came in she looked up and smiled.

"Hi," she said. "Would you like to come for a walk into the village? Go on, it's a pity to waste such a nice day."

I hesitated, "Would it be safe?" I asked.

"Of course it is, silly." She replied. "He wouldn't dare come anywhere near here. Certainly not with Nain and Uncle Cadfan staying here." She had already got up and was heading out the door. Even then I couldn't help but notice something which would become ever clearer over the break. Here, in her own world, where she could be herself, Myfanwy was different. At school she was reserved and withdrawn, always careful and defensive. Here she was filled with an eager joy which was quite infectious. At school her face was normally solemn and her smiles occasional. Here she smiled and laughed readily. It gave me an insight into how much of a strain it was on her to keep her talents hidden.

We strolled out across the causeway and up through the birch wood. This day the gate acted like a perfectly normal gate and we entered onto a winding country lane. The view from the lane was not great since there were grass banks and hedges either side but soon we could see the square tower of the village church and it was not long after that we came into the village itself. It was small and picturesque with shops and whitewashed, thatched cottages arranged around a square common. Our lane entered from the south and there were two much larger roads to the north and west. As soon as we got into the village my mobile phone started to buzz, telling me that I had a text message.

As I pulled it out Myfanwy looked across idly and said, "Those things don't work up at the abbey. Uncle doesn't like them. Who's it from?"

"Oh, nothing." I lied. "Just the Met messaging service telling me about delays on the underground." What the message really said was: "Contact us immediately. Can't find u. Need 2 talk 2 u urgently. Send address and we will pick u up. u r in real and immediate danger. Smith and Jones."

I turned the phone off and put it in my pocket but I didn't delete the message. I looked across at Myfanwy. She was casually looking in some of the shop windows. The message was deeply troubling. Were they referring to the ongoing threat of Apophis or did they know something dark about Myfanwy or her uncle? Did I have a public duty to tell them what I knew about the magic community? But if I did, wouldn't that be a betrayal of Myfanwy's trust? It seemed to me now that I was being caught between conflicting loyalties and that I wasn't really being faithful to either. Myfanwy noticed my troubled expression.

"Delays on the London underground can't really trouble us here you know." She said smiling. "Why don't we get an ice cream?" We went into the small grocery store and selected out ice creams from the freezer. I said I'd pay and went over to the counter where a narrow faced woman with a sour expression took my money. She looked with evident dislike at Myfanwy.

"You staying up at the Abbey?" she asked. I nodded. "You stayed there before?" I shook my head and said that this was the first time. "Well take my advice which I give you for free." She said. "Don't mind how pretty she is, you go and book into the Howard's B&B across the square. My Fred did some work up there and he could tell you some tales!" She leaned forward and whispered, "The place is haunted."

"I'm sorry," I said, "but I don't believe in ghosts." She drew back and gave me a very haughty look.

"You will, young man. If you stay at the abbey, you will." She said.

As we were leaving the shop I could see that Myfanwy was trying not to laugh. Outside, I asked her what was so funny.

"Oh Thomas," she said, caught between laughing and speaking. "You do not believe in ghosts! You believe in a guy who can throw around buses with his mind, you believe that I can take your hand and we can travel instantly to somewhere miles away, you believe that I can slow down time but you don't believe in ghosts. I think that's hilarious. What are your grounds for disbelief?" I thought about it as we walked back down the lane.

"Ghosts are creepy," I said at last. "I don't believe that the spirits of the dead stay around here. I think they move on to wherever they're going." She was silent for a while after this, concentrating on eating her ice cream. She finished as we turned down through the birch wood and onto the causeway.

She started to say, "You are right about the dead…" but was interrupted by the sound of horses' hooves behind us. We moved over to the side and three mounted knights rode past – three mounted knights in armour, with shields and lances. They vanished just before the end of the causeway. I stood rooted to the spot, once again unable to make sense of what I had seen - caught between panic and disbelief. It was a feeling I was becoming used to.

"As I was saying before we were interrupted," said Myfanwy. "I think you are right about the spirits of the dead but you are wrong about ghosts."

After we got back, I went up to my room to rest and clean up before dinner. It was just before sunset, with the eastern sky outside my windows already dark, when I made my way down to the dining room. Somehow, I must have taken a wrong turn because I found myself in a room I had never seen before. It was long and narrow with a tiled floor and bare stone walls. At the other end of the room was an open, pointed archway and coming through this was an old monk in the black habit of the Benedictine Order. He looked almost as surprised to see me as I was to see him. He looked somewhat forbidding with his black robe, his bald head and his face deeply lined by age. Then he smiled and his face was transformed to a picture of welcome.

"Dominus vobiscum, the Lord be with thee!" he said. "Pray, how may I help thee?"

"I'm sorry brother," I said. "I must have taken a wrong turn somewhere. I was looking for the dining room."

The monk shook his head. "Thou art conflicted over a matter which, for all thy worry, thou canst bring to a conclusion. If t'were not so, thou wouldst not have found thy way to this room." He said. "Come, sit thee down and I shall give thee what advice I may." He indicated a bare wooden bench along one wall. I hesitated for a moment but this did not feel like magic, it felt normal. I decided to go with the flow and sat down on the bench next to the monk. He looked at me with a deeply lined but kind face and gentle, brown eyes. I started to tell him about my conflicted loyalties between DIAP and Myfanwy and her people. I found it very easy to talk to him and I found myself telling him details that, until that moment, I had not admitted to myself. He was silent for a while after I had finished.

Then he said: "Hast thou sworn an oath to the princes of this land?" I told him that I hadn't and that I wasn't even from this country. In fact, not even my ancestors were from this country.

"Then thou dost owe them no more than the obedience of law and the maintaince of order. Ask thyself this: Hast thy friend, by the faith that she has shown thee, a right to thy loyalty and protection? Wouldst thy heart rather place thy trust in her or in these prince's men? Faith and trust, it is only upon these foundations that love can be built." Just then a bell started to toll. The monk got up from the seat.

"Pax, my son," he said. "Peace be with thee. I must go now. I am being called to Vespers." He turned and walked towards the archway.

"Brother!" I protested. "I need advice on a practical problem. I didn't say anything about love." He turned and looked me with a broad smile and laughing eyes.

"My son," he said. "Since thou hath been here, thou hast spoken of nothing else."

With this he walked through the archway. I stood there for a moment listening to the opening chants of the monks' evening prayer, then I turned and walked out the door. The way down the stair was now clear and I went down to the dining room. When I got there, the other three were already seated.

"I'm sorry I'm late." I said. "I got caught up talking to one of the monks. Actually, how is it that there are still monks here?" All three of them went very still and silent.

After an awkward pause, Myfanwy spoke: "Thomas, Henry the Eighth closed the monastery here in 1536. There have been no monks here for nearly five hundred years." Nain and Professor Rhys looked at each other.

"Brother Theophane," Nain said.

Professor Rhys nodded and said, "Now that is interesting, very interesting."

CHAPTER 10
Recreation and Attack

"Cadfan!" Nain said loudly, "Do you seriously propose that the four of us should eat in this hall designed to sit fifty? Is this some sort of practical joke or don't you realize how ridiculous this looks?" Professor Rhys looked surprised and Nain gave a snort of derision.

"Clearly not," she said. "Come on everyone, the kitchen is much more homey." Professor Rhys put his hand on my arm and then the three of them disappeared and I was left alone in the dining room. This was even more disconcerting since all the candles went out and the fire started to die down as soon as they left. Myfanwy reappeared a couple of seconds later.

"Come on slow coach" she said. Then she took my hand and immediately we were in the kitchen. Nain and Professor Rhys were in the middle of a conversation.

"…I can understand that and yet he will travel with Myfanwy." Nain was saying. As soon as she noticed us she turned towards us with a beaming smile and said, "Sit down my dears. This is a far more comfortable place to eat." Indeed it was. The kitchen was still large but it had a low ceiling and the normal, crowded informality of a functional room. One wall was almost entirely occupied by a large wood-fired stove. I assumed that the small door next to it led to the pantry. Along the opposite wall there were various modern stainless steel kitchen appliances. Along the inside wall there was a large dresser with plates and things while the outside wall had washtubs, windows and the door out to the garden. In the centre of the room was a simple wooden table with four chairs. On the table were four plates with a proper home cooked meal of roast beef, vegetables and gravy.

As we were sitting down, Nain looked across at Myfanwy without any trace of a smile and said in a most serious voice, "Remember Myfanwy that you must be careful, you more than anyone else." It sounded like a warning. Suddenly the holiday Myfanwy was gone and the school Myfanwy was back, with her solemn face and her reserved, slightly aloof manner.

As we started to eat, Myfanwy asked in a rather cross voice, "Who is Brother Theophane and how can Thomas talk to him?"

Professor Rhys answered, "Brother Theophane was, or rather is, a monk who lived in the monastery here in the fifteenth century. He was renowned for his holiness and wisdom and people would come from all over the country to ask his advice. The story goes that as he was dying he asked a special favour of God. The favour was that he should continue to be able to advise those in special need. It is said that ever since then, when some individuals come into either the monastery ruins or this house, they find their way into the presence of Brother Theophane and he will listen to them and advise them on their problems."

"So he is not like the ghosts," I asked, "Not like those knights who passed us on the causeway?"

"No" Professor Rhys said. "Those are simply visible echoes of the past."

"You can't talk to them" Myfanwy interjected.

"No." Professor Rhys continued. "Brother Theophane is very much alive and living in the fifteenth century. He has just been given the ability to interact with the people who need him wherever they might be in time. This has nothing to do with ghosts or magic. It is something far more powerful. The interesting thing is that his interviews are very rare. Do not be offended that you have not come across him Myfanwy. He chooses his clients with great care. That is why it is so interesting that he spoke to you, young Thomas."

The rest of the meal passed pleasantly, except that I was told off very sternly by Mother Perpetua for not calling her "Nain"- a nickname that I think means grandma in Welsh. That night I took my mobile phone from my pocket, deleted the DIAP message and buried the phone at the bottom of my bag. Faith and trust were things I shared with friends - not with a government agency.

The next morning I woke to find two men in my bedroom. They were dressed in calf length coats, large hats and long leather boots. One was cleaning what appeared to be a muzzle loading musket and the other was sharpening a sword. They vanished as soon as I cried out and jumped up in my bed.

Breakfast was a large meal of eggs and cockles fried with bacon and sausage. It was a combination I had never had before. After breakfast, this being Sunday, everyone headed off to the village church.

This surprised me and as we were walking down the lane I said to Myfanwy, "I didn't think magical people would be Christian – or even religious."

Myfanwy shrugged. "Shows how much you know." She said. Then she relented and explained a little further. "It was part of the trouble back in the fifth century. My family had embraced Christianity while Morgana and her people stayed with their particularly bloodthirsty version of the old religion. It is even part of the problem today. Apophis has no sense of accountability. The old religion died away many years ago and Apophis has now given up on all religion, even his previous worship of himself."

"I guess if you were raised to think of yourself as a god, it must be hard to discover that you are just human after all - a false god maybe." I said, as we walked into the village.

Myfanwy nodded but she looked worried. "Normally," Myfanwy said, "We would go to mass at Belmont Abbey in Herefordshire. There is a gate there that we can go to and it's the kind church that is traditional for my family. We still tend to follow the old church ways and are more at home in the monastic setting. However, Apophis would be expecting that and we were afraid that it would put both you and the monks in danger. So we decided to go to the local village church instead. It would be hard for him to attack us here, so close to Aelred Abbey."

I'm sure the vicar tried hard and meant well but the service was pretty awful. However, the church was old and beautiful and Myfanwy, as usual, sang beautifully. In fact, I noticed one lady nudging her husband, foghorn volume and same variation in pitch, to be quiet so she could hear Myfanwy better. Coming back over the causeway, we found our way guarded by a group of men dressed the same way as the ones who had been in my bedroom that morning.

"Royalist chevaliers," whispered Myfanwy. I looked around, seeing only marsh, forest and fields.

"Do you ever see the ghosts of Cromwell's men?" I asked.

"No," she replied. "The land doesn't seem to remember them."

After lunch it started to drizzle. Then it started to rain. Then it started to seriously rain and blow a gale at the same time and it kept doing this for the next three days. The library became our almost constant home. At first we tried to play games but this proved to be impossible. How can you play a board game with someone who can make the dice come up with any number they want? How can you play cards against someone who can change the way the cards shuffle? In the few games we played Myfanwy would solemnly promise not to cheat. Then I would get an unbelievably good hand only to find that she had one which was even better. She seemed to think that this was very funny. We ended up sitting in armchairs by the fire reading books. This worked well, especially as we had a large number of books to choose from and Nain would periodically make mugs of hot chocolate with marshmallows appear.

Occasionally our reading would be interrupted by some strange visitors: knights and men at arms, royalist civil war defenders and once a medieval theatre troop with an acrobatic jester. I asked Myfanwy how we could see these people, these ghosts.

"To understand that you must understand the nature of time," she said. "You think of time as traveling in a straight, unchanging line, but I see it differently. It is more like a river which sometimes and in some places flows faster or slower. In some places time seems to eddy around particular events and these events then seem to echo down through time. What we see are those echoes. You were right. The spirits of the dead have long since gone to wherever they were going. All we are seeing are glimpses of things that happened long ago. All sorts of people can occasionally see these things in all sorts of places but they tend to happen more commonly whenever my people live in a place for any length of time. We have used this house as a base in England for a long time so the past echoes are very frequent here. That's why the locals say the place is haunted. I guess they're right. It is. It is haunted by its past."

On Thursday the rain let up and a weak, wintery sun broke through the clouds. Myfanwy took me to the place where Brother Theophane would have been buried. There was not much to see – just a grassy area with a few trees. Over the years all the grave markers had been vandalized and forgotten. We explored the ruins of the cloister which at one stage had been used as stables. There was now no roof or floor and many of the walls had fallen down. The echoes of the past were strong here. Not that we saw anything but even I could feel it – a deep sadness that flowed from the very stone. We walked over to the ruins of the monastery church. This was in much the same state as the cloister but it still had a certain grandeur and it still felt like a church should – a place of sacredness and silence. It was as if all the centuries had not been able to wash away the prayer. Neither Myfanwy nor I spoke as we explored the ruin, except towards the end.

Myfanwy came over to me a said in a whisper, "Don't be sad, Thomas. Nothing that is good or true or beautiful is ever really lost. They share a reality that lasts forever." She then did something that surprised me. She stood in the centre of what would have been the nave and made a deep bow towards where the altar would have been. At once we were surrounded by monks sitting in their stalls and bathed in multi-coloured light. The church around us was whole again and the sun was streaming in through the stained glass windows.

"The king's commissioners had those windows destroyed," Myfanwy said. "Claimed they promoted superstition." I turned to look at the western window and there was a magnificent portrayal of Christ rising from the dead. The monks began to chant their prayers and we walked towards the great western door. Like all my people before me, I am a Catholic and as a Catholic there are some things you just do by instinct. As we got to the door I turned and genuflected to the altar and then blessed myself from the holy water font as we walked out. Myfanwy smiled at me in a sort of exasperated fashion.

"They are only echoes of the past Thomas." She said. "You can't interact with them." However, when I held up my right hand, it was wet from the holy water. Behind me the church was once again a ruin but I could still hear the monks chanting their prayer.

That night it snowed and the next day was wintery cold with a few lingering snow showers. Professor Rhys was surprised. He said that it was very rare for it to snow as heavily as this in this part of England. I didn't really care. Like most Australians, I did not have a lot of experience with snow. So of course Myfanwy and I went out to play in the stuff. We built a snowman, which is harder than it looks on television, and had a very brief snowball fight. It was very brief because a snowball fight with Myfanwy is a very bad idea. It doesn't matter how well you throw the snowball at her, it always veers off at the last second and misses and sometimes it even veers back and hits you. It also doesn't matter how poorly she throws hers, they always hit. Again, she seems to think this is hilarious. Tobogganing down the track through the birch wood proved to be much more fun.

It rained the next day and all the snow turned to slush. We once again retreated to the library to read. That afternoon, sitting by the log fire and with the rain drumming against the windows, I finally asked a question that had been on my mind over the last few days.

"Myfanwy," I said softly, "Why shouldn't I be afraid of you?" Myfanwy looked at me, surprised. I hurried to explain.

"I mean why shouldn't the world be afraid of you and your people? You have a power that no government or law could control or check. You could lay waste armies and render their weapons useless. Why shouldn't we be afraid of you?" Myfanwy was quiet for a long time, starring into the fire. I had expected her to be annoyed but when she answered her voice was just sad.

"I will answer you with a counter question," she said. "Why is it unreasonable for us to fear you as we do? There are less than a thousand of us and there are over 14 billion of you. You have armies and weapons of enormous destructive power. If our homeland lay open to you, would your world leave us alone or would they seek to take control? Yes, we could devastate armies and leave them powerless, but not all of them. Some soldiers would be skilled enough and determined enough to survive. Yes, we could make your planes fall from the sky, but not all of them. Some pilots would be cunning and courageous enough to survive and those who survived could destroy our people." She turned to look directly at me. "Thomas, over fifteen hundred years ago our people separated from yours because of the bloodshed that our interactions had caused. The result has been the slow death of our people. So, why is it unreasonable that we are afraid of you?" I nodded, there was logic in her argument, but she continued, "and why should I, Myfanwy Ferchwyn, not be afraid of you Thomas O'Malley?"

"Me?" I asked surprised. "Why would anyone be afraid of me?"

She looked at me, exasperated. "Tom, I have seen your skill in the martial arts. I have no doubt that you could kill without the need for a weapon and that ninety percent of the population could do little to stop you. So, why shouldn't I be afraid?" I shook my head.

"That's not the same," I said. "I would never hurt you."

"Nor would I hurt you," she replied, "and I am not afraid of you because I trust you. Are you afraid of me, Tom?" I shook my head.

"No," I said. "I know you would never seek to hurt anyone." Faith and trust, I was beginning to understand. Over the next few days Myfanwy and I talked a lot about her people and their power and I almost got to the point of accepting magic as normal.

When the weather finally let up and we took the opportunity to go for a walk along the beach. We walked a long way, to the end of the beach and up onto the cliff top path. There was a cold wind blowing from the west so we sat behind the broad trunk of an oak tree and ate our sandwiches looking out to sea.

"Thomas," Myfanwy said. "there is something you need to know about my people…" She stopped suddenly and looked around her, alarmed. "Quick Tom, run! We have to get back to the house. He's coming. I can feel him trying to dampen my power." I didn't need to ask who 'he" was and I needed no second urging to run after her back down the path. We were too late. Apophis was already standing on the beach before we got to it.

"My dear Myfanwy," he said. "How fortunate to meet you like this. What's wrong? Can't teleport anywhere? Someone stronger than you stopping you? What a pity, but then we can't have you running off to get help now can we. Do you remember when we were children? How we would play together? You were my only childhood friend. Now, I'm afraid, I get to play a game called death and you get to die: you and that unnatural abomination of an ape man." With that he made the same double handed gesture at Myfanwy as he had made outside the school and Myfanwy again moved into the same warding action. This time I was going to take a hand in events, there were no buses to throw at me here. I sprinted across the sand and caught Apophis in a tackle straight from the Australian Rules football manual. We both went down heavily and then scrambled to our feet.

"You ape! You dare to touch me!" he yelled. Then he pointed his finger at me and screamed "Die!' It all looked and sounded very dramatic but the only effect was to allow me to grab his arm and throw him over my shoulder onto the beach. He didn't know how to fall and I think he probably broke something when he landed. Certainly, he got to his feet incoherent with rage. I noticed with relief that Myfanwy had taken advantage of Apophis' distraction to get away. Apophis pointed his finger towards the sea in a twirling motion. A huge sea spout rose up out of the water and headed towards me. Less than a second later a few hundred ton of water landed on my head and I was pressed flat onto the beach. I couldn't breathe, I couldn't see and beach was being eroded away beneath me, so I found myself trying swim through a slurry of water, sand and gravel. Fortunately, when you surf you learn to hold your breath and you are used to a whole lot of water landing on top of you, but I was rapidly approaching my limit. Then everything just stopped moving, the water hanging still in the air, and I was able to scramble and claw my way out of the water column. As I lay on the beach gasping for air, Myfanwy let time flow again and an old ship's anchor thudded into the beach, inches from where I lay.

I heard Myfanwy running across the beach towards me calling out "Tom! Tom!" I looked up towards Apophis and saw him turn towards Myfanwy and raise his hand. I tried to move but my body was too slow to respond. Suddenly there was a kind of filmy, iridescent wall, almost like the wall of a soap bubble, between us and Apophis. Apophis gave the same animalistic howl that he had given outside the school and disappeared. I turned around and there was Nain standing at the top of the beach looking cross and worried.

I was almost on my feet when Myfanwy ran up to me and threw her arms around me. Then she quickly drew back, afraid that she might have hurt me.

"Are you hurt?" she asked anxiously. I shook my head.

"No, I'm fine. Nice timing by the way." I said indicating the anchor. "Thanks for that." She then threw her arms around me again and hugged me tightly, wet and all as I was. When she pulled back this time she was sort of crying and laughing at the same time.

"Oh Tom," she said. "Next time run away from the bad guy, not towards him. Promise me, next time you'll run away." I shook my head. I didn't say anything but I thought:

"If he tries to hurt you again, I will break his neck." The funny thing was that at the time I was not afraid at all, even though I had nearly been killed. Later that night I had nightmares and spent much of the night shaking with fear, but at the time I wasn't afraid – I was angry.

CHAPTER 11
Something Tom Needs To Know

Nain came down the beach. She had stopped looking worried and was now just looking cross, very cross. She started speaking when she was still about ten meters away.

"What did you think you were doing walking so far from the house? We go to all this trouble to protect the two of you and then you go wandering off to meet Arawn on your own!" She looked at us fiercely. "You two are just trouble waiting to happen. Come on, back to the kitchen. Myfanwy, bring him." Myfanwy took my hand and we were suddenly in the kitchen standing next to the warm stove which had a bright fire going in the fire box part. Nain was there ahead of us.

"You," she said, pointing at me, "Are dripping on my floor. Be dry." Nothing happened. I was still as wet as I had been before. Nain sighed and said. "Myfanwy, make him dry." Myfanwy smiled and nodded and both my clothes and I were instantly dry, although there was still a lot of sand and seaweed where I'd really rather it wasn't. I desperately needed a long, hot shower. Nain turned to Myfanwy.

"My girl, you were supposed to be looking after him. Why on earth did you stray so far? You could both have been killed." Myfanwy was looking down at the floor and very contrite. I noticed that she had kept hold of my hand. I wondered if she thought we might need to make a quick getaway.

"I didn't think he would come anywhere near the house," she said. "I thought it would still be safe and I wanted somewhere private to tell Tom about…about what we discussed last night." This aroused my curiosity as I was not privy to any late night discussions.

"Bah!" said Nain. "It is perfectly straight forward and you do not need anywhere private to discuss it. Thomas sit down and Myfanwy let go of his hand and go stand over by the window, out of arms reach." We did as we were told. I sat at the table and Myfanwy went over to the washbasins and stood looking out the window. Nain came and stood across the table, looking down at me.

"Thomas, there is something you need to know about our people." She said, unknowingly copying Myfanwy's earlier speech. "When we join we join for life." She held up her hand. "Now I know, whatever you say, that this is not so with your people. You can have multiple romantic attachments. It is even considered normal or healthy to have a number of boyfriends or girlfriends before you marry. Some of you even have multiple wives or husbands. This is a recent development among your people and I think not a happy one," she said rather primly. "Whatever of that, it cannot happen with us. The magic in us will not permit it. The part of us that does magic is linked to our understanding of relationships. If we tried to have a romantic relationship with more than one person, more than one person ever you understand, then the magic would go haywire and it would cause utter disaster for all concerned. Do you follow me Thomas? For all concerned, magic and non-magic alike. I mention this because you and Myfanwy seem to be very close friends, perhaps too close. You need to know the cost of forming any romantic relationship. Do you understand?"

I nodded and looked across to where Myfanwy was standing, still looking out the window. She was just wearing an old rugby sweater and jeans, her hair was messed up and her face was still streaked from where she had been crying but when she turned to look at me her eyes were as green, as warm and as soft as a summer meadow. She gave that little half smile she uses when she's not sure and I smiled back, trying to ignore, or deny, that little voice deep inside that said, "Too late Nain, way too late."

Across the table Nain threw up her hands. "I don't know why I bother talking!" she said. "I'm an old woman. I should stick to making scones. I don't know why I bother talking at all."

That night, after I had had a gloriously long shower, Myfanwy and I were sitting on the small gravel beach in front of Aelred Abbey and watching the moon rising over the sea. Behind us the ruined church seemed to be lit by flickering candles as the monks chanted their night prayer. At the top of the tower a guardsman wearing chain mail and carrying a spear was watching the sea for raiders. I think we were both thinking of Nain's talk, warning really, of that afternoon. It made the situation a little strained.

"So," I said to break the awkward silence between us. "You have never had a boyfriend then." She shook her head.

"No." She said. "No 'romantic attachments'. I've had friends who were boys, of course, but not like that. Just as Nain said, I need to be very careful."

"Like when you and Arawn were playmates," I suggested.

"Arrgh! No," she replied, recoiling in mock horror. "No! He only says that as a kind of sick joke. We could never stand each other. When I was little he would go out of his way to scare me in really nasty ways – thought it was funny. As I grew older I just thought he was creepy. I know now that he is both - creepy and scary." She paused in thought before she continued. "I think he is an example of what can happen when the magic goes wrong. His power is eating at his mind, at his soul. All of his relationships are messed up. His relationship with his father, with other people, with the world around him," She looked over her shoulder to the ruins of the monastery where the monks were just finishing their prayer, "His relationship with God. All messed up. But, thank heavens, none of that has anything to do with me, except that he hates me almost as much as he hates you." We sat in the same awkward silence for a while before she spoke again. "What about you? Do you have a girl pining for you in Australia?"

I shook my head. "I'm a bit slow in that area I guess." I said. "I also tend to be a bit arrogant and judgmental, especially about things like thick make up, stupid clothes and idolizing vacuous movie stars. I think that puts a lot of girls off." Myfanwy laughed. I didn't think it was that funny.

Still laughing, she said, "Yes, you can be arrogant and judgmental. You can also be really obtuse. You are sensitive, humorous, and courageous and you are a good looking boy. I think that there were probably girls throwing themselves at you and you just didn't notice."

I shook my head. "Actually there aren't all that many girls in Angle Creek." I said. She laughed harder. It took her a while to stop laughing. When she had finished, the silence between us was comfortable rather than awkward,

"It hasn't been easy for me at school, you know." Myfanwy said very quietly. "I have always had to hide who and what I was. I could never let anyone get too close. Then you came along and I couldn't hide from you. At first that really scared me. But then I was glad because I had a friend who knew me as I really was and was still my friend." Unlike Horace and co. who also have an inkling of your talent, I thought.

"What if I had just been normal?" I asked. "What if I froze, and forgot and didn't notice like all the others?"

"I have already told you Thomas." She said. "You are sensitive and courageous, you have a dry sense of humour and you are a good looking boy. I think we would always have been friends Thomas."

"That's good," I said, "Because, due to the actions of a certain party, my mother is way more than half convinced that you are my secret girlfriend."

"Oh," she said, "The goodbye kiss. Sorry about that but I could see her putting two and two together, and getting a number way above four, so I just couldn't resist sending all those hares running. I'm sorry I embarrassed you but I still think it was funny." I looked at her in the moonlight. She was looking at the moon with a slight smile on her face. I could feel my heart thumping hard in my chest, my palms started sweating and I was already blushing furiously in anticipation of what I was about to say.

"There is no need to apologize for kissing me Myfanwy. I just wish you'd done it because you liked me and not to aggravate my mother." I said. She turned to look at me.

"I do like you Thomas." She said. I leaned towards her… Just then someone wearing leather leggings strapped to the knee walked between us. I looked around, startled. A Viking long boat had pulled up on the beach and men in chain mail and carrying axes were creeping up the beach. Myfanwy sighed.

"Echoes, Thomas. Just echoes of the past." she said as she stood up. "They are Vikings. They are going to kill the monks and burn the monastery. Not the one you can see, the one that was here before it. They will steal the sacred vessels and melt them down for the gold and silver they contain. They are Vikings, it's what they do. It all happened a long time ago. You can't do anything about it. You can't interact with them in any way." A couple of the Vikings walked so close to me that I almost had to move out of the way.

"Phew!" I said. "They really smell bad!" Myfanwy had started to walk back to the house.

"Yes," she said in a very annoyed voice. "They stink and so does their timing."

The next few days were not the most relaxing. Myfanwy was in a bad mood and Nain was constantly hovering over us like a very large mother hen. These two things may not have been unconnected. The weather was cold and showery but there were fine patches. I spent most of these practicing my Tai Chi Chuan forms in the tower forecourt. Sometimes

Myfanwy would come to watch but somehow Nain could always arrange to find something else for her to do. On the last day Myfanwy did manage to get away and sat on the steps and watched as I went through some of the more advanced and complicated forms. Okay, I may have been showing off, and I did make quite a few mistakes, but it was a pretty good workout. When I practice my forms I tend not to think of anything else. I just concentrate on the movement and the flow of the form. Not that I am consciously thinking about what comes next, it's more that my mind and my body are both aware of the next step and move to carry it out. In the time I am doing my forms, I have nothing else on my mind. Nain came out and looked and Myfanwy.

"Yes, I know," she said. "He has the grace of a dancer, the balance of an acrobat and the strength of a blacksmith. Now come in and get your lunch." She looked up at me. "Both of you." I assume this was meant sarcastically because my best friend in all the world wouldn't say I had any of those things.

I went to go in with Myfanwy but she held her nose and said, "No. Shower first. Go!" Her native tongue is Welsh and sometimes she reverts to a very simple form of English.

That night Professor Rhys came down with the car so that he could drive me home early the next morning. Over dinner we discussed the attack by Apophis.

"He is getting reckless." Professor Rhys said. "To dare to come that close. He could easily have been captured. If you hadn't been so occupied with the welfare of the young ones, he would have been." He paused thoughtfully. "I wish I knew where he goes to. He has a bolt hole somewhere and it is very well protected because I have been unable to find it."

"Perhaps he goes back to your country, or place, or wherever it is you come from." I suggested. "Perhaps he is not in Britain at all."

Nain shook her head, "No," she said. "There is only one way into Annwn and if he used that we would know. All the same I don't trust Cadell. If you can't find this refuge then I think he must've had a hand in its formation."

"Anyway," Professor Rhys said. "We have made more permanent arrangements for your safety. Your school now has a new mathematics teacher, a Dr. Bryn Williams," Here Myfanwy groaned. "And your mother, Thomas, has a new neighbour. I think these arrangements should deter him for a while."

The next morning I packed up my bag and loaded it into the car and all four of us headed off. Myfanwy sat in the back with me while Nain sat in the front with Professor Rhys. The house shut itself up behind us. As we were driving out across the causeway, I saw several of the monks stacking what seemed to be bodies onto a large pile of wood.

"Don't look. It's too sad," said Myfanwy. "They are plague victims. During the worst of the plague people came to the monastery because the monks were the only ones who would still care for them. They still died of course and their bodies were burnt. Unfortunately, that meant that most of the monks died too." Despite Myfanwy's warning I watched and saw the bodies of small infants being placed next to those of their mothers. I quickly looked to the front.

"You are right," I said, trying to stop my eyes from tearing up. "It is too sad." Myfanwy took my hand and gave me a sad little smile. At least that was alright. Whatever had caused her bad mood over the last few days, she was not mad with me.

We had the same dream run going into London as we had had coming out. As we sped at impossible speed through the outskirts of London, I sat back and thought about the last two weeks. I was going to miss the castle. I was even going to miss the inconvenient ghosts. All this time Myfanwy was chatting about the coming half term and I was making a few half-hearted replies. I realized that most of all, I was going to miss spending time with Myfanwy.

After a ridiculously fast trip, we pulled up in front of my house. Professor Rhys went to knock on the door while I went to get my bag out of the boot. Myfanwy came with me. I didn't see what happened to Nain but she was gone by the time I pulled my bag onto the footpath.

Myfanwy lent over a whispered in my ear. "This time it will be because I like you."

Mum was chatting to Professor Rhys as I pulled my bag up the steps. There were the usual greetings and motherly carry on. Then Professor Rhys and Myfanwy took their leave.

"I'll see you at school Tom." Myfanwy said. Then she reached up and very deliberately kissed me on the cheek. "Goodbye" she said cheerily. My mother looked at me quizzically.

"Just a friend," I said rather loudly to my mother. "Not a girlfriend, a friend who just happens to be a girl." Myfanwy stopped as she was getting into the car.

She turned to look at me and I saw her expression change from hurt to anger. She got in and slammed the car door. I had a kind of sick, sinking feeling in my stomach.

My mother was shaking her head and looking me with pity. "You are so like your father," she said. "And you just blew it big time."

CHAPTER 12
The Submarine Incident

The next Monday, school started with a particularly long and tedious school assembly. We were introduced to our new mathematics teacher, Dr. Bryn Williams, who had to be appointed in a hurry after the previous mathematics teacher had won a lottery and decided to retire to the south of France. Dr. Williams was a short, fat and balding man who tended to sweat a lot. I have no idea what the headmaster said. I wasn't paying any attention. All through the assembly I was trying to catch Myfanwy's attention but she wouldn't look at me. She was always very reserved at school but today she stood stiffly to attention in her determination not to look at me. I felt really miserable. Why couldn't I have just kept quiet?

In the home room period she managed to sit at her desk in front of me without giving me a single glance. She went off to her French class without the slightest backward look. It was as if she were saying that I had ceased to exist for her. At lunch she not only wouldn't look at me or talk to me but if I said anything to anybody, she would withdraw from the conversation. Once I had been ignored into silence, she would go back to happily chatting with everybody else. It wasn't subtle and everybody noticed it. It also went on all week. By lunch time on Friday I was feeling desperate. Even Horace noticed.

"Hey Skippy, you look awful. I think the witch-girl is winning," he said. I didn't have the heart to reply. My mood wasn't made any better by the outbreak of pairing up which seemed to have broken out in our class. Horace had lost one of his henchmen who now preferred to sit and have intimate conversations with Ida Bruin – a girl with improbably blond hair and a nasal voice. Even Phil and Gabriella had taken to sitting by themselves and chatting. This I couldn't understand. I couldn't imagine a romantic conversation centred on soccer and I couldn't imagine Phil having a conversation centred on anything else. Wilson just seemed to think it was a very poor return on all his tutoring in mathematics. At home Mum was being very sympathetic and wanting to have heart to heart, mother and son talks. I took to pretending that I had a lot of homework to do.

That Friday Wilson sat next to me and said, "Horace is right. You do look awful. I don't understand why the two of you can't get on. You have this sort of hate/hate relationship going and it just makes both of you miserable." I looked at the unappetizing goop on my plate. It perfectly matched my mood. I had never felt this way before. It seemed like my whole image of myself was just washing away.

"I don't know about her," I said. "But Wilson, I'm as miserable as a bandicoot – and don't ask me what that means because I haven't got the heart to explain."

"Can't you just apologize to her?" he asked.

"How?" I asked. "She won't even look at me let alone talk to me."

"So this time you really did do or say something you need to apologize for?" he asked. I pushed my plate out of the way and put my head on the table in utter misery.

"Yes!" I replied. "I said something stupid which I really regret. I'd give anything to be able to take it back."

"See," said Wilson. "He is sorry. He does want to apologize." I looked up to see Myfanwy standing there with her lunch tray, looking at me in silence.

She turned to Wilson. "Not good enough," was all she said. She then put her tray down and began to walk quickly back out of the dining room. I decided that this had gone on for long enough. I stood up and went after her.

"Myfanwy!" I called out. "Myfanwy, I need to talk to you." The whole dining room went quiet and all eyes were turned first on me and then on Myfanwy. Myfanwy stopped but didn't turn around. I decided to plough ahead.

"Myfanwy, please give me leave to apologise." I know that may sound strange but I felt that I needed to ask this first. She must have known from the first that I would say sorry but she needed to be willing to accept my apology. There was a lot of laughter and a few cat calls around the room as I said this but they all went to silence as Myfanwy stopped time and turned around.

"Everyone heard you say that you know," she said. "The whole school will be talking about this."

"I don't care," I replied. "I don't care if they broadcast it on the BBC. Myfanwy, please let me say I'm sorry." She looked at me for what seemed like minutes although in reality it was probably only a second or two. It was difficult to read her expression but her eyes were hard.

At last she said, "You have my leave to apologize." I knew I had to make this good and I had already worked out what I was going to do and say. I had modelled it on those medieval romances that I knew she liked to read.

I dropped to one knee and bowed my head and said, "My Lady Myfanwy, I most heartily apologize for the offence that I have caused you…"

"Oh get up," she said, "You look ridiculous." I hadn't got very far through my prepared speech but when I got up I noticed that some of the hardness had gone from her eyes. There was even the faintest hint of a smile.

"Myfanwy," I said. "I didn't mean to hurt you. I just wasn't thinking. I said what I did partly out of habit with my mother, if she doesn't know anything she can't pester me about it, and partly because I was sort of panicked by all that stuff that Nain was saying. The thing is: you are the closest friend I have ever had and I need to be your friend in the same way that I need to breathe."

Myfanwy looked at me angrily and she came up and stood close to me. "Listen Thomas O'Malley from Australia," she said fiercely, poking her finger in my chest for added emphasis. "I will always be your friend. It doesn't matter how mad I am at you or what silly thing you've said or done. I will always be your friend. Always! Do you understand?"

I nodded. "Does this mean you forgive me?"

"Of course I forgive you," she said. "But I'm still mad at you. You have a lot of work to do mister. You wanted 'friend', you got 'friend' but it will be a long time before I kiss you again." At this I broke into a huge grin. "What are you grinning about?" she asked.

"That means that you will," I said. "If it's a long time before you do, it means that at some stage you will – kiss me again." She rolled her eyes and turned to walk out of the room.

"Um…Myfanwy. Could you perhaps fix the memories of the people here a bit?" I asked.

"No, I don't think so," she said airily. "I don't think I've ever held up time for this long before. It's very tiring. I don't think I can do any more magic today. Besides, you said you didn't care." With that, time started to flow again, the laughter and the cat calls continued and she walked out of the room.

"Hey Tom, come over here. We give you leave to sit with us," one of the 'in' girls called out.

"Yes," called another. "We will give you leave to do a lot more than she ever will." Amid the general laughter that comment caused, Horace rose to make a public announcement.

"Today the witch-girl has vanquished the kung fu warrior. Will he get his revenge? Tune in next week for the next exciting instalment!" In the midst of all this hilarity I kept my eyes straight ahead and walked back to finish my lunch.

"Well, that didn't go so good." Wilson said. I shrugged and kept my face non-committal. Inside I was singing.

That night mum was talking excitedly about our new neighbor. Apparently she had introduced herself a few days ago and today had brought over a lunch of fresh baked bread and vegetable soup. Mum chatted happily about her. I think she was just glad to have a change from my gloom of the last few days.

"She's a very cheerful person but I am a bit worried about her health. She is very overweight and I don't know where she gets those awful floral dresses she wears. Apparently everyone calls her Nain – which I think is Welsh for 'grandma'. Anyway, she's just house sitting. The owner is between tenants at the moment and she's just there to make sure the house doesn't get invaded by squatters." She looked at my somewhat dishevelled school uniform. "You should get cleaned up and changed. She has invited us over for dinner." Of course I knew who it was but I didn't know how I was meant to play the situation. Was I supposed to know Nain already or not? This question was answered immediately when we went over for dinner.

"Thomas!" she said. "How nice to see you again. Fancy you living next door." We explained to mum that Nain was the Professor's housekeeper and that she had been looking after us over the holidays. Over our dinner of leek soup and shepherd's pie, mum asked a lot of questions about Aelred Abbey. Nain was happy to oblige with a complete description and historical background.

"Oh, it's a wonderful place." She said. "Full of history…"

"Yes," I interjected. "History really seems to come alive there." Nain shot me a warning look before continuing with her own commentary. That weekend I found out how very trying it can be to have two fussy women trying to look out for your welfare. One good result was that I really did get a lot of study done because I retreated to my room for long periods.

The next Monday I was surprised to find myself called up onto the stage by the Headmaster. As I made my way to the front I could hear the Headmaster at his pompous best explaining that care for our fellow students had always been one of the hallmarks of St. Agatha's school. This was not something that I had noticed personally. As I got to the stage I found that I was being used as an exemplar of this noble characteristic.

"During the regrettable bus accident that occurred just before the term break, this student, Thomas O'Malley, at some risk to his own life, stopped to pull an incapacitated fellow student out of the way of one of the rampaging buses. For this he is under consideration for a bravery medal from the Royal Humane Society and their board member Mr. Piercedale is here to interview those concerned." Coming onto the stage from the opposite direction I saw Director Smith of DIAP. They went through the complete charade of asking for student cooperation. Since when were these things done in such a public way? If the Headmaster hadn't been so sycophantic to anyone from officialdom and hadn't been so focused on the honour of the school, he would have seen what a charade it was.

Afterwards, instead of going to home room I was taken to the administration reception room to share drinks and snacks with Director Smith, in his guise as Board Member Piercedale of the Royal Humane Society, and senior school staff. After a while 'Board Member Piercedale' asked to speak to me alone and, of course, the Headmaster agreed. We soon had a corner of the staff room to ourselves.

"The proposal for the medal is quite genuine by the way," the director said. "This investigation is obviously a bit of a sham, a distraction if you like, but the medal proposal is genuine. Well deserved too, if I may say so. I have to ask, where have you been? We completely lost track of you and we have been trying to text you without reply."

"I've been in hiding," I replied truthfully. "I suppose you know that the bus accident was the work of our friend in black?"

The Director nodded his head. "We didn't have any evidence but we guessed as much, especially since you disappeared so soon afterwards," he said.

"Well he found out who I was and where I went to school and he tried to kill me." I said. "I went into hiding and I won't tell you where because I am not sure that it wasn't from your files that he got the other information. I have decided that the less people know about me the better."

The director looked at me thoughtfully. "I wish I could say that I'm sure you're wrong," he said. "But I can't. I think your reticence is probably well advised. Especially given what happened the week before last. We promised to keep you informed, Thomas. Well, our black robed friend has moved on to bigger things. He attacked a Royal Navy trident submarine, took over the missile control station and tried to launch a nuclear missile strike on Norfolk. He killed several of the crew including the First Officer and the Officer of the Deck." He went on to explain how the captain, after he realized that the missiles were about to fire, had almost destroyed his submarine by crash diving it to a depth where the missile doors wouldn't open and how the crew had risked their lives and physically intervened with axes and wrenches to stop the firing sequence.

"In the end I think it was the complexity of the system that defeated him," he concluded. "He just couldn't control everything he needed to make the system work. Especially since the crew, who understood the system far better, were working against him. Eventually he teleported off the submarine and the captain and crew were able to re-establish control." I was shaking by the time he had finished. I knew why he had done this. He was trying to kill Myfanwy and me in a way that Nain couldn't stop. I thought of the shop lady, the vicar, the fog horn singing man and his wife. They all would have died just so that Apophis could be sure of killing me.

"If he'd succeeded, how many would have died?" I asked.

"It is hard to estimate," He replied. "But it would have been in the many hundreds of thousands."

It was lunch time before I got free and returned to the student body. I was still white and shaky as I walked into the dining room. As I went in there was some laughter and calling because of the events on Friday but I was in no mood to care. I spotted Myfanwy sitting at a table with Wilson and another girl I didn't know very well. I made straight for them. Horace noticed and announced to the rest of the room,

"Look folks! The warrior is going back to engage with the witch-girl. Is it romance or is it stalking? The next instalment continues…" I didn't take any notice of him or anybody else.

Myfanwy saw the expression on my face and stood up, alarmed. "Thomas, what is it? What's wrong?" she asked.

"We need to talk and we need to talk now." She nodded and time froze around us. We were now, in the middle of a crowded dining room, the most private people on the planet.

"Myfanwy, something very bad has just happened and something absolutely terrible almost happened. I need to talk to your uncle and Nain but it is going to take some time to explain. Can you bring them to dinner at my place tonight?"

She nodded. "I will bring them but Thomas, you're scaring me." She said.

"If I'm scaring you it's because I'm afraid, very afraid." I said. "I'll explain tonight."

Myfanwy let time flow again and there were a few comments from Horace and his mates which caused some laughter but I didn't pay any attention to them. I was too focused on what I had to do. I called my mum on my mobile phone to ask if I could invite all of them over for dinner tonight. I said I wanted to have a celebration dinner for the proposed bravery medal and I let her conclude that I wanted to try and make things right with Myfanwy. She agreed of course, like a good mother.

I didn't pay any attention to the rest of that day. I was still too shocked at the evil he was prepared to do, just to kill me.

CHAPTER 13
An Offer of Sanctuary

That night Nain was already at my house when I got home. She had come over earlier to help my mum prepare the dinner. Myfanwy and her uncle arrived at 7.00pm precisely. Dinner was a strange affair, although the food was very good. The others were, of course, anxious to hear why I had called them here while mum was chatting happily about her brave son and how she wondered if she would meet the queen at the medal award ceremony. She even tried to help me with Myfanwy, in a backhanded sort of way, pointing out that my good points probably outweighed my social ineptitude. She wasn't particularly subtle about this and a few times I could see Myfanwy struggling to keep a straight face. After dinner we retired to the lounge room. Nain took my mother by the arm and led her to the largest of the armchairs.

"You look tired dear," she said. "Why don't you sit down here and go to sleep." My mother instantly fell asleep in the chair. Nain nodded and said, "Poor dear. She really does need the rest." Professor Rhys got straight to the point.

"Now Thomas, what is so important that you called us all here at such short notice?" I took a deep breath before replying. This was not going to be easy.

"I'm about to tell you things that I promised I would never tell anyone and I'm about to break the law and commit a serious crime against national security." I said. "Today I was talking to the director of DIAP, the Division for the Investigation of Anomalous

Phenomena. DIAP is a secret government agency whose mission is to try and track the activities of the magical community and to bring them under the rule of British law. This was the third meeting that I've had with them. The first was after they realized that I was immune to Apophis' attack on Westminster Bridge." I now had their complete attention.

"What have you told them about us?" Professor Rhys asked in a strained voice.

"I haven't told them anything about you or your community." I replied.

"How can we know that?" he asked. "How can we trust you when you have kept this secret? If you have not betrayed our trust, why didn't you tell us about this DIAP earlier?" Professor Ap Rhys had got up and was pacing the room in anxiety. Nain was looking at me so hard you would think she was trying to bore through my head with her eyes. I had known that this was going to be difficult and it was. I didn't dare look at Myfanwy.

"I didn't need to tell you about them now but I have, even though by doing so I've seriously broken the law." I pointed out. "I've told them nothing. The secret of your existence is safe with me." Professor Ap Rhys stared at me in fear, anxiety and growing anger.

"How can I know?" he asked loudly. "Your mind is just this infernal blank to me. I can't read you!"

"I can," said Myfanwy softly. "Not by magic but by knowing who he is. He is perhaps the world's most arrogant, insensitive, inept, infuriating…boy! But I don't think he would betray us. I don't think he would betray me." I turned to look at Myfanwy. Myfanwy with her crooked half smile, her soft green eyes and her hair flowing down her shoulders. Faith and trust, Brother Theophane had said; faith and trust. I nodded to her, but quickly looked away. This was not the time for personal feelings.

"All of this is beside the point." I said. "They're not really interested in you. They're tracking Apophis. They don't know who he is but they know the destruction he has caused and has tried to cause. They know that the accident at the nuclear power station up north was his work. They know that he boarded a nuclear missile submarine and tried to launch a nuclear strike against Norfolk. What they don't know is that he did that because he badly wanted to kill Myfanwy and me and he had just been stopped from doing that. He was prepared to kill hundreds of thousands of people and to turn a large part of Britain into a radioactive ruin just to make sure that Myfanwy and I were dead!" I heard a horrified gasp from Myfanwy behind me.

"How was he stopped?" Nain asked quietly.

"The crew stopped him," I replied. "The crew, who risked their lives to try and physically stop the missiles with axes, wrenches – anything they could find. The captain, who crash dived and nearly destroyed his own submarine to stop the missiles. The helmsmen, who obeyed their captain's orders even though it could mean their own lives. What did you say Professor about him finding that normal people had a greater strength of spirit than he had? Well he might be the 'over man', he might have the 'will to power' but that crew had the 'will to save' even if it meant losing their own lives and they stopped him. A lot of them died, trying to rush him, but they stopped him.

They stopped him – not with magic but with straight courage and self sacrifice!"

At the end of this I found I was shouting and I was crying. It was just so unfair that brave people should be killed so casually. There were mothers without their sons, there were widows and orphans, there were lovers who would never get married, just because Apophis wanted to kill me. I couldn't speak anymore. I just sat on the couch and held my head in my hands. Myfanwy came and sat next to me. She put her arm around me and lay her head on my shoulder, for a long time no one spoke.

"This is the worst possible news." Professor Rhys said eventually. "Apophis has gotten way out of hand. His attacks are getting worse and his pathological hatred for you and Myfanwy means that you both represent a constant danger to all around you. We must act to isolate you from attack and we must find where Apophis is hiding. Thomas, how do these DIAP people track Apophis?" I was calmer now as I looked up to answer his question.

"They never told me in any detail," I said. "But I gather that they look for what they call 'anomalous events' in the information flow across the internet, things which don't make sense. The volume of information is so great that no one, not even you, can hope to change it all. The system is so complex that no one can know all the pathways but they have some way of monitoring that information flow. They don't detect you and Myfanwy because you don't cause things which get much publicity – Apophis does and they can use it to track him. I think they can track him better than you can."

Professor Rhys nodded thoughtfully. "I think the time may have come to change tactics," he said. "I may need to organize a visit to the Prime Minister…"

"We have time," Nain interrupted. "The attack on that submarine would have taken a huge amount of energy. To travel to a submerged and moving submarine and then to teleport off after it had crash dived, I'm amazed that he was able to do it and survive. He'll be exhausted and he'll need time to rest and to plan. In four weeks the young ones will be on their spring holidays. I think we are safe until then. Cadfan, there is only one way we can ensure that nothing like this madness happens again. We must take Thomas and his mother with us to Annwn." Myfanwy sat bolt upright next to me.

"Really?" she asked surprised. I was glad that there was no disguising the happiness in her voice. I, however, had no idea where or what Annwn was. I looked quizzically at Nain.

"Annwn is the place we retreated to when we withdrew from the common world," she said. "It sits alongside this world and nothing that happens in this world can harm you there. This not only means that we can protect you, but also that Arawn will have no cause to attack any part of this world, since such an attack would not effect you. At the moment, when he attacks you he destroys the lives of those around you. If you were in Annwn he would not be able to do this. Your mother must come too. Otherwise he might lash out at her when he couldn't get to you. We very rarely allow non-magical people to visit Annwn and when we have done so in the past, it has not always turned out well. I think, however, that this is the best solution in the current circumstances."

Professor Rhys nodded. "I agree," he said, "although it is complicated and only short term. In the longer term we must capture Arawn."

I must have looked concerned because Myfanwy said, "Don't worry Thomas. Annwn is a wonderful place. It is absolutely the very best place for a holiday."

The rest of the evening involved waking Mum up and reassuring her that no one thought it rude that she went to sleep and that I had been a good host – something she seemed to consider unlikely.

When they had all gone I said, "Mum, you've been working too hard. I think you might need a holiday."

The next few weeks at school were taken up with assignments and tests as we prepared for the end of the Spring Term. Dr. Bryn Williams may have been effective in protecting us but he was a truly awful teacher of Mathematics. You learnt from his class that he could do the problems very easily. What you didn't learn is how he did the problems. The one positive aspect of this was that Wilson was suddenly very popular, with people crowding around him at every break so that he could explain what they needed to know. Even Horace and co. were sometimes seen hanging around the edge of the pack. Brains always win out in the end. Now that the weather was clearing up, slowly, Phil and some of the other soccer fans had taken to playing a goal scoring game, with Gabriella and some of the other girls looking on. This meant that Myfanwy and I were sometimes left alone to sit under one of the remaining trees and talk. She would ask me all sorts of questions about life in Australia and I would try my best to answer.   However, whenever I asked her anything about Annwn she would say, "No. It's best that you wait and see it for yourself." This hardly seemed fair.

All the classes were preparing for the end of term. In Physics we were winding up our study of classical physics and Special Relativity in preparation for Quantum Mechanics next term. This was being handled efficiently, if without any great enthusiasm, by Mr. Robertson, a tall thin man with short, grey hair and a neat moustache. Everyone assumed that he had once been an officer in one of the armed forces but no one really knew anything about him. He concluded by giving us a series of talks on 'the stochastic behavior of apparently deterministic phenomena.' The end result of which was to say that in our complex universe, even things which we thought we understood well, like the movement of the planets, can prove to be unpredictable. He concluded that our universe is a strange and wild place. This was something that I now knew very well indeed.

For reasons best known only to herself, Mrs. Brown decided to start our transition from the metaphysical to the romantic poets by reading one of her favorite poems aloud to the class. It was perhaps the most famous of Elizabeth Browning's sonnets and she read,

> "How do I love thee,
> Let me count the ways…"

At this point Horace could be heard very loudly saying, "One, two, three, four …"

Amid general class laughter, Mrs. Brown could be heard, hurt and indignant, telling Horace that that just wasn't funny. I felt sorry for her but it was actually kind of funny. Even Horace has his moments.

At home, Nain was using her supposed status as a house sitter with not much to do, to spend time with my mother. She would make coffee and lunch when mum was working in her studio and other things like that. My mum really appreciated her assistance, but Nain was actually doing something else as well. She was planting the seed of the idea that we needed a holiday away from all modern distractions. She was also weaving a complex spell deep in my mother's mind. I didn't know this at the time but it became very evident later. Eventually my mother came up with the idea, apparently on her own, that what she needed was a holiday somewhere quiet, with no internet, or twitter or mobile phone. Nain was then able to say that Myfanwy's mum and uncle lived in a very large house on an island off the Welsh coast and she was sure they wouldn't mind if we wanted to spend the holidays with them. A quick phone call to the professor and the whole matter was settled very quickly and with a minimum of fuss. As always, I was annoyed at the deception but I could see the need. I also had to admit that, deep down, I really wished I could manipulate my Mum that well.

On the last Wednesday of term, Myfanwy invited me for dinner because Professor Rhys had something he needed to discuss with me. I asked what it was about but she said that she didn't know. So that Wednesday night, instead of catching the bus home, I went with her to the gate next to the wall of the old church. Myfanwy opened it and invited me to step through. Once again I found myself in the birch wood, with the path leading down to Aelred Abbey. Crossing the causeway, I again tried to find out what the professor wanted to talk about but it became pretty clear that Myfanwy really didn't know. The door to the tower seemed to be guarded by two men at arms dressed in chain mail with shields and heavy spears. They were looking anxiously about them but didn't see us as we passed. Nain was waiting for us in the hall.

"Welcome home dears," she said. "Myfanwy, could you come and help me in the kitchen? Thomas, I think Cadfan would like a word with you in the library." In the library, the professor was sitting in one of the large armchairs by the fire. He motioned me to come over and join him.

When I had sat down he started speaking slowly and seriously, looking into the fire, "Thomas, I must first tell you that what I am about to say is most uncertain. I mentioned to you before that we have knowledge of only one other like you, the warrior you know as Sir Percival from the Arthurian legend. I must tell you that, towards the end of his life, we know that he somehow lost his invulnerability and did fall under an enchantment. We also notice that you can travel magically with Myfanwy, although not with anyone else. We are concerned that as you become exposed to magic, as it becomes part of your everyday experience, you may lose your unique talent. We believe this is what happened to poor Peretur." He turned to look at me directly. "Thomas, you are preparing to go to Annwn. It is a place thick with magic. No one goes there and returns unchanged. We don't know what staying there will do to you but there is a chance that the next time you meet Arawn, you will not be protected. There is a chance that if you go with us to Annwn, if you maintain your close friendship with Myfanwy, then the next time Arawn points his finger at you and says "Die", your heart will explode in your chest and you will be dead. You need to know this before you go on." I sat still for a long time, trying to absorb and analyse this information.

Eventually I said, "If I stay in London he will try and kill me. I may keep my protection but I would be putting the lives of many others, perhaps thousands of others, in danger. I can't do that. I can't let other people die just so I can stay safe from magic."

The professor nodded, "I thought you would say something like that," he said. "But it was my duty to warn you." Then he brightened up and said, "Let's go into the dining room. Surely dinner is served by now. Can you find your own way? I'll just pop into the kitchen and let them know we are ready." Then he disappeared.

I wasn't happy as I left the library. Sure, I wasn't keen on the idea of facing a psychotic wizard without any protection, I knew what the outcome of that encounter would be. I just didn't think I had any choice in the matter. However, what I was really worried about was what a change of status would do to my relationship with Myfanwy. My ability had given me a unique window into her life. What would happen if she could close that window completely anytime she wanted to? Perhaps I wasn't concentrating but I found that apparently I had once again taken a wrong turn because I found myself in a long, narrow room with a tiled floor and bare stone walls. Brother Theophane was sitting on a wooden bench. He greeted me as I came in.

"Ah! Thomas, thou hast come. I have been waiting for thee. T'is but a short time to Compline, or night prayer as thou wouldst say, so thou must be quick with thy dilemma." This time I knew precisely what I had to say and I told him of my conversation with the professor and of my fears.

"This lady, she will know that thou hast given up thy prowess for the common good?" I nodded and the old monk smiled broadly. "Then Sir Thomas, if she doth not love thee more for thy deed than she did for thy ability, then I doubt much thy judgment in matters concerning women. But I do not doubt thee. That thy enemy may vanquish thee, this may be true or false, but that thy lady will love thee: this I know to be true. Come, kneel now and I will pray with thee. Perchance the Lord will grant thee his favour." I knelt as the old monk prayed over me. When he left, the room was dark and cold and empty and I had trouble finding my way back to the hall.

CHAPTER 14
Leaving London

Myfanwy was waiting for me when I got to the dining room. The candles were lit on the table but there was no one else there.

I must have looked a bit puzzled because Myfanwy started to explain, "There's been a disagreement. Nain insisted that we eat in the kitchen against Uncle Cadfan's wishes. I've been sent to fetch you. Where have you been by the way?"

"I think I got lost in the dark," I mumbled, which was sort of half true. I noticed that she was looking at me expectantly and not making any move to 'fetch' me to the kitchen.

"You may have noticed that my uncle is a very formal and reserved person," she said. "He can even have a formal meeting with his niece's best friend without telling his niece anything about it. I just got shunted off to the kitchen so that you two could have your chat in private and I want to know why. What did you talk about?" I did toy with the idea of being mysterious and not telling her, but one look at the determined expression on her face made me decide that that path was going to be a lot more trouble than it was worth. I told her about what the professor had said and about my decision. She looked at me with a worried frown.

"My uncle is a fusspot," she said. "I don't think that will happen to you. This thing of yours is not just some superficial ability, it's a real part of you. Even if the worst did happen, I could still protect you from

Apophis." She kept looking at me intently and I sort of shrugged and looked away.

"You're worried though," she said, "and I don't believe that you're afraid of Apophis. You should be but I don't believe you are." She spoke slowly and uncertainly, as if she was teasing out an idea as she spoke. "Why? Thomas, I need to know." I hesitated for a long time. Then I sort of blurted it out quickly, to get the embarrassment over and done with.

"I'm worried because it was my ability that drew us together. What'll happen if that goes away?"

"Arrgh!" she cried. "You silly boy!" She grabbed the lapels of my school blazer. "How many times do I have to tell you? I will always be your friend. No matter what happens to you, even no matter how silly you are, I will always be your friend."

I looked down into her fierce, green eyes. "Okay Myfanwy, I believe you." I said softly.

"Good," she replied. "Because it would make no difference. My mother has no magic at all and yet I love her more than anyone on the planet. It is you, not your abilities, but you that I…that I…" She seemed to become confused and embarrassed and blushed deeply. Suddenly we were in the kitchen and Myfanwy hurriedly let go of my lapels and stepped back.

"What kept the two of you?" Nain asked.

The dinner was quite cheery, given that the evening had gotten off to a very gloomy start. Myfanwy at last started to talk about Annwn and it was immediately clear that she was in love with the place. I pricked my ears up when she spoke of waves crashing on the beach.

"There's surf there? Could I bring my board?" I asked. Myfanwy gave a great smile, but there was a lot of mischief in it.

"I think that would be wonderful," she said. "I think you would be the first human ever to surf those waves." The emphasis she gave to the word 'human' should have warned me to be cautious but I was so caught up in the idea of riding the uncrowded waves of a pristine beach that I thought of nothing else. As I was being taken home that night, passing two armoured knights practicing their sword craft, I was thinking of waxing my board. I know now to be wary when Myfanwy gets that mischievous expression. Her sense of fun has a habit of getting me into trouble.

After school had finished for the term, I walked down to the bus stop with Myfanwy. She was as happy as I have ever seen her. She was humming and almost skipping. When I asked her what was so good, all she said was, "Tomorrow I get to take you to Annwn."

The Professor's classic Rolls Royce pulled up in front of our house at precisely nine o'clock on the Saturday morning. Mum was rightly worried that our luggage wouldn't fit in the car. She had two large cases and I had one smaller one, and I also had my surf board. Simple geometry would tell you that there was no way they could all fit in that boot. Of course they did, even my surf board. I looked at my mum to see her reaction to this impossibility but all she said was,

"Isn't it wonderful the way they made these cars so spacious back then." This made no sense but I decided to just let it go for now. Myfanwy rode up front with the professor while I sat in the back with mum. We had the same impossible luck with traffic and traffic lights and soon we were speeding through the countryside and along the motorway to Wales. Even here, the rest of the traffic seemed to pull over into the left lane to let us through. We were also driving way too fast. I actually don't think that car could physically do the speed we were going, even when it was new. We were soon travelling through hilly country and on smaller roads but the Professor kept the same mad speed, not even slowing down for the sharp turns of a winding country road. An F1 driver would have been white and shaking at the experience but my mum, who was never a good passenger, just sat quietly looking out the window and occasionally remarking on how beautiful the countryside was. I had barely had time to ask "are we there yet?' before we were slowing down and coming into the village of Tenby. We parked the car in a garage on the outskirts of the pedestrian area and walked into the town where tall, brightly coloured buildings crowded round a steep walled stone harbour.

It was high tide and the professor led us over to a large fishing boat which was pulled up at the stone wharf on the western edge of the harbour. He introduced us to Owen Ap Bryn, the skipper of the boat. Owen was a small, dark man with a woollen cap pulled down tightly on his head and a black, curly beard. He also had green eyes but they seemed to have been faded by the sea. To my mother and me, Owen proved to be a man of few words but he chatted amiably in Welsh with Myfanwy. The professor explained that he spoke little English. Our luggage was already on the boat and stowed away when we arrived – another remarkable occurrence that my mother didn't seem to notice. We wasted no time in catching the high tide out of the harbour and heading off down the Bristol Channel towards the open sea.

There was a stiff breeze blowing in from the south west. I stood near the bow of the boat to feel the fresh saltiness of the wind. All my life in Australia I had lived near the sea but I hadn't been near the open ocean since I came to Britain: the tame English Channel off Norfolk doesn't count. The salt spray, the gulls, even the motion of the boat as it cut through the choppy waves of the Bristol Channel; these were like the greeting of an old friend. Myfanwy came up to the bow with me. She was looking forward with real eagerness and I knew that she was looking for the first sight of Annwn – of her home. I felt a pang of irrational jealousy that she could go home and I couldn't. Sure, my home was only a timber bungalow on a hill at the back of Angle Creek but I suddenly felt homesick for the wide Australian sky and the hard clarity of the Australian light. Myfanwy looked across at me.

"You look sad Thomas. What's wrong?" She asked.

"It's nothing," I replied. "It's just that watching you being so eager to get home made me feel a bit homesick for Australia."

"Don't worry," Myfanwy said. "You will love Annwn. It's a place like no other. The land itself is alive. The weather is always what you need it to be and the days are always the length you need them. Time itself flows differently there. If we wanted, these four weeks could last a year." I thought about this for a moment.

"You mean that it's like the stories of Tyr na nOg, where you go there for a day and come back to find centuries have past?" I asked.

"Ah, I forgot your people were Irish." she said. "The same idea but no, we don't let time run that slowly and while you're there we will make sure it comes out about even with the rest of the world. We don't want your mother to miss any of her appointments." I thought about this idea of variable time a bit more and another thought occurred to me.

"Myfanwy, how old are you?" I asked. I saw her stiffen and she kept gazing out to sea while she answered.

"That is not a polite question to ask a lady." She said. "Anyway, you know how old I am. I'm in your class. I have lived through sixteen years, just like you."

"Yes," I said. "You're in my class but you don't watch TV; you don't have a mobile phone; you don't go on facebook or surf the web; you speak very formally. All in all, your approach to the world is a bit old fashioned. I know you've lived sixteen years but what year was it in London when you were born?"

She turned around to face me and said defiantly, "It was the 7th of September 1884. There! Is that too weird for you, too spooky?" I put my hands on her shoulders and looked directly into her eyes. I was surprised to see that she was really worried.

"I understand about the difference in time," I said, "but even if you were a thousand years old, I'm still your friend. No matter how weird or spooky things get, and you must admit things can get pretty weird and spooky around you. " I paused for a moment. "Besides," I said. "You look really good for someone who is 127 years old."

"Urgh!" she said thumping my chest in annoyance. "I am not 127 years old. I am sixteen. I was just born 127 years ago and if you had gone to school with everyone calling you witch – girl, you would understand why I can be a bit sensitive." She paused, "Still," she said. "You are right. I should not have doubted you." Then a brilliant smile lit her face,

"Do you really think I look good?" she asked.

"Sure," I said. "For someone born in 1884, you look great! My mother thinks you're gorgeous."

"Your mother thinks I'm gorgeous! Did your mother tell you that?" she asked sarcastically. I nodded and was about to say that I agreed with her when Owen, the boat's skipper came forward to stow some rope in a locker. I looked up at the wheelhouse. It was empty. Owen said something to Myfanwy in Welsh.

"He says that we should get back from the bow. We are going to hit a bit of swell in the Irish Sea and there's weather on the way." I looked up at the sky. There were white clouds scudding across a blue sky with some high cirrus. There was no sign of rain.

"It's good to be able to travel in a magic boat." I said. Myfanwy looked at me puzzled. "Well, it can hold its course with no one at the wheel and the skipper knows about weather changes long before they are obvious." Myfanwy burst out laughing and said something to Owen in Welsh. Owen also found this very funny.

"No, No boyo," he said. A long stream of Welsh followed which Myfanwy, who clearly still found this whole thing very amusing, translated.

"He said that the boat steers itself because he turned on the autopilot and he knows about the weather because of the radio and the radar." Here she pointed to the modern weather radar antenna rotating slowly on top of the wheelhouse. "He also says that it is powered by two Volvo diesel engines, made in Sweden and maintained by a mechanic in Tenby. Thomas, Owen is a fisherman and he has to interact with the outside world all the time. If the boat didn't have this technology it would look odd and attract attention in fishing ports and if you must have the technology, why wouldn't you use it? We use whichever is easier, magic or technology." Just then the boat pitched as it hit the start of the ocean swell and we quickly retreated back from the bow as a heavy spray splashed over us. Owen said something in Welsh as he walked back to the wheelhouse. I didn't need Myfanwy to tell me that it meant 'I told you'. It wasn't long after this that a line of clouds appeared in the west, trailing a grey curtain of rain. We retreated back into the wheelhouse where Mum and the Professor were sitting at the table and sipping coffee. Myfanwy and I went and stood next to where Owen was sitting down, steering the boat with one hand and holding a coffee mug with the other.

After a while of staring through the rain, Myfanwy pointed and called out, "There! There it is!" I looked where she was pointing but all I could see was a low, dark smudge near the horizon. As we got closer, the smudge resolved itself into some low rocks, bare of any vegetation and covered in sea birds – hardly the ideal location for a holiday. Myfanwy looked at my troubled expression and smiled.

"Don't worry," she said. "Appearance can be deceiving." We pulled in very close along the lee side of the largest rock and then turned sharply into what appeared to be a small cleft, a cleft far too small for the boat to fit. As we did so, a whole new vista opened up before us and we were sailing into a wide bay backed by green hills and forest, with steep mountains in the distance. At one side of the bay there was a stone harbour with a small group of thatched and whitewashed cottages. Just outside the harbour a broad, shallow river entered the sea. At the other end of the bay was a wide, sandy beach with breakers curling in from the point. The rain had stopped and a bright sun was shining. Myfanwy smiled at me and said,

"Welcome to Annwn."

CHAPTER 15
Myfanwy's Country

As we came into the calm waters of the bay I moved up to the bow again to get a better view of our destination. Off to our right there were some flat rocks at the foot of a cliff with what I at first thought were seals sunning themselves. When I looked closer, however, I saw that the figures were human, mostly female, with long silvery hair. They certainly behaved like seals, diving freely into the water and swimming swiftly and acrobatically. Once in the water they even looked like seals. I was leaning over the side of the boat to get a better look when I felt a hand grabbing me by the shoulder and pulling me back. It was Myfanwy. Owen stuck his head out of the wheelhouse and said something laughingly in Welsh. Myfanwy replied quite crossly, also in Welsh. Owen pulled a face and escaped back into the wheelhouse.

Myfanwy turned to me and said, "They are Dylan's children. They may look human but they are wild sea creatures. Your Irish ancestors would have called them selkies. You don't want to get too close to them. Despite what the stories say, they don't generally make good wives."

I looked at her surprised. "I don't want to marry them." I said. "I just wanted to get a look at them."

"Yes, that's how it starts," she replied. "Then the next thing you know you have a litter of doe eyed children who can swim really well. It has happened before." She turned to look at the wheelhouse and shouted something in Welsh but Owen took no notice.

The entrance to the harbour was formed by this cliff on one side and the end of the curving stone wharf on the other. At the end of the wharf was a small lighthouse with a grey, slate roofed cottage attached. Owen came forward as we entered the harbour and picked up the end of the mooring rope that lay coiled in the bow. I watched the wheelhouse as the wheel turned to counter the currents and the engines throttled themselves to bring us expertly alongside the wharf. Owen threw the bow rope over a mooring post while the stern line secured itself.

"That's a very good autopilot you've got there," I commented sarcastically to Owen. "Every boat should have one like that." Owen looked quizzically at Myfanwy, who translated.

Owen laughed. "Hard to get, that one," he said in a thick accent. "Rare indeed they are."

There was a woman waiting for us on the wharf and as soon as the boat was secure, Myfanwy ran up the stone steps, threw her arms around her and hugged her tightly. I guessed this was her mother. She was taller than Myfanwy and she had long brown hair and soft brown eyes. She was wearing a long but fairly modern sort of dress. I had half expected her to be dressed like someone from the 19th century but she obviously tried to keep up with fashion. The professor went up after Myfanwy and I followed my mother. As I got to the top of the steps the professor was formally introducing my mother to Myfanwy's mum. She interrupted him by coming up and kissing my mother on the cheek.

"You are most welcome my dear," she said. "You must call me Helen. We are very isolated here and it is wonderful to have someone I can talk to about all the latest happenings in London and someone who works in the fashion industry too. I am so pleased you could come." She then caught sight of me and she looked at me with a piercing and critical gaze. I felt a bit like a piece of livestock being judged at an agricultural show. However, when she spoke her voice was warm and welcoming. "You must be Thomas. My, you are tall and strong for your age by the look of you. I thought that my Myf's letters may have exaggerated, to her everyone is tall." Myfanwy rolled her eyes and pulled a face but her mother ignored her and started to gesture that everyone should walk down the wharf. "Come, come," she said. "We can have a late luncheon up at the house." As we walked down the wharf, my mother was looking around with a kind of rapt expression on her face.

"But this is so beautiful," she said. "It is all so unspoilt, so untouched by that awful commercialism." It certainly was. The collection of cottages at the end of the wharf didn't really constitute a village. There were no signs to indicate that any of the cottages were shops or had any purpose other than as a place to live. The space between the cottages and the wharf was paved but it wasn't really a road. It was just an empty space where cargo and livestock could be kept while being loaded or unloaded from the boats. There was a paved path leading away from the wharf along the river but it was clearly designed for walking and not for vehicles. It was overhung by large oak trees and lined by a confusion of berry bushes. We walked along this path with my mother and Helen chatting together like old friends. Myfanwy took my hand in hers and started to swing it, like a little girl skipping along. She smiled the most brilliant smile and her whole person seemed to radiate joy.

"You are in my world now Thomas. Here magic surrounds you." She said.

"I am used to it," I said. "Remember, I spent last holidays at Aelred Abbey."

She laughed as she replied. "No, no. Aelred Abbey is just a place in your world that my people own and use. This is our world! These hills, these trees… all of this, this is the land of magic and you Thomas, who once refused to believe in ghosts, will have to change your way of thinking. This is the land where magic is normal!" Once again I could hear the echo of the strain she felt at the separation her nature caused between her and her fellow classmates. I looked around. Certainly the countryside was very pretty and the natural life seemed very vibrant. Not only were there a large number of birds in the trees but there were little red squirrels running along the branches and chatting to each other.

"It's beautiful," I said. "But it looks pretty normal."

"Appearances can be deceptive," she said, still laughing. "Take a closer look at the river." At this point the river had eroded the bank and ran swiftly and deeply near the path. As I looked, I realized that what I had taken to be strands of river weed was in fact the long green hair of a large, transparent woman lying submerged in the water. When she noticed me she gave a start and disappeared, merging into the river, only to reappear a bit further from the bank. She looked at me with a coy curiosity. Myfanwy waved and the water lady waved back before merging back into the river. Everything now looked normal.

"That was Sabrina, the river maiden," Myfanwy said. "She's an old friend of mine." I stared at the river intently but it remained just a river. The long strands of green river weed remained just that. I shook my head. On top of the selkies, this was getting to be a bit too much.

"That can't be real. Even with magic, how can things like river maidens or water nymphs exist?" I asked. I really intended the question to be rhetorical but Myfanwy took it seriously.

"Well," she said thoughtfully, "She doesn't really exist in the same way that you and I do. The river exists and she is the personification of it. So her existence is sort of secondary – derived." I shook my head again. Secondary or not, I was having a hard time accepting that such a thing could exist at all. All through this my mother had been chatting amiably with Helen and hadn't noticed a thing.

After about half a kilometre, we turned off the river path and onto some broad stone steps that took us up a hill and through an open meadow. The pasture was about knee high and some black faced sheep watched us without any real interest. The meadow was dotted with what looked like clumps of ancient fruit trees, mostly apples, only just coming into blossom. As we climbed higher we found ourselves under the contemplative gaze of some shaggy, long horned cattle. We all stopped as we got to the crest of the hill and I caught my first sight of what was, perhaps, the most unusual building I had ever seen.

"Welcome to my home," Myfanwy said. The house was large and built of a grey, slatey stone. I think that it had originally been a kind of round fortress but it had been added to and altered in many different ways and with no regard for overall design. It was still mostly round but windows of many different styles had been cut into the stone and in positions that didn't seem to make any sense. In some places the top was a castled walkway and in others it was roofed with the same grey slate. On the ground there was a large glass conservatory at one side and a large terrace with a stone balustrade at the other. The most obvious addition was a large tower with a conical roof that looked a bit like an oversized chimney. It was in a park like setting, surrounded by dark, evergreen trees. The house didn't look ugly. It didn't look beautiful. Mostly, it just looked odd, impressive but odd.

"What an interesting house," my mother said. "Do you know who designed it?"

Helen laughed. "I'm sure that no one did." She said. "It's very old and it was added to and changed as people saw a need. When my husband was alive I was always suggesting that we should change it to a more normal configuration, make it square, add a neo-classical façade and so on. But he would have none of it and now I just keep it this way because it reminds me of him. It certainly does have a lot of character and a lot of its own quirky charm." As we started walking down the path to the house she added as an afterthought, "It's also very comfortable, once you get used to it."

Myfanwy leaned across and whispered in my ear, "You had better love this house or we can't be friends anymore!"

"In that case," I said, "I'm sure I will – once I get to know it." There was no door to the house, just a massive archway that led into a cobbled tunnel. This tunnel ran right through the house to the inner courtyard where the green light of a garden could be seen. A number of doors of different sizes led off this tunnel on either side. As soon as we arrived a small figure came running down this tunnel, yelling in a high pitched cry. It turned out to be a small girl about eight years old.

"Myfwy! Myfwy!" she yelled. Physically Myfanwy did not look much like her mother, although she did resemble her in other ways, but this noisy little person was a miniature carbon copy of Helen, except that she had the same vivid green eyes as Myfanwy. I knew, of course, that it could only be Gwyneth, Myfanwy's younger sister. She caught Myfanwy in a limpet like hug.

"Gwen, it's only been a few Annwn weeks since I left!" Myfanwy laughed. But she returned the hug with enthusiasm nonetheless. Helen took her and formally introduced her to my mother.

"Mrs. O'Malley, this is Gwyneth, my youngest daughter. Her brother is also around here somewhere but I'm sure he'll show himself when he's ready." My mother paid Gwyneth some conventional compliments but she wasn't listening. She had spotted me and was studying me with a disturbing intensity. Once again I felt my worthiness as Myfanwy's companion being judged – this time by an eight year old. I had to struggle not to smile, which would have been a fatal faux pas, as she came over and very formally introduced herself.

"I am Gwyenth, Myfanwy's sister," she said. "You must be Thomas. Myfanwy has written to us about you." She thrust out her hand which I shook with the utmost formality.

"I am pleased to meet you Gwyneth," I said. She nodded in formal acknowledgement and then leaned forward with childish impulsiveness.

"Girls don't curtsy to boys anymore," she whispered. "It's about equality."

"I know," I whispered back, "and anyway, if you curtsied to me, I would have to bow to you and I'm not very good at that." She giggled, then she touched my forehead with her finger. I saw a shadow of doubt and fear pass across her face.

"You're strange," she said. "Your mind is all shiny and hard – like steel. Are you going to be my friend?" I was a bit surprised by the directness of the question but I answered,

"Of course I will be your friend, if you want me to be. How could I not be the friend of Myfanwy's sister?"

"That's good," she said, "because I think you would be a bit scary if you weren't my friend." I knelt down so that I was on her level and could look her straight in the eye.

"I'm really not scary, Gwyneth." I said. "At least, I don't want to be. But I really do want to be your friend." I held out my hand and allowed myself to smile. "Friends?" She smiled happily as she took my hand.

"Friends," she agreed.

"Come on you two," Myfanwy said. "Lunch is ready." Myfanwy took Gwyneth's hand and Gwyneth grabbed mine so that she could drag us both down the tunnel after the adults.

We entered the house by a big set of double doors, in about the middle of the tunnel. This led to a long, curving corridor which was wide enough for four people to walk abreast.

"You should remember this corridor," Myfanwy said. "Because it is the only one that makes any sense." Gwyneth giggled as Myfanwy explained. "Originally the house was just a large, circular fortress of almost solid stone…"

I stopped dead in amazement and said, "It must be over thirty metres thick! What on earth were you defending yourselves against?"

"That doesn't matter now. I'm trying to explain the house to you," Myfanwy said firmly as Gwyneth continued to pull us on towards lunch. "The corridor was originally a kind of escape tunnel with a few storage rooms. It is circular and runs right through the core of the house at ground level. At the start it had only four exits at each of the four points of the compass. You have seen one of them, the main entrance, the others now lead to the conservatory, the terrace and the walled garden. It is important that you remember these because they are your only reference points in what is otherwise a kind of three dimensional maze. All the other rooms and corridors were added later and without any sense of planning. Because the house was a ring of solid rock, these new additions weren't so much built as tunneled and they go every which way. It is very easy to get lost in this house." I could see what she meant. As she had been talking we had walked past a large number of doors and corridors. Some were wide, some were narrow, some led upwards, some led downwards, some had steps, some entered on the same level, some were of the same rough, dry stone construction as the original building, some were of dressed stone and some were the kind of plastered and carpeted corridor that you would see in any modern hotel. All these entered the main corridor at all sorts of angles and there was no discernible pattern to any of it.

"One more thing," Myfanwy said. "If you can, always walk clockwise around this house." She didn't explain any further and I didn't have the chance to ask why because we arrived at the dining room. This was a large and pleasant room with French windows along one wall, opening onto the stone flagged terrace and with a view across the river and to the forest beyond. It was set up very much like a modern room with a couch and arm chairs at one end and the dining table at the other. Lunch was set out on the table and it was only when I saw it that I realized how hungry I was. After lunch, Mum and Helen settled down in the arm chairs to talk about things fashionable while Myfanwy showed me to my room, which just opened off the main corridor to minimize the chances of getting lost. All my stuff was there already.

"When you've finished unpacking, meet me out on the terrace," Myfanwy said. Then she disappeared.

CHAPTER 16
Myfanwy's Garden

Just as it had been at Aelred Abbey, my room was comfortable and set up much like a modern hotel room. It was large and had a bay window that looked across the forest to the foothills of the mountains. All my stuff, including my surfboard, was already there when I arrived. When I had finished unpacking, I went back to the dining room, where my Mum and Helen were still chatting over a cup of tea. Myfanwy and Gwyneth were out on the terrace sitting on the stone balustrade. As I walked over they stopped chatting to say "hi". The view from the terrace was spectacular, with the river, the fields and the mountains.

I guess you have a lot of questions and we are here to answer them," Myfanwy said. "How's your room by the way?"

"My room is good. It seems to be equipped with every modern convenience. The light switches work and the toilet flushes. Which does raise an interesting question, there is no electricity grid here, so how do the lights work? Also, are there plumbers here? How does the sewage get treated?" Gwyneth giggled and Myfanwy looked exasperated as she replied.

"That's your big question? You come to an ancient house in a magic kingdom and your big question is where does the poo go?" Gwyneth collapsed in laughter as Myfanwy continued. "The sewage gets disposed of in a sanitary and environmentally friendly way and there is over a thousand years of stored energy in this house so it is easy to make the lights work. I would have thought that different questions would have been your immediate concern. Like; 'How come my mother doesn't notice all the strange things going on around her?' But no, you wanted to know about the sewage system." I was a bit put out by this response and not sure how to respond but I was saved when a voice from behind me said,

"The truth is that Myfanwy has no idea how the sewage system works nor has it ever entered her head that such practical matters might be important." I turned around to see a boy of about twelve who stuck out his hand and said,

"Hi, I'm Carwyn, the brother and you must be Thomas, the boyfriend." Carwyn was more like his mother than Myfanwy, except that he had the same look of mischief which Myfanwy sometimes assumed. Carwyn, however, seems to have adopted it permanently. I shook his hand and he looked at me intently. I knew from experience that that look meant that he was trying to read my mind or do some other feat of magic on me. I just stood there and waited for it to dawn on him that it wasn't working.

"Now there's a thing," he said after a second or two. "I've never come across anything like you before. There are those on this island who would find you a bit scary. Not me of course..."

"No, because he's our friend, so it's alright." Gwyneth interrupted.

Carwyn nodded, "Fair enough," he said. "Now, Myfanwy was going to tell all about the wonders of a magical life." He looked across at Myfanwy. "Continue," he said. "Don't mind me."

Myfanwy looked at him with a very stern expression on her face. "Carwyn," she said crossly. "Get over here!" He sauntered over to her. All of a sudden her face broke into one of her broadest smiles and she threw her arms around him in a big hug.

"I haven't seen you for so long!" she said.

"Hey, get off it," he complained as he disentangled himself. "You're invading my personal space. Why do girls always have to be so emotional?" I was interested in these interactions. I am an only child and had always harboured an idea that one day I might get a brother or sister. Of course, now that mum was getting on and with dad still being in Australia, I had kind of given up hope and I felt envious of the obviously close bond between Myfanwy and her siblings.

Carwyn looked at me, after he had re-established his dignity. "Well I can answer some of your questions." He said. "What's the mobile phone reception like? There isn't any. Internet connection? You must be joking. Television? Most people here have never heard of it. There is mail, however. It comes at irregular intervals, whenever Owen decides to go over to Tenby in his boat. Don't go looking for any fast food restaurants, shopping malls or even shops. There is nightlife of a sort but, believe me, you really don't want to know about it. All in all, this place is perfect – not!" I decided to ignore this description and go back to Myfanwy's comment.

"I had assumed," I said to Myfanwy, "that my mother was affected by the same sort of inattention spell you use all the time at school."

"In a way she is." Myfanwy answered. "But the spells I do at school are momentary distractions from minor incidents for people who aren't really interested anyway. They're easy. To do this for a prolonged period in matters that are of central importance to the subject, that's hard. It took Nain weeks of careful work to get your mother to the point where she is completely unable to notice anything magical but is otherwise unaffected. It does mean that her memories of this holiday will be a bit vague but she will be unharmed apart from that. Our mam will be looking after her."

"Okay," I said, "But I'm also a bit confused about the mixture of modern and medieval that goes on around here. What is this place's connection to the modern world and why is it so patchy?"

"That is really hard for us."Myfanywy said. "Time normally runs much faster in your world and it is hard for us to keep up with changes in technology and social customs. We do sometimes get it all very mixed up. That is why my mam is so interested in talking to your mam about fashion. The twentieth century was so violent that we just let it flash by, barely keeping tabs on what was happening. In fact, since the time that Cadell came back from London and... you know. Well from then until I had to go to school we were very disconnected and we had a lot of catching up to do. As Carwyn has pointed out, modern telecommunications, entertainment and commerce are still a step too far for most of us. Although, Uncle Cadfan has a good knowledge in most areas and Carwyn would claim to be an expert."

"That's going to be a problem for you, you know." I said. "As the world gets more complex, it's going to be harder for you to hide. The fact that DIAP knows you exist proves that, especially since you knew nothing of DIAP."

"Perhaps," Myfanwy said, "but at the moment that's not my problem, nor yours." She looked at Carwyn and Gwyneth, who were sitting together on the stone balustrade. "Tell mam I've taken Thomas on a tour of the island. We'll be back for dinner." With that she took my hand and we were on the parapet of the house looking across the fields to the harbour, the river, the beach, the cliffs and the sea beyond that.

I felt the now familiar disorientation but before I could complain Myfanwy said, "Great, isn't it? When I was a little girl, this is where I used to come if ever I was annoyed or upset. I would look at the sea and imagine the world that lay out there somewhere. Can you imagine all the mundane things that I thought of as exotic? Buses, shops, even school; they all seemed impossibly adventurous. While things that the people of your world only dreamed of in their wildest fantasy tales, these seemed to me to be routine and boring." It was a beautiful view and we looked out at it for a while, still holding hands, but something was bothering me.

"Myfanwy, " I asked, "In this tour of the island, are we going to keep jumping…" Suddenly we were on a stone bridge over the river. "…from place to place." I guessed that the answer was yes. Myfanwy smiled but otherwise ignored my comment.

"I would always come to this bridge when I needed to think. The flowing water was calming and I would sort of chat to Sabrina. She's very good at listening but really doesn't say anything at all." As she was speaking, a human face formed in the water with the flow lines of the river forming her hair.

"Hello Sabrina," Myfanwy said, "This is my friend Thomas." The face in the water looked at me and smiled. "Bye now," Myfanwy said. "Can't stay, we're on a tour." Then we were on the beach with beautiful, green waves curling onto the sand.

"No!" I said. "Don't do that. Why can't we just walk?" Myfanwy shrugged,

"This is a magic land," she said. "This is my home. Here it is normal to use magic and walking is just too slow." Then we were at the foot of a huge oak tree which, Myfanwy explained, was used for community gatherings.

"Could you at least warn me when you're going to do that?" I asked.

"Okay," Myfanwy said. "Here we go!" Then we were at the top of a cliff out at the headland, overlooking the beach. I knew that she was showing off and rejoicing in the freedom she had here to use her power but I pulled my hand away and sat down.

"I did give you warning that time." Myfanwy said.

"No more," I said. "I just want to stay in one place for a while."

Myfanwy pulled an exaggeratedly sad face. "Don't you want to hold my hand Thomas?" She asked in a sweet, little girl voice.

"Normally I would love to hold your hand," I said, "but it tends to lead to what Mr. Robertson would call 'rapid and disorienting spatial displacement' and, anyway, I like this place." There was a magnificent view along the coast with breakers rolling in from the ocean and crashing onto the rocks at the cliff's base. Myfanwy sat down next to me.

"I like it here too." She said. "What if I promised not to take you anywhere with magic?" In answer, I put my arm around her shoulder and she leaned against me. We sat like that for a long time. Not saying anything but watching the waves roll towards the coast and listening to them break against the rocks. Eventually my back got a sort of crick in it and I had to straighten up and stretch a bit. It broke the mood. As I looked away from the sea and towards the mountains, something occurred to me.

"Myfanwy, why didn't you take me inland at all?" I asked. "All these places are close to the coast. Why didn't you take me to see the mountains or the forest?"

"It's dangerous," she said. "There are dark things there, things where magic has gone wrong or turned sour, not to mention the wolves, bears and wild boars. Unless we have a very good reason, we don't go any further inland than Friar's Hill." She pointed to a tall hill at the beginnings of the forest which was bare of trees except for a ring of trees around the top – like a friar's tonsure.

"Come on," she said. "We need to do some 'spatial displacement' now if we are going to get home in time for dinner."

The next morning, after my mobile phone alarm had woken me, I followed the instructions I had been given the night before and walked around to the kitchen at the back of the house. As I walked in I was greeted with the delicious smell of frying bacon. Helen was there cooking bacon, eggs and sausages on top of an old wood fired stove.

"Good morning Thomas," she said. "Your mother in having a lie in but breakfast will be ready soon. I wonder if you could go and tell Myfanwy to come. She's out in the garden." The windows of the kitchen looked out into a large walled garden with fruit trees around the edge and some large raised beds of herbs and vegetables in the centre. There were even a few flowers. I said 'okay' and went out through the heavy wooden door in the centre of the kitchen's outer wall. At first I couldn't see Myfanwy but then I spotted her at the back of the garden. She was caressing the branch of a tree and as she did so it came into bud. She walked on and as she trailed her hand across a tired rosemary bush it sprouted fresh, green growth. She went from plant to plant, touching or caressing each one, and each plant responded with life and growth. She seemed to be surrounded by butterflies. I felt very shy and quiet watching her. It seemed as if all the sacred beauty of spring was wrapped up in her and this garden. Eventually she spotted me and called me over.

"How do you like our garden?" she asked.

"It's beautiful," I said, not really looking at the garden. Just then one of the things I had taken to be butterflies landed on Myfanwy's shoulder. It was not, in fact, a butterfly. It was a small humanoid figure about ten centimeters long with large butterfly-like wings. I stared at it in disbelief for a long moment, trying to frame an appropriate reaction. None came to mind.

"Um…do you know that you have fairies at the bottom of your garden?" I said at last.

Myfanwy laughed. "We have fairies all over our garden." She said. She held out her hand and two of them landed and started to preen themselves, one brushing her hair and the other arranging and rearranging his wings. "They are beautiful but silly and vain little creatures. These ones will just have been hatched. They will spend the whole of spring and summer looking for their mate. They will mate in the late summer and then, in the autumn, they will die. It's a sad little tale" I was watching the small creatures, absolutely fascinated.

"It is sad but it is also beautiful in a way." I said. "It's like a fable. They spend their whole lives lost in beauty, looking for the one thing that is important and when they have found it, their life is complete." I held out my hand and some of the fairies came and landed there as well. "Their lives may be short but they are long enough to learn that the one thing that is important is to love and that is something that cannot be measured by time." What was happening to me? How could I just accept these things as normal? Already, I could feel Annwn seeping into my bones. Myfanwy was looking at me strangely. She bent down and touched a rose bush. Immediately it came into flower. She broke off a red rose and gave it to me.

"It's normally the guy who gives the girl flowers." I said.

Myfanwy smiled. "Take it surfer boy. It will feed the poet inside you." She said. "Besides, you left something out. It's not enough to love. You must also be loved and know that you are loved. Otherwise you will wither and die." She put the red rose in my shirt pocket and the whole garden seemed to be full of its fragrance.

"Hey, Where did all these fairies come from?" a small, high pitched voice asked. Gwyneth was standing behind us looking around in amazement and I noticed that we were indeed standing in a large, colourful cloud of fairies. "I knew they always liked you Myfanwy but I have never seen so many." Gwyneth said. Then she drew breath sharply, as if she had just made a discovery. "They like the two of you together. They like the two of you together a lot!" She then had a fit of giggles.

"What is it Gwen? Why are you here" Myfanwy asked in an irritated voice.

"Mam said that you should come in because breakfast is ready and you need to say goodbye to Uncle Cadfan. He's going back to keep looking for Arawan." Gwyneth answered. We started to head back to the kitchen and Gwyneth went skipping ahead of us.

"The fairies like Tom and Myfanwy." She chanted gleefully. "The fairies like Tom and Myfanwy."

"Fairies are known to be sensitive to human emotion." Myfanwy whispered in my ear. I took her hand and this time we didn't pop off anywhere strange. We just walked back down the garden together towards the kitchen.

CHAPTER 17
The Selkies' Song

Later that morning I decided that I would give the surf a go. I told Myfanwy, who was doing something with Gwyneth, and she said she would follow me down later. Her expression said mischief but I really didn't think I could get into any trouble on a surf board, it was my home turf. So I got my wet suit and board and headed off down the trail to the beach. At first it was simply brilliant, alone on a white beach with green curling waves. The water was cold but my wet suit kept me pretty warm. There was about a two meter swell and I would ride down the face with the tube collapsing behind me, no need to worry about collisions or being cut off or priority on the wave. It was just choose a wave and go. Then the first of the creatures that Myfanwy's people called Bryn's Children, the Selkies turned up.

At first I thought it was a seal and surfers don't much like being with seals. They attract the sharks that feed on them and those sharks can all too easily mistake a surfer in a wet suit for a seal. Then it stuck its head out of the water while I was waiting for a wave. The face was that of a fine featured human female with large, dark brown eyes and long silvery hair. She said something to me in Welsh but I merely shrugged, the next wave was coming and I set off to catch it. She set off after me, swimming behind the face of the wave I was surfing. In the water she moved so much like a seal that you would swear it was a seal until she turned towards you and you found yourself looking at a human face where no human face should be. More of them turned up as I paddled out for the next wave. They crowded round my board and started to sing a hypnotic, rhythmic chant that pulled at my mind even though I had no idea what they were saying. The idea started to grow in my mind that I could swim away with them and be free.

This was a terrifying idea both in its absurdity and its power. I knew rationally that I would die if I did that and yet it still pulled at my mind. I caught the next wave more to distract myself than anything else. One of the selkies came out of the wave in front of me and I had to swerve sharply to avoid them. I fell off my board and down the face of the wave. The wave swept over me, pushing me down to the sea floor. I was surrounded by selkies and here their rhythmic chant was even clearer. The idea that I could swim off into the cool, green ocean and be free was almost irresistible. The rational part of my mind was losing function and, even after the wave past, I hesitated on the sea floor. I really think that it was only the fact that my wet suit was buoyant and dragged me to the surface that saved me. I gasped for air at the surface and decided to head for land before the selkies could get at me again.

The next wave broke before it got to me and I got such a surprise that I forgot to try and catch it into shore. I even forgot about the selkies for a while. In the foam of the wave there were horses galloping towards the beach. People will sometimes use 'white horses' as a description of waves breaking at sea but these were real horses. They raced past me and looked so real that I expected to see them gallop up onto the sand. They didn't, they faded back into the water as the wave died away. The selkies started to gather again so I determined to catch the next wave no matter what. By this time I was really too close to the shore, so the wave broke as it got to me but I climbed on my board and decided to ride it in anyway. Once again there were white horses galloping in the foam and I felt like a cross between a surfer and a chariot racer. As the wave died away I could still hear the selkies' chant and felt an irrational desire to turn around and go out to sea with them. It scared me more than I can say.

Myfanwy was on the beach as I ran up the sand. She was laughing at my predicament. Clearly she didn't know how badly things had gone wrong. All my fear turned into anger as I threw my board down.

"Why didn't you warn me!" I yelled. "You knew that something like this might happen and you let me go without any warning." She had stopped laughing and was looking at me with real concern. "Myfanwy, I almost died! I almost swam away with them to drown." She now looked stricken and all the colour had drained from her face. The selkies had started to gather in the shallow water of the shore break and once again they began their chanting. I put my hands to me ears.

"What is it that they are singing? How can I make them stop? I need to make them stop! Their song keeps pulling on my mind." Myfanwy looked puzzled.

"They keep saying the same thing over and over again, in Welsh and in Irish." She said. "They say 'Come back to us boy of the waves, hear the call of the sea.'" Myfanwy looked at me and I could see understanding dawn on her. "It's your wet suit." She said. "It looks like the skin they take off when they want to become fully human. They think you're one of them sort of stuck half way. Take off your wet suit, quickly!" As you may be aware, it is actually impossible to take off a wet suit quickly and my hands were shaking so much that I had to get Myfanwy to help me with the zip. Eventually I was left sitting on the sand and shivering in my board shorts while Myfanwy took my wet suit down to the water's edge and yelled to the selkies in Welsh. They stopped their singing and she waded out to show them the suit. It didn't take them long to turn away in disgust. The selkies song stopped and so did my desire to go drown myself, although the white horses were still galloping in as each wave broke and I felt a strange, empty longing as I looked at the open sea.

I dried myself and got dressed as Myfanwy came back up the beach. When she handed me my wet suit, I took it roughly and threw it on the sand. I was still confused and fearful and angry.

"You knew but you didn't warn me." I said. "All you had to say was "Be sure to come in when the first selkie appears and I would have been fine - but no. You thought it would be funny to see how I coped with those creatures." Myfanwy looked at me with a stricken expression.

"Tom, I didn't know that they would affect you." She said quietly. "I thought you would be immune to them just like you are immune to everything else." I didn't say anything. I just turned around and walked off the beach.

"Tom, how could I have known?" She called after me. "How could I have known that you would be affected by them? Why do they affect you when nothing else does?"

I didn't walk back towards the house but turned to follow the path towards the headland. There I found a rock and sat down, staring at the sea. I was still angry with Myfanwy but it was her last question that really bothered me. Why did the magic of the selkies bother me so much? I was afraid that Professor Rhys had already given me the answer; that my continual and close contact with magic had begun to weaken my defences.

"Woman trouble is it?" said a small voice beside me. I turned to see that I was sharing the rock with a small man in rough, country clothes. He was about two feet tall and had greenish blue skin. This I didn't want to deal with just now.

"Go away." I said. "I don't want to talk about it." I especially didn't want to talk about it with some impossible magic creature.

"Just trying to help," the little man said. "Take my advice and apologize." This was too much!

"Why should I apologize?" I demanded. "I didn't do anything wrong."

"Ah! If only I had a gold coin for every time I've heard that." He said. "It doesn't matter who was right and who was wrong, it's your relationship that matters. Go and apologize." I looked at him critically. Standing on the rock I was sitting on, he still didn't quite make it to my eye level.

"Who and what are you to give me advice?" I asked somewhat sarcastically.

"I am Apple the pixie, at your service," he said with a deep bow. "I give advice to kings and warriors, to wizards and sorcerers, as well as to love lorne teenagers. Mind you, they don't always take my advice but I give it to them anyway. Go and apologize."

"She almost got me killed!" I said.

"Ah! That's serious," he replied. "Did she mean to?" I shook my head. "Then imagine how she must feel now with you storming away in anger. Now, don't tell me you didn't storm off. How else would you come to be sitting by yourself on a rock in the middle of nowhere? Go, forgive her, apologize to her and comfort her. Trust me, it'll be the best thing you ever do." As I thought about it, I could see that he had a point. Myfanwy must be feeling pretty awful about now and she didn't really deserve that. I felt my anger draining away. I stood up.

"You're right," I said. "I need to go back." Apple looked pleased and surprised, I got the feeling that not many people took the advice he offered. He threw a handful of fine, metallic looking dust at me.

"Pixie dust for luck," he said. "If you are dealing with the family of Owyn Ap Rhys, you are certainly going to need it." With that, he scampered off into the heath and was gone and I set off on the long walk back to the house. When I got back to the fields in front of the house Helen was there with a painting easel while mum was setting up one of her large format cameras on a tripod. Gwyneth was sitting on the grass watching them. I sat down beside her.

"They are both going to do landscapes." She said.

"Gwen, Have you see Myfanwy?" I asked.

She looked at me with a kind of evil grin and asked, "Did you have a fight?" I nodded and pulled a sad face. "Then she'll be up on the parapet of the house. She always goes up there when she's sad."

"How do I get up there?" I asked.

Gwyneth looked puzzled. "I don't know," she said. "My mam never goes up there and none of the rest of us would bother using all those stairs and passageways. I don't even know if you can." I said thanks and got up to go to the house. "Don't get lost," she said as I walked away, "and remember to always walk clockwise."

I stood for a moment studying the house, looking at where the parapet section was in relation to the central tunnel. I figured out where I should enter the side passages if there was a straight stairway and then doubled the distance back around because I knew a straight stairway was too much to hope for. I went into the central corridor and paced out the distance to my calculated entry point. There I found a crooked little passageway. It was leading downwards but I took it anyway and sure enough it soon led to a steep set of stairs going up, then to a wide passage going right and left. I soon found I had entered a kind of maze of passages. I have a very good sense of direction but I swiftly lost confidence in the twists and turns of those passages. I ignored any entrance with doors, since these probably led to rooms and I was not interested in rooms, and I always kept turning to the left to try and obey the instruction to walk clockwise. Whenever I could, I went to the left and I went up. I don't know how long this actually took but it seemed to take a very long time and I nearly despaired of ever finding my way out – let alone to the parapet. Then I found myself at the foot of a small wooden staircase with a heavy wooden door at the top. Daylight was coming from under the door. When I went up and pushed the door open, I found myself at one end of the parapet walkway with Myfanwy at the other.

When she saw me she turned away and said, "Go away. Go right away. In fact, go back to Australia. You'll be safe. I don't think Apophis will follow you there."

"I'm not going anywhere Myfanwy," I said. "I'm certainly not running away from Apophis but I yelled at you and I'm sorry…"

"I don't want an apology Tom! I'm not mad at you, I'm ashamed of myself. I'm the one who nearly got you killed. You're in my world and I should have looked after you but I didn't. I was reckless and you nearly died. Uncle Cadfan must be right. The longer you stay here, the longer you stay with me, the weaker your immunity becomes. Today the Bryn's Children were able to get to you. Tomorrow maybe Apophis will. Please just go away. I can't have anything happen to you." By this time I was standing next to her.

"I'm not afraid of Apophis," I said, "and I'm not going anywhere." She turned back to me and I could see that she had been crying. There were still tears in her eyes. Suddenly, she threw her arms around me and held me in a tight hug, sobbing into my shoulder.

Between sobs she said, "What if you died because of me?"

I hugged her back and said, "That's not going to happen but we do need to find out why the selkies could get at me that way."

"Then you need to go and talk to Friar Daffyd," said a voice behind us. We both turned and Carwyn was standing there with a carefully neutral expression on his face.

"Carwyn!" Myfanwy said in an exasperated voice. "What are you doing here? Can't I have any privacy?"

Carwyn pulled a very contrived expression of puzzlement. "In this house? In this family? No, I don't think so," he said. "Anyway, you really do need to go and talk to Friar Daffyd and Mam wants me to tell you to come down because dinner's ready."

CHAPTER 18
Friar Daffyd's Hermitage

The need to know the meaning of the selkie incident pressed heavily on my mind and I didn't sleep well at all that night. The same was clearly true of Myfanwy because next morning she was determined that we should take Carwyn's advice and set off to visit Friar Daffyd. Mind you, setting off with Myfanwy means that she grabs your hand and you are suddenly somewhere else. In this case we were at the edge of the forest near the foot of Friar's Hill. A steep, rocky path wound its way up towards the top.

"Is there a reason why we materialized at the bottom of the steep hill?" I asked. "If we have to do that weird teleporting stuff, couldn't we at least teleport to the top of the hill?"

"Friar Daffyd doesn't let people just arrive at his hermitage. He values his privacy. You should be happy surfer boy, from here on up we have to walk." Myfanwy said smiling. "Come on, it's a nice morning for a stroll."

The path was steep and rough and it took us most of the morning to climb to the top. Myfanwy chatted almost continuously all the way up, mostly telling me about the people who lived in Annwn and pointing out their houses. I think she was trying to cover up the nervousness she felt about the selkies. Most of the time I wasn't really listening but I did learn that the people of Annwn tended to live in small, separate cottages with no real towns. The large house of Myfanwy's family was very much the exception. This did raise the question of the status of Myfanwy's family in this society.

The views from the path were spectacular and just kept getting better as we climbed. When we finally got to the top, I could see that the ring of trees I had seen from the headland was actually more like a fence of trees. In fact, the trees had grown so close together that they formed a kind of hedge. They were mostly fruit trees, particularly apples, although there were also Yew and Oak trees mixed in. Other things, like blackberry and hawthorn bushes, were growing between and around the trees so that there were no gaps and there did not seem to be any way in.

Myfanwy kept walking along the path which continued around the outside of the hedge until we were on the inland side of the hill, looking out over steep, rocky mountains and thick forest. There a small wicker gate led to an avenue of hedge, and I realized that the hedge formed not a circle but a portion of a spiral. Myfanwy opened the gate and walked through. I followed. We were now walking with the hedge on either side of us. After a short while we came to another gate which led us to a broad open space at the top of the hill. This was surrounded by the tree hedge as if by a wall. In the centre of the space was a small lake whose waters were dark and still. There were a number of chickens who were scratching around under the hedge, and a goat who was looking at us with mild interest as it continued chewing.

I had the immediate impression that I had walked into somewhere special, somewhere different. This may seem strange since I was already in Annwn, which was itself a very different sort of place, but here there was a feeling of silence and stillness, of timelessness and peace, that the rest of Annwn didn't have. It was as if time and change were disconnected. Time still ran but nothing here really changed. Years could pass but the chickens would still be there scratching and the goat would still be there chewing.

There were three buildings around the lake, all made of stone with thatched roofs. The one closest to us was clearly an animal shelter, to house the chickens and the goat. The building across from us had a cross on top and looked like a small chapel while the one on our right had a small chimney from which a thin stream of smoke could be seen curling into the still air. Beside it there were the raised beds of a small vegetable garden. It was from this last building that a figure emerged. It was a short, balding man dressed in the rough, brown tunic of a Franciscan friar. He held out his arms towards us.

"Myfanwy! My dear girl. How wonderful to see you," he exclaimed. Myfanwy ran over to him and gave him a quick hug then she turned and introduced me.

"Ah, so you are Thomas. Let me see you," he said. He placed a hand on each shoulder and looked me directly in the eyes. I now had enough experience of meeting magical people to know that he was testing my immunity to magic. Finally he pulled back.

"Remarkable," he said simply. "Myfanwy my dear, my vegetable garden needs a bit of care. I wonder if you could have a look at it. Thomas, why don't we go over and have a chat by the lake?" Myfanwy pulled a face which clearly showed that she knew she was being disposed of but she went with reasonably good grace. We went and sat on a small stone bench at the edge of the pond. The friar seemed to belong in this place. There was a stillness about him and a habitual silence that fitted the peacefulness of the hermitage. It felt easy to tell him about what had happened with the selkies, about my reaction and about the fears I still had. He sat and gazed into the still waters of the lake and listened and I think he would have been content to sit like that for a long time. However, I was impatient to get answers to my questions.

"How is it that the selkies can affect me when no other sort of magic can?" I asked - demanded really.

He gave a small shrug and said, "That's not much of a mystery. Cadfan, or even Myfanwy, should have been able to work that out. The answer is that the enchantments of the selkies are not magic in the same way as Cadfan's forgetting spells or Myfanwy's relationship with nature." I looked across at Myfanwy who was walking slowly through the friar's vegetable garden and having the same effect on plant growth that she had had back at her own house. "This is because the selkies, as you call them, are not really magical creatures," Friar Dyffad continued. "Rather, they are mythic creatures. You see Thomas there are three basic ways of understanding the world, of approaching reality. There is the mundane, practical understanding which most people use most of the time. Now it may seem strange to you, but the magic of myself, Cadfan, Myfanwy and of all our people fits into this understanding. We use energy to manipulate the physical world just as your engineers and scientists do. Different in some ways, yes, but the same basic idea. Indeed, if we were to allow them to study us, I'm sure your scientists could come up with a physical explanation of what we do." I nodded, thinking of Dr. Jones and his discussion of quantum uncertainty. "However, the selkies would utterly confound any such explanation because they are creatures from a different way of understanding the world, a mythological understanding. This view of the world derives not from the intellect but from the deep longings of the human heart and while your engineers might be confounded, I think your poets would understand.

The existence of these creatures - the selkies, the fairies, the pixies, the water maidens and the rest – is dependent on human mythological understanding." As he was speaking the dark waters of the lake seemed to shift and change and images of the creatures he spoke about, and others that I couldn't name, drifted to the surface and faded into shadow. "This is why they have largely disappeared from your world where the practical understanding has become so dominant that people have lost their capability for mythological thought. They survive here because our people do not have such a rigid understanding of the world."

"That doesn't explain why the selkies could affect me," I interrupted. "They affected me so badly that I almost went and drowned myself. Even now I hear this one phrase of theirs over and over in my head. I don't even know what it means and yet it still pulls at me in way I have never experienced before. It sounds like: an glaoch na mara." Friar Dyffad looked at me thoughtfully.

"Interesting," he said. "Irish, a language I have not heard for a long time. It means 'the call of the sea' and there is your explanation. Thomas, you are from the Clan O'Maille and your ancestors lived on the west coast of Ireland. For over a thousand years they were fishermen, traders, explorers and, yes, pirates too." Again the lake shifted and images of a wild sea coast with men dressed in rough woolen clothing and sailing leather covered boats drifted to the surface. "They lived by the sea and from the sea. The selkies and their enchantments would have been no surprise to them. You have clearly retained some of their mythological sensibility. This may well be the reason you are so keen on surfing." Once again the waters shifted and I gasped in surprise - there was an image of me surfing the point break at Angle Creek. The image was from years ago when my dad was just teaching me to surf. I could see him sitting on his board so clearly that I wanted to reach out and touch him. "The reason the selkies could affect you is that they are a part of you. They are a personification of something deep in your heart. This has nothing to do with magic, this is a part of who you are. The sea will always call to you Thomas."

"So Professor Rhys is wrong?" I asked. "I won't lose my immunity to magic through constant exposure?" He put his head on its side and gave a small shrug.

"Cadfan's theory is certainly possible," he said. "It depends on what you are. You are a puzzle to us Thomas. Your resistance to magic is so complete and so effortless that it seems to be almost magical itself. It's hard for us to believe that such a thing is possible. There are rare souls who are so integrated and certain of their own self that magic will have only a limited effect. This can even be taught to some extent. But if you are such a person then you are the most complete since Peretur and have this quality to a remarkable degree." In the lake I could see the face of a young man with close cropped hair, wearing the uniform of a Roman officer. "If this is so, then as your mind accepts magic as normal, you may lose your protection. In that case your close friendship with Myfanwy and your coming to Annwn may well have placed you in danger. However, you can rest easy about the events of yesterday. The call of the selkies is not evidence of this happening." He was quiet and still for a long time, staring thoughtfully into the still waters of the lake. When he spoke again he spoke so softly that I had to strain to hear him.

"There is another possibility," he said. "One that would be even more remarkable and hazardous. You may be what we call a wild talent and this ability of yours may itself be magical. If that's so, then no one can predict what may develop from your friendship with Myfanwy and your coming to Annwn. Cadfan is certainly right about one thing, no one comes to Annwn and goes away unchanged, you least of all." This didn't sound very encouraging so I decided to change the subject.

"Um…Friar Dyffid, you said there were three ways of understanding the world. You have only mentioned two. What's the third way?" I asked. He smiled and indicated the rough tunic he wore.

"The third way is the most important. It is the way of understanding so dear to my beloved Francis. It is the spiritual understanding, the religious dimension. Your world is in danger of losing this understanding as well and yet to be fully human you must have all three, each in its proper order and balance. To be fully alive a person cannot just be mind and hands, they must be heart and spirit as well." He then smiled broadly. "And they must eat. Come, let us go and get some lunch."

Myfanwy joined us as we went up to the hermit's hut. The anxiety that had been plaguing her all morning showed in her nervous smile.

I smiled to reassure her and the friar said, "Oh, don't worry Myfanwy. All your immediate fears are groundless. Your Thomas remains as stubbornly resistant to magic as ever. You, however, need some reminding of the difference between myth and magic." You could almost see the anxiety fall away from her like a weight. Her smile broadened to light up her whole face and she almost skipped the rest of the way to the hut.

The inside of the hut was unlined and spartan. There was a small bed in one corner and a bare wooden table with benches either side in the middle. The only other furniture was a tall cupboard which acted as a pantry and a smaller cupboard whose top acted as a workbench. A spare tunic and a cloak hung from a peg on the wall. There was also a small iron stove with a fire burning brightly. It had a large pot and a camp oven on top. Friar Daffyd urged us to sit down and then went to get bowls and plates. We were then served a thick and spicy vegetable soup from the pot and a type of bread from the camp oven. The bread was almost like a scone and in Australia we would have called it Damper, I don't know what the Welsh call it. I was hungry after the long morning's work and the soup and the bread tasted good. A number of small mice ran quietly and confidently under the table to collect fallen bread crumbs. Clearly, they didn't bother the friar and he didn't bother them. Myfanwy saw them and pulled her legs up a little but had no further reaction.

"You aren't going to make these ones dance?" I asked. As I said this, the friar looked sharply and severely at Myfanwy.

"Myfanwy," he said. "I hope you remember that even the smallest living thing has a dignity natural to it which must be respected. They are not things to be used for your amusement." Myfanwy hung her head with a sheepish expression.

"I do try to remember brother," she said meekly. She then kicked me hard under the table. I quickly decided that a distraction was in order.

"Friar Daffyd, forgive me for asking this," I said. "But are you a real Franciscan?"

The friar laughed. "You are well named, Thomas the doubter," he replied. "Yes, I am a Franciscan, although I haven't been in touch with my Order for nearly four hundred years and I think they would be a bit surprised to hear from me now. When the time came for me to be educated I was due to go to the Benedictine Monastery on Caldy Island, as was the practice of my family. However, we found that the monastery had been closed years before by King Henry so I was sent to the Franciscan Friary at Timoleague in the south west of Ireland: a place that the English soldiers found very hard to access, although they certainly tried. There I fell in love with Francis, with his love of life and with his poetry, and I joined the community. I stayed there until 1629 when the English finally destroyed the friary and the community was scattered. I came back to Annwn and took over the hermitage. I have been here ever since."

"I'm sorry I asked," I said. "It's just that in my world there's a big conflict between religion and the people who believe in magic – witches and so on." Myfanwy rolled her eyes and gave a contemptuous snort but the friar merely nodded.

"Telling the future, talking to spirits, love potions - things like that?" he suggested. When I nodded he explained, "Even if all that were possible, and I don't really believe that such things are, it would be very dangerous. What these people are trying to do is to manipulate the world of the spirit as if it were the mundane world of cause and effect. This robs their spiritual understanding of its essential nature and leaves them trapped in their own illusions and imaginings." He looked at me very seriously. "I hope you realize that the talents of Myfanwy and the people of Annwn have nothing to do with this sort of nonsense." I nodded. I really did know. It was pretty obvious when you thought about it. I couldn't imagine the government setting up a secret agency like DIAP to investigate the activities of "Glynda the white witch and star lady".

After lunch we set off for home. We had a long walk ahead of us. As we were leaving, Friar Daffyd stopped me and spoke to me very seriously. "You are a mystery to us Thomas and, I think, to yourself also," he said. "We do need to get to the bottom of this mystery. It will take me a few days but I intend to call a meeting of the Nobles of Annwn. We will meet at the Meeting Tree and I think you should be there. In fact, I think it is essential that you should be there. I will let you know when the meeting is ready." I nodded in agreement. I didn't know who the Nobles of Annwn were but if I was going to face Apophis I needed all the information I could get and these sounded like the people who could answer my questions.

CHAPTER 19
The Trial

The next few days passed quietly. In the morning I would practice my Tai Chi Chuan forms in the field in front of the house, watched sometimes by Myfanwy. In the afternoons Myfanwy would take me exploring her island. Much to my relief, we went more slowly than on that first day because we went on foot, often accompanied by Gwyneth or Carwyn. As Myfanwy introduced me to the people of the island, I learned that Annwn held a diverse community: there were farmers, healers, herdsmen, weavers and metalsmiths. The cottages down by the harbor mainly held the fisherfolk and on the edge of the forest there lived the quiet, dark people who were hunters. It was while we were visiting the hunter people that I noticed that the river road continued on deep into the forest. When I asked Myfanwy where it went, she would only say that the forest was dangerous and wouldn't discuss it any further. She wouldn't even look down the road.

In all of this, I couldn't help but notice the respect in which Myfanwy and her family were held: a whispered "The family of Owen Ap Rhys" ran quickly through each household we visited. Myfanwy and Gwyneth were both normally addressed as "my lady", something which delighted Gwyneth and embarrassed Myfanwy. The reaction to Carwyn was even more interesting. He was simply met with a silent bow which he would return with an amused grace. To the extent that politeness would allow, they mostly ignored me.

During this time people started to arrive from the other world and Owen's fishing boat began to operate more like a ferry. Nain was the first to arrive and Myfanwy and her whole family went down to greet her. She then disappeared, off on business of her own. The next day a tall, muscular man with flaming red hair arrived. I had never seen him before but I noticed that Myfanwy was very wary of him and kept well out of his way. He strode off to the north, to a part of Annwn we had not visited. Professor Rhys came a few days later and came to stay up at the house. He left early the next morning to talk to Friar Daffyd. That night at dinner he made the announcement I had been waiting for,

"There's going to be a community meeting tomorrow, Thomas. I think you might find it interesting. Would you like to come along?" I nodded my agreement but my mother looked uncertain. She didn't know if she had been asked as well and if she could say no without giving offence. Helen leaned across to her and said in a loud whisper,

"I don't think we need to go dear. We've been to too many meetings and we have a lot of work to do on our exhibition." Mum smiled and said that was true. Everything was settled.

Apparently it was considered very bad manners to teleport to a community meeting, so the next morning we walked down to the river. As we got to the stone bridge, Professor Rhys asked us to stop.

"We must wait for our guest," he said. I looked at Myfanwy but she seemed as puzzled as I was and just shrugged her shoulders. It wasn't long before the guest appeared. A white boat came up the river. It moved swiftly against the flow even though it had no obvious means of propulsion. It was a canoe covered in white leather and with a frame of light coloured wood. It had a high prow and elegant, sweeping lines. The boat, however, was no more remarkable than the figure which stood easily amidships. He was about my height and had reddish hair about the same colour as mine, although his was long and swept back from his head. He was dressed in a vivid green tunic, trimmed with gold which came down to his knees. He wore a belt of ornate leather and a bright plaid cloak around his shoulders. Around his neck was an ornate ring of gold and at each hip there hung a short sword in its scabbard. There was no one else onboard although the boat was large enough to have held a dozen men.

As the boat pulled up to the bridge, he stepped easily ashore, leaving the boat to ride in the river. Without any mooring, it stayed exactly as he had left it. He called out a greeting to Professor Rhys in Welsh and had a broad smile on his face as he walked up to meet him. I heard Myfanwy give an exclamation that seemed half exasperation and half disgust. I turned to look at her and she seemed very annoyed but there was also something like admiration in her expression.

"Who is he?" I asked.

"His name is Declan," she answered. "He is one of the Tuatha De Danann and he has come from Tir na nOg off the west coast of Ireland. We must have asked him here because of your ancestry. He is also a great showoff." She looked at me closely and then laughed. "You don't see it, do you?" She asked. I just sort of shrugged, not knowing what she was talking about. "He won't like that. He has put a 'glamour' on himself. It is something all the De Danann are good at. When anyone looks at him, anyone except you that is, they see him as the most beautiful man in the world with a bright halo of light about him. It's a trick they used at one time to get people in Ireland to worship them." I turned and looked back at this Declan. He was not ugly but he was nothing special either and there was certainly no bright halo.

"But…You don't see him that way, do you?" I asked. "You know what he is doing."

"That's the really annoying thing," Myfanwy answered. "I know what he is doing but his spell still works. To me he just looks magnificent." Beside her, Gwyneth gave a soft sigh, almost of adoration. I decided then that there was ample reason not to like this Declan of the De Danann. He walked up and bowed deeply and extravagantly to Professor Rhys, who was standing in his neat business suit, with his bowler hat in his hand. The professor returned the bow rather stiffly.

"You must stop all this nonsense you have cast about yourself Declan," he said. "It is not seemly."

"Ah! I only did it to impress the young ladies. You can't blame me for that," Declan replied. He turned and gave a bright, friendly smile to Myfanwy and Gwyneth. Myfanwy gave a snort of disgust and disappointment replaced the rapt expression on Gwen's face. To me he had not changed at all but I assumed that the 'glamour' had gone.

"I am, of course, your guest Cadfan, and I mean no criticism but why do we speak this mongrel of a language?" Declan asked.

"Thomas knows nothing of the ancient tongues," the professor replied. Declan looked at me then and there was genuine sadness in his face.

"No, I don't suppose he does," he said. "The wonder is that he is alive at all. The tale of his people is a sorry one." His smile returned as he walked over to me but I watched him warily. At first I thought he was about my age but the more I looked at him the greater my doubts became. Something about him made me think that guessing his true age might prove problematic. His eyes were not the emerald green of Myfanwy's people but a deep, royal blue.

"Hi, I'm Thomas O'Malley," I said, offering him my hand. He shook it with enthusiasm.

"Declan," he said. "So, you are Thomas. The one who has caused me to leave Tir na nOg and cross the wild sea," He looked at me intently and the smile quickly left his face to be replaced by a thoughtful and wary look. "You are one of the west people, right enough Thomas and I think we have seen your like before. It was people like you who caused the end of our age in the world. Cadfan, I wonder if you know the risk you have taken in bringing this one to Annwn."

"We had little choice," the professor replied. "Arawn was hunting him and was prepared to kill thousands in order to get at him." From the wary look on his face, I'm not sure Declan wouldn't have been prepared to let him. However, his smile returned as he greeted Myfanwy and Gwyneth with exaggerated and slightly mocking courtesy. He too made a silent bow to Carwyn which Carwyn returned rather grudgingly. The professor indicated that we should continue our walk to the meeting and set off with Declan beside him. The two made an odd pair, Declan in his long cloak and tunic and the professor in his business suit and bowler hat.

We arrived at the meeting tree, which was a huge oak tree in the middle of a grassy meadow, about mid-morning. There was already a crowd gathered of all the different peoples of Annwn. There was a small group off to one side. This consisted of Nain and Friar Daffyd, whom I knew, and the tall red haired man who I had seen getting off the boat. There were three others who I had never seen before: an old man in a sky blue robe, a young man dressed as a fisherman, in jeans and a thick woolen jumper, and a lady with long, blond hair who was dressed in white. Professor Rhys and Declan went off to join this group while Friar Daffyd came over to greet us.

"Bless you all," he said. "It is good to see you. Gwen and Carwyn, you haven't come up to see me for a long time. I will expect a visit soon." He took me by the arm. "I'm afraid I must ask you to stand over here on your own Thomas. What happens now is that each of the nobles of Annwn, and our Irish guest if he so chooses, will conduct a test of their own choosing to determine the nature of your strange ability." He gave a wry smile. "It will seem a little odd to you I think, because my guess is that you will simply stand here with everyone watching and with nothing happening. The council of nobles will then try to come to an understanding of your ability."

"You are not one of the nobles then?" I asked.

"No, no," he answered. "I am just a simple friar. I am here only as what I think your people would call a technical advisor. Those six are the nobles." I looked across at this group of nobles and they were certainly a strange group. Nain was there wearing one of her floral dresses and an old straw hat. She was smiling at everyone as if she really was everyone's grandmother. Professor Rhys seemed wildly out of place, standing erect and solemn in his business suit and bowler hat. The red haired man was dressed in very fashionable but casual clothes and had a look of slight irritation. The old man in the blue robe seemed distracted by the clouds and the guy dressed as a fisherman had silvery hair and large, deep green eyes. It was clear that there was more than a little selkie blood in his ancestry. The pale woman was the strangest figure of all. She had long, ash blond hair, very pale skin and was wearing a long white gown with a silver belt around her waist. The only colour about her was the brilliant green of her eyes. Her face had such an expression of ethereal calm that it was slightly unnerving. After greeting the group, Declan had gone a little way to one side and sat down. He seemed to be simply enjoying the morning sunshine.

"My lady," Nain said. "Before the formal testing begins, there is something I would like to demonstrate to the council. Friar Daffyd, will you please travel with Thomas to the river bridge." Friar Daffyd took my arm and then disappeared. He was back almost straight away.

"I'm afraid I can't make Thomas travel with me," he said.

Nain nodded. "Very good," she said. "Myfanwy, will you please come and travel with Thomas to the river bridge." She came forward nervously and took my hand. We were then on the stone bridge over the river with Declan's boat still where he had left it. Myfanwy suddenly let go of my hand and hugged me tight.

"Don't be afraid Tom," she said. "Don't be afraid."

I pulled back and looked at her curiously. "Until you said that, I didn't think I had any need to be," I said. "What should I be afraid of?" She just smiled nervously and took my hand and we were back under the oak tree. There was a general buzz of comment from the crowd when we arrived back. Nain turned to the rest of the council as if to say "See!" and the lady in white nodded slowly. I noticed that Declan had also taken a sudden interest in the proceedings.

The formal examination that followed went pretty much as Friar Daffyd had said it would. I stood there with everyone looking at me in silence while nothing happened. Occasionally I got an itch on my forehead, near the top of my nose, but that was about it. Eventually the council all sort of looked at each other and the pale lady began to make an announcement.

"Thomas O'Malley you may go. The council will now…"

"Wait!" a thin, broken voice interrupted. "Am I not still a noble of Annwn? Do I not still have a voice in the council? Do I not still have the right to test this abomination that stands before us?" There were loud gasps and a stifled scream from the crowd. Declan sprang to his feet with his hands on his swords. Coming towards us was something from a horror movie. There was a withered, old figure dressed in a tattered black robe and seated in a carved wooden chair. Somehow, this chair had the living legs of a deer attached and was walking towards us. It was flanked on either side by two enormous wolves.

"Cadell, you are the abomination. You foul the very air we breathe," the red haired man said in a deep and powerful voice, "but you do have the rights and protection of custom. So do your test and be gone, because no one on this council will ever listen to anything you say."

The figure in the chair smiled a thin, mirthless smile. "If my test succeeds there will be no need," it said. Professor Rhys had looked away and was visibly shaking. I realized that this was Cadell, the father of Apophis, who had killed Owen Ap Rhys, his brother. I looked over to Myfanwy who was holding a sobbing Gwen and trying to comfort her. Carwyn had interposed himself between the monstrous group and his sisters and was glaring at Cadell with all the precocious courage of a school boy. I noticed that Declan's eyes never left Cadell nor did his hands ever leave his swords.

Cadell stretched out his hands towards me with his fingers outstretched. Around me the air started to crackle and there were flashes of light. These became more intense until I was surrounded by a sphere of light and white noise. The sphere started to expand and I noticed that the grass under my feet had died and turned to dust. From somewhere outside this sphere I heard Myfanwy scream. I don't know how long this all took but eventually I felt a presence pressing in on me, like someone I didn't like invading my personal space. Instinctively, I drew back but the presence kept pressing in. Then I got angry. What right did anyone have to force themselves against me like this?

"No!" I yelled. "No more!" with that yell all the anger and revulsion I was feeling flowed out of me in a rush and the presence and the sphere of light and noise vanished. I found myself standing under the oak tree with my right hand pointing towards Cadell. Cadell was lying on the ground. His chair was broken, the legs were dead and unmoving and the wolves were running away, back to their forest. In that moment I looked at a pitiful, crippled old man. Then he snarled at me with an animal hatred. He tried to stand on his crippled legs and then he vanished, presumably back to his house. Suddenly, I felt very tired.

CHAPTER 20
A Decision Is Made

There was complete silence for a while, nobody moved. Then Declan started to clap and the crowd joined in, clapping and cheering. Myfanwy came running over and hugged me. Carwyn came running up and shook my hand, all the time cheering. Myfanwy was not cheering, she was sobbing into my shoulder.

"He tried to kill you Thomas," she said. "His test was a death spell, the worst one he could think of. He changed the foundations of the world around you so that nothing could live. He thought that that would kill even you."

"What he did," said Carwyn with a gleeful superiority, "was to change the ratio between the strong nuclear force and the electromagnetic force by the tiniest fraction and just in that small area. Of course, if you do that then chemical bonds start to become unstable, biochemistry becomes impossible and no living thing can survive. That's what all the light and noise were about, molecules in the air becoming unstable and releasing energy. I still don't understand how you survived or what happened at the end but it was great to see Cadell humiliated!"

However, when Friar Daffyd came up he had a very serious expression. "Carwyn, would you please take Gwen home," he said." and tell Helen that there may be something of a celebration tonight. Myfanwy, could you please take Thomas directly to my hermitage. Don't worry about the protocols, you have my permission. Please just take him directly there."

Then we were in the hermitage and everything was still and quiet. The chooks were scratching around under the fruit trees, the goat was contentedly chewing and the still waters of the pond reflected the bright, spring sky. Once again I was struck by the peaceful power of this place. Here peace was an active and positive force. Myfanwy still had a tight grip on my arm, as if she was afraid I was going to disappear. We went and sat on the bench by the pond.

"That was the spell that…"Myfanwy stopped, unable to get the words out.

"That was the spell that killed your father?" I asked. She nodded. I put my arm around her and drew her towards me. All the fear and grief came flowing out and she cried softly as I held her close to me.

It was sometime later that Friar Daffyd returned to his hermitage. Myfanwy had cried herself out and we were just sitting together watching the clouds reflected in the waters of the pond. He came over and sat with us.

"The council is deliberating," he said. "Not about you, there is no longer any mystery about you, Thomas. Paradoxically, it seems that your immunity to magic is itself magical. You have a strange, wild talent and a powerful one at that. Declan says that the DeDanann have encountered it before, that it is rare but not unknown among your people. I'm not sure that I believe him. I have never encountered anyone like you.

No, the council is now deliberating about the action to be taken against Cadell. That was a dreadful spell, a complex, subtle and dreadful spell. Only Cadell would have the skill or the daring to do something as dangerous as that. But you surprised him Thomas. Not only were you able to maintain the proper order of the world around you but when pressed, you were able to project you negation of magic outwards to defend yourself. I think that for a moment there Cadell found himself without any magical ability or perception at all. You see, Thomas, we can not only do things normal people can't, we see the world in a different way." He picked a small flower from the grass. "If I were to drop this flower you would see only one possible outcome, it would fall down. However, we see a whole range of possibilities. It might, for example, stay floating in the air." He let go of the flower and it didn't fall. It just stayed floating where it was. "It's like a musician. A musician will be aware of the most probable note to resolve a chord but he will also be aware of other possibilities, some in harmony and some discordant. Reality is like that with us. For every event we see a myriad of possibilities, not just the most probable outcome. You took away from Cadell not just his power but his perception also. He was forced to see that there were limits on his existence and power. He was made painfully aware not just of his humanity but of his mortality. It must have shaken him to his core."

"But I didn't really have any control over that." I said. "It just happened."

"Not conscious control, no." the friar said. "But at some level you do have instinctive control. I think this is why you can travel with Myfanwy and with no one else. At some level you want to travel with Myfanwy. You want to go where she goes and you can control your immunity to allow it to happen. This is not something of your conscious mind but a deep desire of your heart."

"But she could take me places even before we were friends, while I was still really afraid of her power," I objected. The old friar smiled.

"Yes," he said. "Isn't that interesting? The heart has reasons the mind doesn't know. The bond between you is strong and it is deep: deeper than either of you can yet understand." He slapped his hands against his knees and smiled, obviously changing the subject.

"Anyway," he said. "I had to get you away from that mob or you would still be there and I think after that effort you deserve a quiet lunch." We joined him in his hut for a lunch of soft cheese and warm bread. After lunch Friar Daffyd asked to speak to Myfanwy on her own, so I set off to explore the hermitage grounds. Eventually I found myself in front of the chapel. I hesitated but then walked in. I found myself in a silent and still space, a sacred space. It was dimly lit with two candles at the front and a red sanctuary lamp to one side. There was a small alter in front a large icon of the crucifixion which dominated the chapel. I knelt down to pray, something I had not really done since I left Australia. Here in the silent chapel, I finally accepted what Annwn had been trying to teach me. Yes, I was Tom the schoolboy surfer nerd from Australia but I was also a warrior of the Clan O'Maille, sent by fate to Myfanwy's people, and there was a task that only I could do. The choice was before me.

By the time Friar Daffyd came looking for me I had made up my mind. I knew what I needed to do. If the council would not support me, I would do it alone.

When the friar eventually found me in the chapel, I turned to him and softly asked, "Friar Daffyd, were you ever ordained a priest?" He looked at me with a look of surprise and puzzlement.

"Yes I was, to serve my community, many years ago. Why do you ask?"

"Because I need you to hear my confession," I said. Without further comment he went over to a cupboard at the side of the chapel and took out an ancient stole, huge and heavily embroidered. He placed this over his head and indicated a bench along one wall of the chapel. There we sat while I made my confession. When we had finished, he looked at me with real and deep concern in his face.

"Thomas," he said, "In my years in Ireland I have heard the confession of many a young warrior and I know when a man is preparing to go into battle. What is it that you are planning to do?" But I just shook my head, this was not the time or the place. More and more, I was becoming convinced that I would have to do this alone.

Myfanwy was waiting for us beside the entrance. I expected her to ask questions but she seemed to be distracted, as if she was thinking of something so important that what was happening here and now didn't seem to matter much. All the way down the hill she was strangely distant. She would nod and smile occasionally but she clearly wasn't following my attempt at conversation and didn't really answer any of the questions I asked her. At the bottom of the hill she kept walking along the path until I pointed out the time.

"Myfanwy, much as I hate that rapid spatial displacement of yours," I said. "If we have to walk home we will be very late." She smiled then and came back to take my hand.

"Ah! I see my advice has worked," said a small, gruff voice behind us. "Advice and a liberal dose of pixie dust – always does the trick" We turned around to see the pixie, Apple, sitting on a rock.

"What advice and who's been using pixie dust?" Myfanwy asked. Then it dawned on her and she turned to look at me with an accusing expression. "That's how you found me on the parapet that day! I couldn't figure out how you got up there through all that maze of tunnels that no one's used for years. You were using pixie dust!"

"Oh go away with you!" Apple said. "The boy has no more knowledge of using pixie dust than you do of surfing. He just looked a bit down on his luck when last I saw him, so I gave him a liberal dusting. But it was the advice that worked, my advice…"

"And what was your advice Apple?" Myfanwy challenged. "To always apologise, no matter what?" She started to laugh and it was so good to hear her laugh again that I didn't even mind that she was sort of laughing at me. "Oh Tom," she said. "Never take advice from a pixie, especially not that one!"

Apple drew himself up to the full dignity of his twenty four inches and was preparing to disappear in a huff when I bowed to him and said, "Thank you for your help, Apple. It was much appreciated, by me."

Apple seemed a little mollified and he returned my bow. "In that case, I will give you some further advice," he said. "Do not attempt what it is in your mind to do. You are not a champion yet and not even the hunt and the hounds of Annwn could accomplish such a task."

Myfanwy stopped laughing. "What did he say?" she asked. "Apple, what did you say about the hunt?" But Apple was gone. She turned to me but I simply shrugged.

"You said it yourself," I said. "You should never take any notice of what a pixie says." She looked doubtful and would have pressed me further but I held out my hand and said, "Time to go". Reluctantly, she took my hand and we were back at the house.

The dinner that night was pretty much like the big, magical feast that I had first imagined when I visited Aelred Abbey. It was in a room I had never been in before; a room lit by flaming torches along the walls and with a huge vaulted ceiling held up by massive stone pillars. A real feast appeared on the polished wood table in the centre of the room. It started with little, spicy appetizers. These were followed by a cold potato soup, then a kind of seafood stew with crab and cockles, then roast venison with leeks and a red wine sauce, and finally wild berries and sorbet. The silver goblets were full of a kind of fruit juice that I could not identify but they were refreshing and never seemed to empty. My mother looked a bit confused each time a new dish appeared but she quickly recovered and was chatting happily to those around her. No one mentioned why we were having such a feast and Nain was the only member of the Council of Nobles, other than Professor Rhys, to attend. However, there were several of the farmers and artisans that I had met with Myfanwy seated at the table.

After dessert we left the table to go to another room where cheese, chocolates and cups of coffee or cocoa were laid out and waiting for us. It was here that I was finally able to talk to the professor alone.

"Professor," I said. "The Council has to follow up with Cadell. He is the key to finding out where Apophis is and what he is up to. He is Apophis' father, he must know something of where he might be and what he is planning."

The professor shook his head and said, "He has gone back to his house and his house is a fortress with enormously powerful magical defenses. He is beyond our reach."

"Not if you were to use me," I said eagerly. "I could use my talent to get you through the defenses."

Again he shook his head. "I'm afraid not Thomas," he said. "Through your bond with Myfanwy, you are seen as being closely allied to my family and such a move would be seen as giving my family too much power and influence. The council would not allow it. They think that we have too much influence already."

"There are things at stake here that are more important than the politics of Annwn," I insisted. He gave a sad, twisted sort of smile.

"For some on the council there is nothing more important than the politics of Annwn," he said. He was only confirming what I already feared: the council would do nothing and I would have to do this alone. I found it difficult to enjoy what remained of the party.

Myfanwy had seen me talking to the professor and as soon as she could get me alone, she dragged me off to a corner of the room. She looked at me with a fierce anxiety.

"Thomas, I know you are planning something," she said. "What are you planning to do?" I shook my head. Her features softened and her voice dropped almost to a whisper.

"I'm worried about you Thomas," she said. "I'm worried that you are going to go off and do something stupid. Annwn is not a place where you can play around. There are no police here to protect you. You could get yourself badly hurt or even killed." She looked up at me with her vivid green eyes and I thought of how right my mother was: she really was beautiful. I think it was the first time that I had ever really thought that about a girl. At least, I didn't just think it but felt it in a way I never had before.

"There is no need to worry," I said. "I have no desire to meddle in the politics of Annwn." She looked a little relieved but still doubtful. I gently brushed a bit of wayward hair from her face. "Myfanwy…"I started, but then I stopped. There was so much I wanted to say but I had neither the words nor the courage.

"What?" she asked anxiously. I smiled to reassure her and said,

"It's nothing; it's just that my life has been a lot more interesting since I met you." Soon after that I said I was tired, which was certainly true, and Helen showed me the way back to my room.

CHAPTER 21
A Walk To A Ruin

I used my mobile phone to wake me early the next morning and I went quietly down to the kitchen. There I put some bread, some cold meat and fruit into a small day pack and filled up my canteen with water. I still managed to get out of the house without waking anybody. The sun was just starting to come up over the horizon as I made my way across the field and down to the river. I didn't know precisely where Cadell's house was but I knew it was in the forest and I was pretty sure the track along the river would take me in the right direction. As I got down to the river, I found Declan sitting on a rock and whittling a short, wooden staff that he had just cut from one of the trees.

"Good Morning Thomas," he said, still whittling the stick. "I've been waiting for you."

"How did you know I would be here?" I asked.

"Oh, I know you and I know what you intend to do," he replied brightly. "I have seen men like you before. Let me see if I can reconstruct your thinking. It is your duty to stop Apophis, Cadell is your only possible contact with Apophis, so it is your duty to seek out Cadell. Now, once you have decided that this is your duty nothing, not personal danger, not social embarrassments, no political tangles, not even love will turn you away. I believe your people have a saying that covers this situation – something about a bull in a china shop. Do not do what you are planning to do."

"I have been told that before," I said. He looked at me quizzically. "By Apple, the pixie."

He laughed and said, "You shouldn't listen to pixies but you should listen to me. Do not do what you plan to do. Even if you succeed, it will bring you misery. Do you know the story of Oisin and Niamh?" I nodded, I had read it in a book of Irish fairy tales my grandmother had given me.

"Niamh was a princess of Tyr na nOg who fell in love with a young Irish warrior called Oisin." I said. "She took Oisin to Tyr na nOg where they lived happily for a year but then Oisin became homesick and he travelled back to Ireland on a magical horse. However, when he got there he found that three hundred years had passed and everyone he knew was now dead. While helping some men move a rock, he slipped off the horse and again touched the soil of Ireland. Three hundred years then came upon him in an instant and he died a short time later."

"Good," he said. "The old stories have not been completely lost. Perhaps there's still hope. I don't need to point out the warning that story carries for you. I told them that your talent was rare but not unknown. I don't think they believed me but it is true. Although, I have known only one other. His name was Brendan and he came with his monks to our island and there was nothing we could do to stop him. He came, he prayed, he preached and he left some of his monks behind. They are still with us, still praying their prayers in their monastery. The whole nature of Tir na nOg has been changed by their presence, in ways that Brendan could not have understood. Be careful Thomas. There is a delicate balance in this island and you are like a wild, summer storm. Remember that the story of Oisin and Niamh always has a sad ending."

"No it doesn't," I said. "The story goes that St. Patrick himself was nearby when Oisin fell and he came as quickly as he could. Oisin lived long enough to meet Patrick and to talk with him. Of all the great warriors of the Fianna, Oisin was the only one who lived long enough to be baptized and become a Christian. It is a happy ending."

"Not for Niamh and not for me," he said. "I never got to know my father. Can I persuade you not to go looking for Cadell?" I shook my head. "I didn't think so. Then, will you accept this walking stick as a gift from a friend?" He held out the short staff he had been whittling, it was by now almost completed carved with intertwining animal and plant shapes. "You may need it. There are more things in that forest than Cadell. There are bears, wild boars, wolves and some dark things of which I will not speak and which have no name. This may help you ward them off."

I took the staff from him gratefully. I had no doubt that it would be useful. I looked at him then with his light, bright smile, with his vain manner and casual charm, and knew that he was playing a role, that he was being much less than he could be. I don't know what made me say what I said next. It was not like me at all, but on that morning I wanted him to be my friend and I wanted my friend to be the best he could be.

"I have a gift for you also," I said. "It is this: when you return home, you must go to talk to one of Brendan's monks. There is a happy ending available for you Declan, but you must seek it out. You are not the immortal you pretend to be." I touched him on the shoulder and suddenly the ageless youth vanished and the oldest man I have ever seen was sitting on the rock.

I quickly withdrew my hand and Declan returned to his former, ageless self. His face was serious but calm.

"That is a powerful gift you offer," he said. "I pray that you are never deeper in my debt because I don't know that I would survive the repayment. Annwn is changing you Thomas. I wonder what you will be by the time you leave."

I smiled and said, "What greater gift could I give you than the awareness of your own mortality? Thanks for the staff." I then turned and walked off down the river path leaving Declan sitting on his rock.

At first it was simply a pleasant morning walk along the river, past groves of fruit trees and herds of black faced sheep and shaggy cattle. Then the trees started to grow closer together and the fruit trees were replaced by oak until the path became a precarious thing, perched between the fast flowing river on one side and the deep, green wall of the forest on the other. The forest was not silent. There were scrabbling's and other animal sounds in the undergrowth and a large number of birds in the branches. Red squirrels often ran across my path and I saw one fox returning late from his night's hunting. However, none of this disturbed me and I made good time walking deeper into the forest.

After I had been walking for about an hour or two, I noticed something dark at the foot of a tree. It turned towards me and I found myself staring into the large, brown eyes of a black bear. I froze, adrenaline pumping through my body. The bear, however, took no notice of me and shuffled off deeper into the forest. I realized that this was a truly wild forest and Myfanwy was right: I could get seriously hurt here. After that I walked with a lot more caution and paid greater attention to my surroundings. I think it was this that saved me when I came across a herd of wild boar scratching around the bank of the river. I noticed them before they noticed me and I stopped and held Declan's walking stick out in front of me defensively. As a weapon, it seemed pretty pathetic.

When the herd noticed me, most of the sows ran off into the forest but one large male, with very large tusks, faced me and stood his ground. Green light raced along the carvings on the stick and I found myself holding a long halberd with a wicked steel spike on the end of it – with a weapon like this I had a better than even chance against the beast ahead of me. I grounded the butt of the halberd and faced the boar, neither of us moved. I slowly slipped my hand into my pocket and pulled out my mobile phone. Moving with painful slowness, I pointed the camera towards the boar. It was dark under the trees and this model had an inbuilt flash. Sure enough, when I took the picture the flash went off and this startled the boar. It ran off into the forest after the sows and the halberd turned back into a walking stick. As I put my mobile phone back into my pocket I thought, this is s remarkably useful stick.

It was not long after this that I noticed a path leading off to the right and heading up into the mountains. By now it was early afternoon, so I sat down in the middle of the path and ate some lunch. I considered my position. The path along the river seemed to just keep going without any change and I knew that you turned up just such a path to get to Myfanwy's house. Also, where else would a path be going except to a house and, other than Cadell, who would have a house this deep in the forest? I decided to leave the river and head off up the path.

At first the path climbed steeply through a dark, green tunnel of forest. It was slippery under foot and I found the going very hard. I didn't think anyone had been along this path in a long time. After a while it leveled out a bit and, as I climbed higher into the mountains, the forest was not as dense and the ground was rockier. There were also other trees now mixed in with the oaks. I was still climbing, however, and as the afternoon wore on I was breathing hard and sweating. I was also taking more frequent rests. It was during one of these rests that I first heard a wolf howl. It was a long way away and I didn't really think much about it. I just got up kept walking along the path.

The next time I heard a howl it was closer and this time it was answered by a howl from the opposite direction. It occurred to me for the first time that I might be being hunted. I started to move forward faster and to look for possible trees to climb. By now I was moving through an open forest of pine and birch trees and there didn't look to be many easy candidates. More wolves joined in the howl chorus and they were getting closer. Then they stopped. I didn't like that. Then I heard the swift padding of paws behind me. I swung Declan's staff around and turned to face the wolf. There was a flash of green light and I found myself holding a two meter long fighting spear with a long leaf shaped spear head. This must have been razor sharp because when it struck the lead wolf across the nose, it sliced it open. The wolf yelped and ran off into the forest. I swung the spear around my head in a figure eight pattern and the other wolves decided to take a watching approach, keeping just out of the range of my spear. Occasionally they made runs at me, often in twos or threes from different directions, but after I had wounded several of them they held back, wary of the spear and content to wait until I got tired.

I kept walking along the path as I held the wolves at bay. After a while I became aware that they were trying to herd me off the path. There were a significant number of large wolves directly in front of me and none at all to my right. I decided that I really didn't want to go where they wanted me to go, I didn't think they had my best interests at heart, so I charged the wolves in front of me, swing the spear as if it were a long handled sword. The wolves scattered but I heard heavy paws rushing up behind me. I turned and thrust in the same motion, catching a gigantic wolf clean in the chest. The force of his charge pushed me over and drove the spear deep into his body. I rolled to me feet and turned to face the rest of the wolf pack but they didn't follow.

I had rolled out of the forest and into a landscape of barren rocks. The contrast was sudden, it was as if there was a line, on one side forest and on the other rocks. The wolf pack would not cross the line. Even the wolf I had speared, though mortally wounded, was trying to crawl back to the other side of that line. As I looked around me, I saw a scene of utter devastation. Scattered among the rocks were the trunks of dead and uprooted trees, the rocks themselves were shattered and broken and, in the distance, the very sides of the mountains were scarred where great slabs had been torn away. I remembered what Professor Rhys had said during my first visit to Aelred Abbey; "They were both powerful and skilled and the battle between them was epic. It tore apart the forest, it tore down the sides of mountains…" I had come to the site of the battle between Owen Ap Rhys and Cadell.

I walked on along the path, through a landscape of dead trees and shattered rocks. Here and there I could see the white of skeletal remains. Most of these were dear or other wild animals that had been caught up in the battle. Occasionally there were strange, misshapen forms that made you wonder what had gone on. Sometimes these misshapen forms had a human aspect, which was even more disturbing. Several times, as I was walking, I felt a vague itch in the centre of my forehead followed by a kind of "pop" feeling. I had experienced this before and figured that I was passing through Cadell's magical defenses. The "pop" feeling was new but I guessed that it was because some spell, intended to be permanent, was being destroyed by my negation of it. I was surprised by the extent of the devastation. It took me a long time to walk across it and it was late afternoon when I climbed up the final ridge, looked down into the valley and saw the ruin of a massive gothic palace: the family house of Cadell and Apophis.

I took some time to get the layout of the house before I went down into the valley. The house was an architect's gothic nightmare. There were tall arched windows, turrets and flying buttresses but all without pattern or order, as if some demented child had been playing with a giant, gothic Lego set. It was a ruin. The windows were empty, the arches broken and the towers fallen. There was no sign of life anywhere. It took me a while but I eventually noticed a small portion of the house where the roof was mostly intact. I decided to make towards that area but I was really hoping that Cadell would come and find me. I didn't fancy searching around this ruin in the dark.

Despite actually wanting to be found, I couldn't help but try to move silently through the ruins. Every step I took, every time I dislodged a stone, the sound echoed in the stillness and vague shadows seemed to stir in the corner of my eye. The whole place gave me the creeps. It was not a nice place. You could feel that terrible things had been done here. The entry to the small roofed area was at the end of a very large room which now stood open to the sky. I thought it must once have been a ball room or a very large eating hall but now its columns and windows were broken and the large flagstones of its floor, huge slabs of rock two meters square, were covered with dust. As I walked down its length, I could see that there was a sort of platform at the end and I realized that actually this had once been a throne room. In the darkening shadows of the evening, it took me a while to realize that the throne was still there and that Cadell was sitting on it. He had obviously been watching me for some time and when he noticed that I had seen him he called out,

"You! You foul abomination! How dare you enter my house as if it were a public park? What right do you have to insult me with your presence?"

"Look, calm down. I just want to talk Cadell," I said reasonably. "I have come about your son. He has lost his grip on reality and is hurting innocent people who know nothing of Annwn or your people. This will not end well for him. I ask you, for the sake of the love you have for your son, for the honour of your family, help me to put a stop to what he is doing." I felt the vague itch that indicated he was trying to cast a powerful spell on me. I pointed at him in anger and stopped his magic. I was getting to be good at that.

"Surely," I said as forcefully as I could, "even if you do not care about your own son, you do not want the last heritage of your family to be pointless pain, death and destruction!"

"But that is precisely what he does want," said a voice behind me. I turned around and there, emerging from the shadows, was Apophis.

"Pointless pain, death and destruction: that is an excellent summary of why I was born, of why he raised me. Did you imagine that you were coming to talk to a loving father about his wayward son? Your naivety is as pathetic as your arrogance is foolish." Green light flashed along the carvings on Declan's staff and once again I was holding the fighting spear. Apophis laughed. "Do you imagine that I am going to fight you warrior? How stupid do you think I am? How arrogant! You come to the house my family has lived in for over a thousand years. Do you know how much energy is stored in these stones? There is no place in existence where I am more powerful. Yet you calmly come in here to get what? Information about me?" Apophis laughed and, on his throne Cadell cackled. "You are a child and you want information. Well then, I will give you a child's rhyme of my plans,

> There is a ring which seeks it beginning
> But which can only find its end.
> And in its end all endings be."

"Arawyn!" Cadell called from his throne. "Stop this foolishness and kill him!"

"What are you going to do?" I asked. "Throw some of your family's house at me? I'd be careful, there's not much of it left."

"No," he replied. "I will not throw my family's house at you but I will throw you from my family's house!" At that, he pointed to the floor and the flagstone on which I was standing accelerated suddenly into the air. I was forced down by the g-force. I could barely breathe, so rapidly did the stone accelerate away from the earth. After what seemed like minutes, but was probably only a few seconds, the acceleration suddenly stopped and I was in free fall. The flagstone fell away from me and I could see that I was thousands of feet in the air, over forested mountains painted red by the light of the setting sun.

I spread-eagled my arms and legs, like I had seen skydivers do on TV. I knew that it wouldn't really do any good and I fully expected to be dead in a few minutes. Strangely, I didn't really feel afraid. My main emotion was concern for those who would be hurt by my death. I even wondered what story the professor would come up with to explain my sudden demise – fell while mountain climbing in Wales probably. For a while nothing much seemed to happen. I seemed to be sort of hanging in the air with a strong breeze blowing past my face. Then the ground started to get noticeably closer and I could make out where I was going to hit. As I watched it rush ever faster towards me, it suddenly seemed to be covered in huge soap bubbles. I blinked in surprise just before I hit the first bubble, it hurt badly before it burst. Then I hit the second and the third and the fourth, each time it hurt. Finally, I hit the ground and was knocked unconscious.

CHAPTER 22
Banished

When I regained consciousness, I was lying on the ground in the dark and every part of my body hurt. I looked around and saw a small fire not far away. It was in front of an old fashioned gypsy wagon and there was a white horse dozing nearby. There was an elderly lady sitting on a log next to the fire and stirring a pot suspended above the flames, an elderly lady in a bright floral dress and with a straw hat on her head. I dragged myself to my feet: it really hurt. Nearby, I found Declan's walking stick and this time I really used it for support as I hobbled over to the fire.

"Hello Nain," I said. "Fancy meeting you here." She scowled at me in a very bad tempered way. "I take it the soap bubble things were yours," I continued. "Thank you for saving my life – again."

"Humph!" she replied. "One of these days you are going to manage to get yourself killed, you young fool. What did you think you were doing?" I winced as I sat down by the fire. "Now there's poetic justice. If you were anybody else, I could fix all your bruises and breaks without a problem. But you being you, I can't help you at all. Think of it as a punishment for arrogant, pigheaded foolishness." She handed me a bowl of the stew from the pot. It was rich, thick and smelt of herbs. "Here get some of that inside you. It will help you get better."

"Thanks," I said. The stew was a bit over spiced and the meat tasted strange but it was hot and thick and I was very hungry. So the stew was very much appreciated. I tried to figure out what the meat was. After a few mouthfuls I looked up and asked "Rabbit?" Nain nodded.

"Fresh caught this afternoon," she said. "You haven't asked how I came to be here." I stopped eating and looked up at her across the fire.

"There are only three possibilities," I said. "Either you spoke to Declan, to Apple the pixie or you figured out what I was going to do the same way that they did. However it happened, I'm just glad that you came."

"Humph!" she said again. "It was a bit of all three. Then when I saw that rock fly up into the sky, I knew there was trouble. I figured Cadell wouldn't be throwing rocks up in the air like that for no reason, so I altered its trajectory slightly, just in case. I'm sorry I couldn't be more accurate. I was aiming to dump you in that pond over there. You would have been wetter but less bruised."

I grinned at her. "At least you missed the big pile of rocks," I said. "Anyway, it wasn't Cadell. It was Apophis." She froze in place and stared at me.

"That's not possible," she said. "He's in Britain. There is no way he can get into Annwn without us knowing about it."

I shrugged. "I don't know about that, but I do know that it was Apophis who rather dramatically threw me out of that ruin of a house," I said. "That was how I got into trouble. I couldn't figure out how to neutralize both of them at the same time and I chose to neutralize Cadell."

Nain nodded. "Probably a good choice," she said. She looked at me closely. "Are you sure?" she asked.

When I nodded, she got up and pointed to the gypsy wagon.

"There's a bed in there. I suggest you go and get some sleep. Lock the door and don't come out until I return in the morning. I have to go and tell the others."

"There's one more thing," I said. "Apophis was showing off and he told me a riddle about what he plans to do. He said, 'There is a ring which seeks its beginning, but which can only find its end, and in its end all endings be.' Does that mean anything to you?" She shook her head.

"We'll talk about this later but now I've got to go," she said. "Remember, go inside the caravan and don't come out until morning. There are things in this forest which you really do not want to meet in the night." With that, she whistled and the white horse trotted into the fire light. She climbed onto its back and then rode off at impossible speed through the forest.

When I had finished my stew, I got up and walked painfully over to the caravan. Inside there were cupboards, pots and pans hanging on hooks and a neat little bunk bed. I closed the door behind me, stretched out on the bed and went straight to sleep. It had been a long day.

When I woke I could tell by the light that it was late morning and the rocking motion of the caravan meant we were underway. I groaned. Everything that had hurt a little bit last night now hurt a lot and what had hurt a lot last night now hurt even more. I slid out of the bunk bed and half crawled, half walked up to the front of the caravan. I took Declan's walking stick and climbed out a hatch and onto the bench at the front of the wagon. There Nain was driving with the same white horse in the traces. We were back down on the river road and heading out of the forest.

"Good morning," Nain said. "Still in pain I see. Good, it'll teach you a lesson. You did a good job of destroying Cadell's defenses by the way. We got to the house without any trouble. You were right, Apophis had clearly been there recently. We still can't figure out how. Unfortunately they had both escaped into the mountains before we got there - must have had some sort of warning system. Don't worry though, we'll get them." I could have pointed out that their previous efforts didn't really inspire confidence but I hurt too much and the sun was too warm. So I just sat there in silence. The horse plodded along at the normal sort of speed you would expect from a horse pulling a wagon. Eventually Nain started talking again.

"You caused quite a panic yesterday. When they realized that you had disappeared, the first thought was that you had gone surfing and the Selkies had tempted you away to Davey Jones' locker. Your mother was very worried but Myfanwy was almost frantic. Then Carwyn pointed out that your surf board and wet suit were still in your room. They then thought that you might have gone to visit the friar. Everyone was relieved until they found out that the friar hadn't seen you since the day before. They were organizing a search of the cliff top path when Apple whispered that I should go and talk to Declan. I found Declan down by the river, totally unconcerned about your disappearance and playing a love song to that hussy of a river maiden. He can carry that neutral observer thing too far. He told me where you had gone but didn't lift a finger to help: just kept playing on that little harp of his.”

“Oh, I don’t know,” I said. “I really like the walking stick he gave me. It is a very useful stick!” Nain looked closely at the intricately carved stick I was holding.

“Humph!” she said. “Declan should know better. The time for things such as that has long past. Still, I suppose giving you a gift doesn’t technically violate his neutrality.”

“Neutrality in what?” I asked.

“Politics,” she said. “There is an ancient treaty between ourselves and the DeDanann. It stipulates that the Irish are not to intervene in the politics of Annwn. Speaking of the politics of Annwn, you have really upset the apple cart. The old balance has been lost and I don’t know how they will forge a new one. In fact, I am taking you to a meeting of the council now.” She held up her hand to silence me. “Don’t worry! Your mother knows you’re safe and I will take you straight up to the house after the meeting.” I nodded and closed my eyes. I must have dozed off because when I opened my eyes again we were approaching the meeting tree and the nobles of Annwn were waiting much as they had been the day before yesterday. Their expressions, however, indicated that the situation had changed. While the white lady had the same expression of ethereal calm, Professor Rhys looked miserable and the red haired man looked like someone who has just won a lottery. The other two just looked uncertain and a little afraid. Declan was sitting on the grass, apparently unconcerned and idly playing a small harp.

The crowd was gone but standing in front of the nobles was a pack of nine dogs and their handlers. These were three bald men, naked to the waist and dressed in leather pants, who each held the leads of three very large and nasty looking dogs: something like Irish Wolf Hounds only thicker set. As the caravan came to halt in front of the group, Nain leaned over to me and whispered,

"That is Iolo ap Huw, the Master of the Hunt, and those are the hounds of Annwn. They are a perilous tool indeed. The council has clearly decided to take decisive action."

As Nain got down from the cart, the dogs howled and lunged at her and were only held back with difficulty.

"Iolo!" Nain called out. "Keep those animals of yours under control. They'll frighten my horse." The central figure of the three laughed. This had to be Iolo ap Huw. He was a little older than the other two and his bald head was tattooed with the markings of an animal skull. His laugh was not entirely sane and not at all pleasant.

"Have no fear grandma. You are not our prey…today." I decided then that he was not someone I wanted to have as a close friend. I climbed down from the caravan painfully and with difficulty, using Declan's stick to support myself.

Iolo watched me and said, "So boy, you are the one who has caused all this trouble. If I hunted you, I think you would find that you are not immune to my hounds." I straightened up and looked him in the eye.

"Maybe," I said, "but I can guarantee that not all your hounds would return."

"Ooooh!" Iolo said mockingly. "He has spirit. I should have known that Myfanwy Ferchwyn would make such a choice. I like that. It makes the hunt much more interesting."

The red haired man cried out impatiently, "Enough of this Iolo! He is not your prey and there has been no choice. You have your task, get to it!" Iolo smiled a smile that would give the bravest nightmares.

"True master," he said. "Today is a good day. Today I hunt one of the nobles of Annwn!" He then gave a loud yell and the dogs were released. They ran off towards the forest at incredible speed with their handlers no slower behind them. I almost felt sorry for Cadell and Apophis.

The council then turned its attention to me. It wasn't welcoming. The white lady's expression didn't change but Professor Rhys wouldn't look at me and the others glared at me in open hostility.

"Thomas O'Malley," the white lady said. "You have abused your status as a guest here and have meddled in the internal politics of Annwn. Some good may have come from your actions but the actions themselves show a reckless disregard for the safety of this realm. Also, the threat of Apophis, which was the reason you were brought here, has passed. The hunt will not give up until they are caught. Therefore, it is the decision of this council that you should be banished from Annwn, never to return. Your belongings are already packed on the boat. Your mother has been informed. Furthermore, in order to preserve the delicate balance of power on this island, this council forbids any further contact between you and Myfanwy Ferchwyn so there is no need to say goodbye. You are to go directly from here to the boat harbor and thence to Britain."

I stood silent and still, trying to process what was being said. Next to me, Nain let out a yell.

"Are you mad?' she said. "Have you taken leave of your senses? This boy has done more for this realm in the last few days than you have over all your long and useless lifetimes. And how can the council come to a decision without me? Am I not still a member?"

"Your vote would have made no difference old woman," the red haired man said. "The four of us were determined that this should be done."

"This is madness!" Nain said. "You cannot separate them. They have already formed a bond! You have seen this for yourselves." She turned towards Professor Rhys. "Cadfan! You must know this." Professor Rhys just shrugged and shook his head sadly, holding out his hands in a gesture of helplessness. "Bah!" Nain said. "You are the old woman not me!"

"All this is pointless," the red haired man said. "The council has made its decision. The bond has not been sealed and we cannot allow the house of Owyn ap Rhys to be so closely linked to a wild talent such as this: a talent which can defeat even the most powerful of us. That is simply not acceptable."

"Bad luck," I said calmly. They all looked at me in surprise. I was hurting all over and it was difficult to stand straight but there was a cold anger burning inside me and I needed to speak. "This is your island and if you ask me to leave I will go but I will never accept your authority and you have no power over me. You have no right to say who I will or will not see. Myfanwy is my closest friend in all the world and I will not be separated from her. Not by this council, nor by any other power on the planet. She is the only girlfriend I have or want and you'll just have to get over it." I turned to Nain and said, "Nain, could you give me a ride to the harbour? I fear I have overstayed my welcome."

On the way down to the harbour, Nain said, "Boy, today you defied the Council of Nobles of Annwn and in doing that you have made a mortal enemy of Alwyn ap Bryn. That was well done. That was well done indeed. I once wondered how Annwn would change you, now I know. The bewildered schoolboy I first met could not have done that." I took it that Alwyn ap Bryn was the red haired guy. I didn't mind being his enemy at all.

Down at the harbour, my mum was waiting anxiously by Owen's boat. She had been told that I had had a fall in the mountains, which was accurate enough as far as it went, and that I needed to be taken to hospital immediately. Given how bruised and sore I felt, this was also probably true. Owen and another fisherman helped me down into the boat and I lay down on some nets in front of the wheelhouse. The boat set off almost immediately with my mother still fussing around me. Neither Myfanwy nor her siblings had been allowed to come down and say goodbye. Even my mother noticed this.

"Tom, did you and Myfanwy have a fight?" she asked. I shook my head. "It's just that she didn't come down to see you off and she seemed to spend much of this morning crying and being comforted by her family." I shook my head again.

"I don't want to talk about it just now mum, okay?" I said. She nodded in an annoyingly understanding way.

"I'll leave you alone for a bit, then," she said and went inside the wheelhouse. I watched the green hills of Annwn slip away. I knew that Myfanwy would be up on the parapet watching for the boat. I couldn't see her but I watched until the boat made a sharp turn around the point and the magical island of Annwn gave way to a pile of insignificant, sea washed rocks.

I got up and walked to the stern and watched as these rocks rapidly disappeared behind the boat. Already, I felt a great emptiness and the world seemed dull and flat. After a while I noticed a small, white boat coming after us. Its motion through the water was very peculiar. It didn't so much cut through the waves as ride over the top of them. It was also moving very fast and rapidly caught up with us. It was, of course, Declan's boat and he was standing in the middle, holding his hands in front of his face with his fingers entwined. As his boat pulled up beside ours, he jumped lightly and easily onboard. Owen came storming out of the wheelhouse and started shouting at Declan in Welsh. Declan pointed his finger and Owen was pushed back into the wheelhouse. The wheelhouse door then slammed shut and stayed shut. Owen's immediate attempts to open the door with magic didn't work and he was reduced to banging on the door, shouting and glaring impotently.

"Hello Declan and thank you for the walking stick" I said. "I have very carefully stowed it in my luggage. It is by far the most useful stick I have ever had." Declan smiled.

"I'm glad you like it," he said. "I've just come to say goodbye before I return to Tyr na nOg. I also need to tell you three things. First, when Brendan came to our land we did everything we could to stop him but we couldn't. He knew where we were so we couldn't hide from him. Remember that if ever you want to return to Annwn. They might have banished you but I doubt that they have the power to enforce it.

Second, you may be surprised by the strength of their reaction but you have scared them badly and scared people often do silly things. You have also upset the power politics in Annwn. There has recently been a dramatic shift in power towards Myfanwy's family and the other families resent this. Owyn ap Rhys was talented himself and he had three children, all of whom are themselves talented. Now that Arawyn has ruled himself out, none of the other major families have any obvious heirs and the council were already afraid that Myfanwy's family will become the undisputed rulers of Annwn. Then you come along and, through your friendship with Myfanwy, offer to her family a power that none of the council could have dreamt of in their worst nightmare. No one could stand against the children of Owyn ap Rhys if they had you by their side. Now, I don't know exactly how things stand between you and Myfanwy but if a romantic bond has been formed then it must not be broken. Myfanwy's magic would go haywire and the result would be disastrous and tragic. Unfortunately, I think the council would prefer that to Myfanwy's family having access to your power."

"What about my magic?" I asked. "Friar Daffyd said my ability was itself magical. Would it react in the same way?" Declan looked me surprised.

"Good question!" he said. "I hadn't thought of that. I really don't know how your strange talent would react." He looked thoughtful for a while. "I also don't want to find out. It could be very bad indeed. If you have hold of her, don't let her go.

That leads to the third thing I want to tell you. I think that the fear of the council is foolish. I think it is simple demographic destiny that Myfanwy's family will one day rule Annwn. The children of Owyn ap Rhys are a formidable force. They will discover just how formidable as they grow older. I think it would be a very good idea if you, with your sense of duty, were a part of that team. I'm a little concerned about what Carwyn might do without a balancing force. Anyway, I'm now away home." I held out my hand,

"Thank you for all you have done Declan," I said. "I am glad to have you as a friend." He didn't take my outstretched hand but jumped lightly up onto the boats side rail.

"Forgive me for not taking you hand Thomas. I am also glad to have you as a friend but I have very bad memories of the last time you touched me. I'm afraid I would much rather keep my youthful beauty. If ever you find yourself in Tyr na nOg I will guarantee a grand welcome indeed. You will find me talking to Brendan's monks." He smiled broadly. "You are right. I do need to seek a happy ending for myself." He then jumped into his small boat which turned and headed off at great speed into the west. As I watched Declan move away across the ocean swell, his words kept repeating in my head like some annoying pop tune: "If you have hold of her, don't let her go." Did I have hold of her? Was the bond between us deep enough to cause these dire consequences? Had I let her go by leaving? What would they do to keep us apart? I didn't know the answer to any of these questions and for the first time I felt not just emptiness but fear.

Owen burst out of the wheelhouse and started shouting furiously in Welsh after the disappearing Declan. He then turned and angrily spat out one word. "Irish!"

"Careful now Owen," I said. "I'm Irish too you know: Australian Irish but Irish nonetheless.

CHAPTER 23
Myfanwy Goes Missing

Owen had radioed ahead and an ambulance was waiting for me when we got to Tenby. I was taken up to the community hospital where they examined me and did a few x-rays. It seemed that nothing was broken although I was very badly bruised. I would be very sore for a while but would make a full recovery in a week or so. One of the doctors gave me a long and very stern lecture about the dangers of climbing alone on the coastal cliffs. He was about to give me prescription for some painkillers and let me go when a nurse came in and whispered something. He looked puzzled but left with the nurse immediately.

When he came back he said, "Well, it seems you must rest here a while. An ambulance is on its way from London to pick you up."

"Why?" my mother asked in a bit of a panic. "What's wrong?"

"Nothing that I can see," said the doctor. "Your doctor in London must be a real nervous Nellie." He shook his head in disbelief. "A real nervous Nellie with connections. This is a terrible waste of health resources. Still, it's not your fault. You just lie there and wait for a free ride back to London." Mum looked very puzzled at this, because we didn't really have a doctor in London, certainly not one who could, or would, arrange such an ambulance trip. This was especially true since we hadn't actually told anyone in London that we were coming back or that I was hurt.

"Professor Rhys must've arranged this," she said eventually. "Otherwise, it doesn't make sense. That was nice. I really liked him." I knew this wasn't true but I nodded in agreement.

"Yes, must be him," I said.

The ambulance arrived a couple of hours later and I was not surprised to see that it was manned by the two DIAP operatives, back in their paramedic uniforms. Dr. Jones was also with them: this time looking like a medical doctor, with a stethoscope sticking out of the pocket of his white coat. They chatted with the hospital doctor and forms were passed back and forth. Then they wheeled me out to the ambulance on a stretcher. I felt a real goose. They arranged it so that Mum rode up the front while one of the operatives and Dr. Jones rode with me in the back. As soon as the door closed and the ambulance started to move, Dr. Jones started with his questions. For a doctor, he did not have a very good bedside manner.

"Mr. O'Malley, where have you been and how have you been hiding from us? We tracked your mobile phone out into the Irish Sea and then lost you. Now you turn up having had a very bad fall and suffering from serious bruising. Don't try and tell me that this was just a holiday accident!" I shook my head.

"No. The fall was courtesy of Apophis," I said. "He figured that he could kill me if he threw me high enough up in the air. Fortunately I landed on something soft."

"Where is he now?' the operative asked. Again I shook my head.

"I don't know. He got away and I was in no real shape to chase him down." I said. I hesitated then, unsure of how much to reveal. "I'm not sure but I think he may be being chased by the rest of the magic community."

Dr Jones nodded. "Maybe, I'm sure they're not too happy with what he has been doing," he said. "Did he give you any clue about where he was going or what he was going to do?"

I nodded. "Actually, yeah," I said. "He's a cocky, overconfident showoff. Before he tried to kill me he gave me a riddle to show how clever he was. I think it's a genuine clue. He would enjoy the fact that he was telling me what I really wanted to know but in a way I couldn't understand. What he said was: "There is a ring which seeks its beginning but which will only find its end and in its end all endings be." Dr Jones looked very thoughtful for a while.

"It must be a word or phrase that ends with the letter B and it begins with a word the means an ending," he said. "This ending word probably occurs again towards the end of the word or phrase to form the ring. This may take a bit of working out." I shook my head doubtfully. He was trying to work it out as if it was a clue in a cryptic crossword puzzle.

"I don't think Apophis does cryptic crossword puzzles." I said. "It's not the way he thinks."

"A ring doesn't really have an end or a beginning," the operative guy said. "Unless he's talking about when it was made. Perhaps he is talking about destroying something shaped like a ring, like the ring road around London."

"I don't know, Fisher." Dr. Jones said. "I don't think that's ambitious enough." They continued to toss ideas around for a while but didn't really get anywhere. Even in an ambulance and with priority lanes on the motorway, the trip back to London took a lot longer than the trip down had taken in Professor Rhys' car. Eventually silence fell in the back of the ambulance and I used the rest of the trip to get some sleep. I woke up when we got into the stop-start traffic of London. To maintain a plausible story for my mum, Dr Jones stuck his head up front and said to the driver,

"I don't know why we were sent down there. There doesn't appear to be anything wrong with the boy that a few painkillers and some rest won't fix. How about we just drop them home?" So we arrived home well before our luggage. This came by courier the next day, courtesy of Professor Rhys.

As soon as mum was in London again she set about organizing the joint exhibition that she and Helen would be holding. We went to the Easter ceremonies at Westminster Cathedral and in the candlelit church, with the glittering mosaics and the domes arching into darkness above me, I felt connected to great power and great mystery. As I prayed, I was confident that no archaic, self-appointed council of weirdoes would be able to keep me away from Myfanwy. But I was left to nurse my bruises alone for the rest of the break and I spent most of the time playing computer games.

There was a shock waiting for me at school, although thinking back on it, I really should have expected it. Myfanwy was not at the opening assembly and when we went to home room her desk was empty.

I felt a knot form in the pit of my stomach. Of course they could separate us. All they had to do was banish me and keep Myfanwy in Annwn, then a magic barrier and the Irish Sea would keep us apart. I kept staring at the empty desk. I didn't want to believe it. Every time someone came to the classroom door I would look up. Hoping that I was wrong and that she had been delayed and was just late for class. However, she didn't come and as the morning went on I just got more and more miserable.

I sat on my own at lunchtime, eating some slop more out of duty than hunger. Phil and his fellow soccer nuts were out kicking a ball around and not paying attention to Gabriella and her friends, which gave them something very satisfying to moan about. Wilson still had his protective little tutor group around him, a group that was becoming more loyal as exams approached. None of my friends were paying any attention to me which suited me just fine. I didn't expect them to. I didn't want them to.

However, a girl from the more vocational subject stream surprised me by coming over and sitting next to me. Her name was Susan Cavendish and she was a pretty girl with blond hair and light brown eyes. She had always seemed nice but I didn't really know her that well. I was surprised that she sat next to me because she had never joined our group for lunch before. For a while she ate her lunch in silence.

Then she said, "I hear that Myfanwy won't be coming back to school."

I nodded. "Seems so," I said and went back to my eating. She then spoke very quickly, as if she just wanted to get this out and over with.

"Look, I know you and Myfanwy broke up and I know it hurts at the moment but that will pass. It doesn't seem like it will but it will." I looked at her in astonishment. Where did she get the idea that Myfanwy and I had broken up? "When the time comes, if you need someone to talk to about it or even just a shoulder to cry on, I'll be around." I stared at her blankly not knowing what to say. She started to look very uncertain but kept going. "Just remember, okay? I'd like to help."

"Um…Okay, I'll keep that in mind," I sort of mumbled. She nodded and walked off very quickly, leaving most of her lunch uneaten on the table. This conversation was so odd that for a while I forgot to be miserable. Where did she get the idea that Myfanwy and I had broken up and, even if it were true, why would my emotional health concern her? The class after lunch was mathematics and it was taken by Dr. Bryn Williams, my sole remaining contact with Myfanwy's world. However, even though I occasionally caught him looking at me intently, he was as dry and incomprehensible as ever.

The days dragged on without Myfanwy. I went to the gate to Aelred Abbey near to the school but it was gone. There was just a normal fence and the wall of an old church. I went to the gate near my house but again it was gone. My world was perfectly normal again: sane and sensible. In another world Apophis and his dad were being chased through the mountains by Iolo and his hunt but this world was once again the safe and predictable place I had always imagined it to be. Only now, without Myfanwy, safe and predictable just seemed colourless and dull. Try as I might, I couldn't think of any way that I could get to Annwn. All I could do was pray.

It was strange that at school I kept running into Susan Cavendish. I had barely met her the whole of the previous term and now we kept meeting in the hallway or on the way to the bus to and from school. She even joined our small lunch group whenever it met. She was attractive, good to talk to and seemed really nice but there was something about the frequency of these meetings that made me feel uneasy. Our lunch group also had another new pairing. Rachael had always been a prominent member of Wilson's 'tutor group'. She now started to take a close personal interest in Wilson which he reciprocated in a rather bemused way. This was a most unlikely couple and I think it was initiated by Wilson's ability to explain how a variety of nuclear weapons would work. I hoped it wouldn't get too serious. The idea of a child with Wilson's brains and Rachael's taste for destruction was truly worrying.

In English, Mrs. Brown was still trying to get the class to appreciate romantic poetry. In many ways this was quite sad. It was clearly something that meant a lot to her and yet she got very little response from the class. Eventually she decided to get us involved by writing our own poem in the romantic style. I couldn't get my head around any romantic thoughts with Myfanwy's empty desk in front of me. I looked out my window in a gloomy mood. It was spring and the old garden was green with new growth but not the same bright, luminous green it had been when the sun had miraculously burst through winter storm clouds. The trees were full of birds singing their hearts out but none came to sit on my window sill and sing just for me. Things like that couldn't happen now that Myfanwy was gone.

I doodled my way through the class and had produced nothing at the end of it, which didn't really matter since we had a week to complete the poem.

As I was leaving the class, Mrs. Brown held me back and said, "I know it hurts but write it down and give it structure. It will help. Trust me, I know." I looked at her in surprise and I saw not a teacher but a person, a person who had been badly hurt and who had survived. Embarrassed, I just nodded my head. It was a shock to see a teacher in that light and I hoped it wouldn't happen too often. The whole incident was strange. She seemed to have some idea about my relationship with Myfanwy but how could she know that and why would she want to get involved?

Even though I was missing Myfanwy, I hadn't given up on trying to solve Apophis' riddle. Sitting in the group one lunch time I gave it to Wilson, the smartest guy I knew. I told him it was a riddle that I had heard but didn't know the answer to. He considered it for a while.

"Well," he said. "The ring part is obviously meant to put you off. The end of a bee is its abdomen or tail…Give me a while, it's nothing obvious. Do you know more of the context?" I shook my head and said no. He was trying to solve it the same way Dr. Jones had, as if it were a word puzzle. I didn't think that Apophis was that subtle. It would be something real, something that was indeed obvious when you knew it. Susan got up from the table to go to her class.

"Well I'm glad to see that you are thinking of something other than Myfanwy at last," she said. "It's time to move on." As she walked away, I turned to the others in the group.

"What is it with her?" I asked. "I barely met her last term and now she's there every time I turn around. I don't get it." Rachael looked at me in exasperation.

"You can't be that thick," she said. "Look, she likes you. She really likes you and now that you and Myfanwy have broken up she's trying to get together with you. Only she's running into this wall of male…thickness!" I looked at her puzzeled.

"What makes you think Myfanwy and I have broken up?" I asked.

Wilson shrugged. "It's obvious, everybody knows it. That's the reason you're so depressed. That's the reason Myfanwy didn't come back from holidays." I looked at him in growing frustration.

"Myfanwy and I haven't broken up," I said. "We are still as close as we ever were. Myfanwy just didn't come back here. Where's your evidence? Look, how many student romances have broken up in this school? How many students have left the school because of that? I'm guessing none. Of the students who have changed schools, how many left because of a breakup? Again, I'm guessing none. Sure, I miss Myfanwy and I wish she was here, but we haven't broken up!" Rachael and Wilson looked at each other,

"In denial," they said together. I gave up. I just couldn't understand why they were so convinced. It was only during the following maths class that I began to understand. Dr. Williams was still teaching us mathematics even though Apophis was being chased through the mountains of Annwn and posed no further threat in London. Why was Dr. Williams still here I wondered. It didn't take me that long to work it out. If everyone else could be made to believe that my relationship with Myfanwy was over, perhaps I would come to believe it too, especially if an attractive alternative presented itself. This was devious and manipulative and I cannot say how angry it made me. People are not puppets. No one has the right to manipulate them in this way, even if they do have the power. After the class I went up to talk to Dr. Williams.

"Sir, could I have a word?" I asked.

"Is it about mathematics O'Malley? Because otherwise I'm very busy," he said. I reached out to touch him with one thought in my mind: no magic. On his face I saw the look of fear and shock that magical people get when I take their magic from them.

"You will stop messing with my life, you will undo what you have done and in none of this will Susan Cavendish get hurt or I will ensure that you will never sense or do magic again. Do you understand?" Bye this time he was on the edge of real panic with beads of sweat starting to form on his forehead. Eventually he nodded and I let him go. I didn't think I would have been able to carry out my threat but I figured he couldn't be sure of that. I was certainly angry enough to try.

After that things did go back to normal. Susan was still friendly but she started spending time with her old friends again.

"You missed your chance there," Rachael said to me one lunch time. "She's decided that you are still too attached to Myfanwy."

"I am still too attached to Myfanwy," I said. "Nothing will change that." She leaned across the table and stared at me with a disturbing intensity.

"Have you spoken to her recently?" she asked. "Because you never mention anything she has said or done."

"No," I said. "Look…it's complicated. Her people don't approve of me and they are trying to keep us separated." Her eyes widened.

"Wow!" she said. "That's so romantic. It's classic. You're fated to be together but are kept apart by cruel circumstance."

I grimaced and said, "It's not romantic. This is not some silly novel. I don't know where she is and I have no way of contacting her. Can you imagine how that feels?"

"Myfanwy's family were always a bit odd," Wilson said.

"You have no idea," I replied.

Mrs. Brown gave back the poetry assignments the following week. I got a very good mark, much better than I had been expecting.

"Most of you have done a credible job," Mrs. Brown said. "Although there were exceptions. Horace, nothing that starts 'Roses are red, violets are blue…' can be considered romantic: certainly not what you wrote after that. Phillip Trenton, I'm sorry but there is no way you can make football romantic. The two just do not mix."

"Yeah, tell me about it," Gabriella muttered loudly.

When the laughter this caused had died down, Mrs, Brown said, "The best poem in the class was written by Rachael. Rachael, would you be so kind as to read your poem to the class please." Rachael's poem was really good, although it did seem to concentrate a lot on unrequited and doomed love enduring through death. If I had been Wilson I would have been a bit worried about this whole romance of death thing. Personally, I have never found death or the grave romantic: sad yes, but not romantic. After class, Mrs. Brown stopped me as I was walking out.

"I actually liked your poem better," she said. "I just didn't think you would want to read it to the rest of the class." She was right. I folded my poem up and put it in the pocket of my school blazer.

"Thanks," I said. It was now five weeks since I had spoken to Myfanwy and her absence still hurt like an open wound.

CHAPTER 24
There is a ring which seeks its beginning.

Somewhat to my surprise, the joint exhibition of my mum's photographs and Helen's paintings was still going ahead. It was opening on the last day of the mid-term break and for most of the mid-term break I was being used as unpaid help, setting lighting and hanging the pictures. I had to admit that the pictures were all pretty good. Some of them were stunning. They were all of Annwn landscapes but there were no identifiable features in the pictures and they could have been of any number of locations in Britain or Ireland. Together with the gallery staff, Mum and I did all of the work setting up the exhibition. Helen didn't arrive until just before the opening. It was interesting that no one raised any questions about the identity of the artist Helen Rhys, even though I figured that the latest Helen could have been born was around 1860. The magic community was obviously very good at laying a false paper trail.

The opening night was a very glitzy affair. I attended to accompany my mother but Helen was accompanied by Professor Rhys: none of her children came. After the opening speeches there was lots of milling round and people dressed in black eating finger food. After a while I found myself alone in a corner with Helen.

"Hello Thomas," she said cautiously. "How are you?" I decided that now was not the time for polite niceties.

"I am miserable," I said. "I miss Myfanwy more than I can say. Separating us like this is just completely stupid." I lowered my voice and said in an angry whisper, "They even tried to manipulate me into forgetting about Myfanwy and hooking up with someone else. How dare they play with people's lives like that?"

Helen nodded. "I know," she said. "We couldn't stop them or even warn you. Both Cadfan and Nain tried but the Council stopped them. Myfanwy was very worried. She misses you too by the way. She also doesn't like her new school very much." It took a couple of seconds for the implications of this reply to sink in.

"You mean that she is back at school somewhere in Britain?" I asked. "She is not in Annwn?" Helen smiled broadly.

"Oops!" she said. "I wasn't meant to tell you that. They were afraid that if you knew that, you would work out that she would be staying at Aelred Abbey and you might try to visit." My heart jumped inside me. This was the best news I had ever heard. I started grinning like an idiot. I wanted to laugh out loud. I wanted to jump about. I grabbed Helen and gave her a big thank you hug, something I wouldn't normally do. Helen was laughing, then her face turned grave.

"I have another message for you," she said. "Carwyn wanted me to warn you that he believes that Cadell and Apophis are also in Britain. I don't quite understand it but he went to their house and found something to do with worms that would let them escape." I thought about this for a while.

"Do you mean a worm-hole," I asked. "A sort of tunnel connecting two different places."

She smiled. "Yes! That was it," she said. "He said he found a worm-hole in the cellar and he thinks they escaped through this rather than off into the mountains. That was why Cadfan could never find Apophis in Britain. He was always escaping back into Annwn through this worm-hole. Carwyn has destroyed this one and he said it would have taken extraordinary skill and a ridiculous amount of energy to construct, so he doesn't think they will be able to construct another one anytime soon."

"Don't worry Thomas," said a voice behind me. "He probably believes you to be dead, so he won't come after you." I turned around to see Professor Rhys. He turned to Helen and said, "Helen, I hope you haven't been defying the wishes of the council."

Helen looked at him dismissively, almost disdainfully, and said, "I am a mother Cadfan. I listen first to the wishes of my children." After that an art dealer came up to discuss some of the paintings with Helen and we sort of drifted apart in the crowd. I had a lot to process but it was all swamped by the knowledge that Myfanwy was back in Britain and I would be able to see her. It was only later that night that I realized that Norfolk has quite a long coastline and I had no real idea where Aelred Abbey was.

School started the next day but I found it hard to concentrate on anything other than the mysterious location of Aelred Abbey. So much so that I almost missed the most vital piece of information I had ever been given. In was during a discussion in Physics class where Mr. Robertson was complaining about the general ignorance of physics. It seems that someone had tried to take legal action to stop an experiment at the Large Hadron Collider, claiming it had the potential to destroy the world.

"The chances of anything like this happening are so small they can be completely discounted," he said. "There is as much chance of this happening as there is of a cooked meal suddenly appearing on everyone's desk!" I was suddenly very interested. "Everyone is talking about "how strange that the freakish summer snow storm in Eastern France is but these things are a billion, billion times more unlikely than that freakish storm."

"Um…I'm afraid I don't really know what the Large Hadron Collider is, Sir," Phil said. "Or why is there problem."

"The Large Hadron Collider is a huge particle accelerator under the French/Swiss border," Mr. Robertson said in his normal clipped and slightly irritated voice. "It is a giant ring of super cooled magnets designed to probe the very beginnings of the universe. It does this by accelerating atomic particles to near the speed of light and then crashing them into each other. The energies are like those in the Big Bang. Some ignorant fools believe that the extreme energies in these particle experiments could cause black holes to form and destroy the Earth or even to collapse the quantum field to a lower energy state and slowly destroy the universe. As I said, the chances of anything like this happening are infinitesimally small." The realization that I had the answer to Apophis' riddle hit me like a brick wall. Wilson made the connection too and looked across at me with a big grin. I gave him a

thumbs-up sign to show that I understood but I wasn't
really happy.

<blockquote>
There is a ring which seeks it beginning
But which can only find its end.
And in its end all endings be."
</blockquote>

The Large Hadron Collider was a ring of magnets
designed to seek the beginnings of the universe, its
own beginning necessarily included, but Apophis
planned to interfere with the experiment so that one
of Mr. Robertson's infinitesimally small risks actually
happened. This would not only be the end of the
experiment. It would be the end of everything.
Apophis was truly mad. He was going to commit
suicide and he wanted to take the universe with him.

Just then the bell went for lunch and I rushed out
to the garden. I sat under the tree where Myfanwy and
I used to sit and talk. I pulled the card that DIAP had
given me on my first visit and dialled the number on
my mobile phone.

"Hello," a bright female voice answered. "Quick
and safe typing service." I had to think quickly. I knew
that a mobile phone was never secure and that DIAP
was paranoid about security so I decided to play along
with the typing service cover.

"Hi," I replied. "This is Tom O'Malley. I'm at
school now but I have a really important essay on
Apophis which needs to be typed very urgently."

"Wait one moment sir," the voice said. There was
silence for a few minutes and by this time some of the
kids were beginning to drift out into the garden to eat
their lunch. It wouldn't be long before someone asked

me who I was calling and I didn't even know if they had understood my message. I didn't really even know that I was talking to DIAP. Then the voice came back on the phone.

"If you could stay where you are sir, we will come by to pick up your typing as soon as possible."

"Thank you," I said and hung up. I had done all I could. Now I just had to wait and hope that DIAP had understood. I waited anxiously in the garden, too nervous and upset to eat lunch. Everything seemed so normal, so stable and permanent, and yet it might all come to an end. I felt sick. Lunch ended and I was just about to return to my class when the deputy headmistress rushed up to me.

"Thomas O'Malley," she said breathlessly. "There has been a family emergency and your uncle is here to take you home. Grab your bag and go quickly, I understand it is urgent." I was about to tell her that all my uncles were in Australia when I saw the DIAP agent called Fisher standing at the door. A few minutes later I was driving away from the school in a new, grey Vauxhall.

"You know, that woman is very naive and the security at that place is terrible," Fisher said. "I think we should move you to somewhere where they take the security of their students seriously." I was too worried to reply. Eventually we came to the same army base, went to the same wooden building and I entered the same ordinary looking office that I had on my first visit. The director and Dr. Jones were there, as was Professor Rhys.

"Hello Tom," the director said. "Let me introduce Professor Rhys. He is a consultant who is helping us with this Apophis matter."

"Tom and I already know each other," the professor said. "Tom was a classmate of my niece." The director immediately looked suspicious but I had no time for either social chatter or security paranoia.

"Look, I know what Apophis is planning to do and I know when he is planning to do it." As I explained my understanding of the riddle, the director and professor looked dubious but Dr. Jones simply walked over to the computer keyboard on the desk and a satellite image of Europe appeared on the screen on the back wall. He zoomed into the border region between France and Switzerland. A large yellow circle appeared superimposed on the image.

"That gentlemen is the track of the Large Hadron Collider or LHC," Dr Jones said. "It is, of course, buried deep underground and it is a very secure facility. They will be running two high energy experiments over the next week: one two days from now at 6.00am local time and the next twelve hours after that. Since he needs the experiments to run as if normal, I think he will attack from the surface without the LHC staff knowing. He will need to be sure of not being interrupted, so I think he will choose the unpopulated western edge – probably just north of the village of Crozet at the foot of the Jura Mountains."

"That's also the area that has just been hit by a freak summer snow storm so that no one is moving around outside and all flights, in and out, are cancelled. How very convenient," the director said. "So you think this is a serious threat?"

"Director," Dr. Jones said. "I think this is perhaps the most serious threat this planet has ever faced."

After that I was thanked and then hustled out of the office. Clearly, they did not intend that I would play any role in the defense of the planet. I was even driven home by an ordinary army corporal. Apparently Fisher and his mate were busy 'kitting up'. Professor Rhys also left quickly, to try and get help from the magical community. I was left to sit in my room and wonder if the world was going to end. This was just plain stupid. I was their most powerful weapon against Apophis and they were leaving me to sit at home and twiddle my thumbs. I knew that I had to get to the LHC and I thought immediately of one person who might just be able to get me there: Myfanwy.

I started by searching the internet for Aelred Abbey. Unsurprisingly, the internet thought there was no such place. It was not going to be that easy. I then searched along the Norfolk coastline using satellite images. It took a while but eventually I found what I was looking for: an old building which matched my memory, a causeway across a coastal marsh and the nearby village. Once I had found these it was a simple matter to work out how to get there. It was late when I had finished and I decided that I would set off the next day. I went to bed with very mixed emotions. Tomorrow I was going to see Myfanwy but the day after that might be the end of the world.

I didn't know it at the time but while I was searching the web for Aelred Abbey, a priest in the Vatican Secretariat of State was puzzling over a diplomatic cable he had just received. It didn't seem to have any origin and the text itself didn't make sense.

He almost threw it out as either a joke or a mistake but decided instead to take it to his boss: the Cardinal Secretary of State. He watched as the cardinal read the message and perhaps saw his jaw muscles tighten and his knuckles whiten.

"Father," his Eminence would have said. "You must forget that you ever saw this message. I will take care of the matter personally."

The next morning I put on my school uniform as usual, although I had no intention of going to school. Mum said goodbye to me rather absent mindedly and left early to see to exhibition business. I wished I could say goodbye properly but that would only make her suspicious. I left her a note, packed my warmest coat and set out to find Myfanwy. Almost as an afterthought I took the walking stick Declan gave me and set out to the centre of the city to catch the train to Norfolk. It wasn't difficult but it did take longer than I had hoped. I got the train to Norwich and there I had to wait to catch a small community train to Cromer and then west along the coast. It was well after lunch time when I finally got off the train. I bought some sandwiches at a shop in the town and then considered my options. I consulted the area maps on my mobile phone. I could wait for a local bus which would eventually take me to the village near the abbey or I could take a short cut and walk to the abbey. On my phone, it didn't look too far. I decided that I was too keyed up and anxious to sit around for over an hour waiting for a bus, so I decided to walk. This turned out to be a mistake as it took much longer than I thought it would and almost certainly longer than the bus would have taken. I spent the next couple of hours walking along minor country roads, through flat, marshy country, always unsure of where I was going and depending on my mobile phone to guide me. It was late afternoon by the time I got to the gate that led to the abbey and walked down the well remembered path through the birch forest. However, as I stood on the causeway and looked at the familiar bulk of Aelred Abbey, I felt a sense of triumph. I had done what they had not wanted me to do: what they had tried to stop me doing. They would not keep Myfanwy and me apart so easily.

Despite being hot, tired and thirsty from my afternoon's walk, I ran across the causeway towards the castle. The great doors were closed but opened easily when I pushed. I heard voices coming from the library, so I went in there. Myfanwy and Declan were up the other end of the room, sitting in the chairs near the fireplace, although the day was too warm for a fire. Myfanwy was dressed in her new school uniform, which seemed to be mostly blue, and her dark hair hung down over her shoulders. My heart skipped a beat when I saw her. When Myfanwy saw me she let out a little scream and ran towards me. I met her about half way and she grabbed me and hugged me tight, really tight. I honestly didn't think she was that strong. After a short while she pushed me back.

"You can't be here," she said. "If they find you here it will cause all sorts of trouble."

"We have a much bigger problem than anything the Annwn Council can dream up." I said. "Apophis is about to bring his plans to their conclusion and if he succeeds…" I stopped, unable to think of the right words. Finally I said, "If he succeeds it is the end of everything." Just then Nain appeared. She was carrying a tray with glasses, a jug of lemonade and some cold pasties.

"I was wondering when you would turn up," she said. "I have been watching. I'm thinking that you will be hungry and thirsty, so here you are." She set the tray down on a small table near the empty fireplace. It is amazing how thirsty you can get walking. I sat down and drank two glasses of the ice cold lemonade before doing anything else.

"Look Thomas, with Myfanwy and me sitting here," Declan said. "It's not what it might look like..." I looked at him with a slight smile and said,

"Declan, I am not worried about you chatting up Myfanwy."

"You're not?" he asked. A frown crossed his unnaturally youthful face, "You know, that's really insulting."

"Well," I said. "If you are Oisin's son, you are old enough to be her great, great, great grandfather."

"You need, at the very least, one other great," Myfanwy said crossly. Declan gave an exaggerated sigh and sat down.

After I had finished drinking, my hunger asserted itself and I started to eat the pasties while I told them about Apophis and the LHC.

"So you see," I said as I finished. "The riddle "There is a ring which seeks its beginning but which will only find its end and in its end will all endings be." is not really a riddle in the sense of a puzzle at all. It's just a flowery description of what Apophis actually intends to do." Nain and Declan looked dubious but

Myfanwy had done enough physics to understand that these things were real and she looked worried.

"This thing could actually destroy the world?" Nain asked.

I shook my head and explained. "Not on its own, but Apophis can use it to destroy the world, perhaps even the universe. Something he could not do on his own. The LHC gives him access to almost unimaginable energy and if he can use his power to just push it hard enough…" I spread my hands in a gesture of hopelessness. "It's the end." There was silence for a while after this.

"Look," I said. "I can stop him. I have told DIAP and Professor Rhys but I don't think DIAP can stop him, they just don't have that capability, and the professor has gone to talk to the council on Annwn who will talk and dither until it's too late."

Here Nain nodded her head. "Only too true," she said.

"Myfanwy," I continued. "I need you to teleport me to just north of the village of Crozet in France. It is near the Swiss border, at the foot of the Jura Mountains."

Myfanwy shook her head. "I can't Tom," she said. "I can't teleport to a place I have never been before."

"But look," I said. "I can show you the satellite images. I have the maps stored. I can give you the precise latitude and longitude." I held up my phone which had all the data stored on it.

She still shook her head. "It's no use Tom," she said. "Before I can teleport somewhere, it has to be real to me as a place. I have to know it …as a place. Knowing the location is no use to me. Think about it.

Your location is always changing. The Earth is spinning on its axis, it's orbiting the sun and the sun is orbiting the galaxy. Where you are now is not where you were a few seconds ago. The coordinates you have are just mathematical abstractions which are based on purely arbitrary points of reference. Magic doesn't work that way. I need to have been to a place before I can travel there by magic." This raised a lot of important questions in my mind but I put them aside. The current problem was urgent and I was starting to feel desperate.

"But the experiment is at six o'clock tomorrow morning and the snow storm has cancelled all flights," I said. "This is the only way I can get there on time."

"Perhaps I can help," Declan said. "Follow me." He got up and walked towards the door.

"Declan remember, you must maintain your neutrality," Nain said. He looked at her with a broad smile.

"Don't worry Holly," he said. "I have no intention of breaching the terms of the treaty."

We followed him outside. He put his fingers in his mouth and whistled. I instantly clapped my hands over my ears and even so the whistle echoed and shuddered through my bones. It shuddered through the very earth and shook the stones of the castle. It lasted for what seemed like minutes and when he had finished everything was silent and still. So silent that I thought I might have gone deaf, but I heard him when he said, "It'll take a while. It's a long way from Tyr na nOg."

I only learned later that it was at about this time that a military transport plane took off from RAF Northolt on a routine supply mission to Afghanistan.

It had on board, however, two passengers who were not listed on its official flight manifest. They were dressed in winter camouflage, heavily armed and equipped for a special operations surveillance mission. They were not on the manifest because they would not be on board when the plane landed. A few hours later, high above the Jura Mountains, the rear cargo door of the plane opened and the two figures leapt out into the night. They fell a long way before their parachutes opened. They took great care not to be seen and no one saw them.

CHAPTER 26
A Ride into Darkness

It was about an hour later that Declan's solution arrived. By this time it was starting to get dark and I wasn't sure of what I saw, but it seemed that there was just a white streak out of the west. When the streak stopped it proved to be a very large horse. It was pure white and looked like a racehorse but it was the size of a big Clydesdale. It had eyes like fire and it's gaze was fixed on Declan. Declan walked over and reached up above his head to stroke the horse's nose.

"Of course I will remain neutral," Declan said. "It's just that I'm not so sure about my horse. His name is Embarr because he is faster than thought. Come over here and let him know where you want to go. Just think it." However, as I got close to the giant horse it reared up and snorted, which was a frightening thing to see.

Declan smiled ruefully. "Sorry," he said. "He doesn't like you. I forgot that he wouldn't be able to read you."

"But he will like me," said Myfanwy behind me. I turned around and she was standing there dressed in a thick woollen cloak over her school uniform. "Put your coat on surfer boy, it's cold where we're going," I hesitated.

"Myfanwy," I said. "Apophis wants to kill you as much as he wants to kill me. I think it would be better if you were safe."

"So do I," she said. "But I am your only way of getting to him on time and if he succeeds in destroying the world I'll be just as dead as everyone else on the planet. So, show me where we're going." I gave in and showed her the maps and images I had stored on my phone. After a while she nodded.

"That's enough," she said. She walked over to the horse, whose size was only emphasised by her small stature. The horse, however, bent its head down to her and whinnied softly as she stroked its nose. I put on my coat and took Declan's walking stick. Myfanwy teleported herself onto the horses back and leaned down to pat its neck. This kept the horse calm so that, with Declan's help, I was able to rather awkwardly vault onto its back. As soon as I was settled behind Myfanwy, the horse took off. I was expecting it to go east, across the channel, but it headed back over the Norfolk countryside to the southeast. Fields and villages, rivers and roads, all flashed by. This made Professor Rhys' car driving seem slow. It wasn't long before we past the coast and were riding over the channel as easily as over a meadow. At one point I had to hold tight to Myfanwy as the horse jumped over a ship. Soon we were riding up the beaches and through the fields of Belgium and on into France. Our speed did not diminish but the whole ride continued on for hours, past fields and vineyards, towns and chateaus, forests and hills. It is a long way across France, from its north west corner to its border with Switzerland. Eventually the horse came to a sudden stop and we slipped off, tired and sore. In a flash of white the horse was gone and we were left alone on the side of a hill on the edge of a snowbound forest. It was still dark but the sky was just becoming light over the mountains to the east.

"It looks like we have arrived early," Myfanwy said. "What do we do now?"

"There's no point in blundering around in the dark," I said. "We'll wait until it's properly light and then go and find him. I could also use some rest." It had been almost 24 hours since I was last asleep in my London bed and I was tired. We found a large tree whose base was free of snow and lay down together. Myfanwy's thick cloak was large enough to wrap around both of us and we were warm, sharing our body heat. I fell asleep almost immediately.

We woke to the sound of gunfire. I jumped to my feet but couldn't see anything. Once again I heard a shout and a single gunshot but it was coming from some distance away to our north east. Myfanwy took my hand and pointed to a hill in that direction.

"Let's go there," she said. Instantly we were standing on that hill and looking down into the field below. There, two armed men dressed in military alpine camouflage uniforms were advancing on Apophis. They were calling on him to keep his arms by his side. He didn't obey. He raised his hand to point at one of the men and instantly they both opened fire. Apophis changed from an attacking to a defensive gesture and the bullets seemed to scatter off some sort of invisible shield in front of him. I tried to reach out to stop his magic but I couldn't. Clearly, I was too far away although not far enough to stop ricocheting bullets occasionally hitting the snow near us. I realized that I would have to get down into the valley.

"It's no use," I said. "I need to get closer. Say a prayer that I don't get accidentally shot."

"Tom," Myfanwy said. "I can't stop time from this distance but I can really slow it down. Do you think you could dodge through those bullets if they were travelling slowly enough?" I nodded.

"I'll certainly try," I said as I started to run down the hill. At first there was no change and I was just running down the hill through the snow with occasional bullets landing near me. Then, as I started to get to the bottom of the hill and the density of bullets got greater, Myfanwy slowed time so that I could clearly see the bullets coming and dodge away from them. I took great care to avoid them because I knew that, even though they seemed to me to be moving really slowly, they still had the same energy and if one hit me it would still be deadly. I would just have longer to think about it. This was emphasized when I misjudged one move and a bullet grazed the sleeve of my coat. It seemed to be going very slowly but it still tore a great gash in my sleeve.

As I was running towards them, one of the soldiers stumbled in the snow and stopped firing for what would have been less than a second in real time. Instantly, Apophis changed his gesture. He kept warding away the bullets from the soldier who was still firing and pointed his finger at the one who had stumbled. The poor man never got up from his stumble. In a single, smooth movement the other soldier picked up the fallen soldiers weapon and kept firing both at Apophis', who was forced back into full defensive mode again. I was desperately struggling through the thick snow on the valley floor. Declan's walking stick was now a battle spear and I was using it to help push my way through the snow. I had to get close enough to cancel Apophis' magic before the second soldier ran out of bullets.

I was too late. I was still about 200 meters away when I heard the firing stop and I desperately reached out towards Apophis with only one thought: no magic. Unfortunately it was still too far. The soldier threw down his empty weapons and drew a knife from his belt. He threw it at Apophis and I could watch it in slow motion, turning end over end, travelling straight towards Apophis' heart. Apophis raised his hand and the knife stopped in mid air. He then smiled that nasty smile of his and pointed his finger. The knife turned around and then flew straight and quickly into the soldier's chest. He gave a small grunt and fell face down in the snow.

Apophis still hadn't seen me and he now concentrated his effort on the ground, stretching both arms straight down by his sides with his fingers widespread. I realized that he was finishing what he had come to do. It was just after six o'clock and hundreds of meters beneath our feet, physicists were running a high energy experiment to probe the origin of the universe. Apophis was now trying to use this to destroy the world.

I was only about thirty metres away when Apophis finally noticed me. He seemed genuinely surprised.

"You!" he said. "Why aren't you dead? Why can an abomination like you not have the simple decency to die when you are supposed to?"

Myfanwy must have exhausted her strength because time was now running at its normal speed. I pointed Declan's spear at him and concentrated on only one thought: no magic. I knew it had worked by the look of shocked surprise on Apophis' face.

"Do you think I am afraid of you?" he asked, his voice sounding decidedly shaky. "Because I'm not."

"You should be," I answered. "You no longer have any magic, so you can't teleport away, and I have a very sharp spear. I also have every reason to use it." I kept advancing towards him with the spear pointed directly at his chest. I saw fear in his eyes for the first time. He looked about himself desperately, probably trying to find a way to teleport. As he was doing this, his eyes followed back along my trail through the snow and fixed on the figure standing at the top of the hill. His expression changed from fear to pure hatred.

"Myfanwy," he said through clenched teeth. "I should have known that she would follow filth like you." Just then I heard a groan off to my side. The soldier who had been hit by the knife wasn't dead. He rolled onto his side and I recognized him for the first time: it was the DIAP agent called Fisher. I was distracted very briefly and only lost concentration for a second but it was long enough for Apophis to teleport. He teleported to the top of the hill and pointed both hands in an attacking gesture at Myfanwy. Myfanwy made a warding gesture in response but I knew that she was exhausted from slowing down time for so long and I wasn't surprised when she quickly collapsed and fell. I felt as if all the energy had just left my body and I stumbled into the snow. When I got up Apophis had disappeared.

"No!" I yelled and desperately started to run back through the snow. I was concentrating so hard on getting to Myfanwy that I didn't even hear the helicopters coming in. I only became aware of them when one landed next to me, swirling the snow into a white blizzard of a cloud. Another helicopter landed on top of the hill where Myfanwy had fallen and four landed down on the field where the two DIAP agents lay. Two attack helicopters stayed airborne and kept circling the perimeter of the area. Soldiers jumped out of all the helicopters that had landed and fanned out to secure the area. I quickly found myself surrounded and Declan's walking stick was taken from me. The soldiers weren't exactly rude but they clearly meant business and I had three very efficient looking assault rifles pointed at me. When I was told to walk back down the hill I really had no choice. I did, however, keep looking over my shoulder to where Myfanwy had fallen. I saw an army medic bend over her. After a while he signalled to a soldier who slung his weapon over his shoulder, picked Myfanwy up and carried her down the hill like a baby, her long cloak trailing in the snow. She showed no sign of life.

Director Smith of DIAP was waiting for me at the bottom of the hill. Nearby, army medics were franticly working on the DIAP agent Fisher. The other DIAP agent, however, was being zipped into a body bag.

"You!" the Director yelled as he saw me. "What on Earth are you doing here? How did you even get here? And why do I have one agent dead and another with his own knife sticking out of his chest?" he was clearly upset so I spoke as calmly as I could but I also owed it to the two agents to tell the truth.

"Your men are dead and wounded because you sent two of them up against a magic user with no defence against magic. They were both brave to an almost impossible degree. They must have known they would probably die and yet they attacked and they kept attacking. Even with his partner dead behind him and out of ammunition, Fisher pulled out his knife and kept attacking. He must have expected to die but he knew he had to try and stop Apophis. Why did you ignore me? I was your best weapon against him. If I had been with them, this would have been very different."

"They weren't supposed to attack," the Director said. "They were a reconnaissance party. They were supposed to report his position and wait for us the engage him. We just got held up with weather and other problems… We were only ten minutes late!" I couldn't help thinking how disastrous that ten minutes might have been for the world.

Just then the soldier carrying Myfanwy arrived. I looked across in fear only to see a pair of brilliant green eyes looking back at me. She was alive! I was so happy I couldn't move. The soldier carrying her came and stood next to me.

"Thank you, you can set me down now" she said, making a small waving gesture with her hand. The soldier shrugged.

"You're welcome…I think," he said and trotted off back to his section, looking very confused. She gave me that tentative half smile she uses when she's nervous.

"Sorry if I scared you,"" she said. "But I just feel really, really tired, which is strange because I think I should be dead." My paralysis left me and I grabbed her in my arms and hugged her tightly to me.

"I was so scared," I said. "I was so scared that he had hurt you."

"Who is this?" the Director demanded behind me. I turned around and answered.

"This is Myfanwy Ferchwyn. She is the niece of your consultant, Professor Rhys." The director ran his fingers through his hair.

"Can anyone tell me what has been going on here?" he yelled.

"Yes Director, I think I can." Doctor Jones was emerging from one of the helicopters with a computer pad. "I just pulled this video off the surveillance drone." He walked over and showed the pad to the Director.

"Fisher and Brown notified us at 5.45 that they had located Apophis. The drone arrived five minutes later and kept station. All is quiet for a while, on the thermal channel you can see Fisher and Brown hidden in the trees and Apophis standing out in the field. They knew that Apophis only had a ten minute window in which to do his thing: after that the experiment would be shut down. When we were delayed and six o'clock came without any support, they decided to attack on their own. They were probably hoping to distract him long enough for us to arrive. You can see that they kept up a rapid fire of high velocity bullets and I imagine that this Apophis character was fully occupied keeping them from hitting him. Of course, they couldn't do this for long: eventually they ran out of ammunition and they had no time to reload. Their attack came to its end at 6.05. Then something strange happens and our friend Mr. O'Malley turns up out of nowhere and engages Apophis with what looks like a spear. At 6.09

Apophis disappears. We owe Mr. O'Malley a debt. He clearly stopped Apophis from doing what he intended to do."

Just then one of the medics attending to agent Fisher called out, "Sir, we have done all we can for him here. We have to get him to a hospital urgently!" The Director nodded distractedly.

"Go!" he said. "And Jones, you go with them and load those data onto our system." Jones nodded and went over to where Fisher was being loaded onto one of the helicopters. They took off immediately and headed south, no doubt towards the nearest hospital. The director looked at us.

"There will be another experiment at six o'clock tonight," he said. "We need to track him down before that. If either of you have any idea where he might be I need you to tell me." Just as we were shaking our heads, a soldier from one of the other helicopters ran over and said.

"We've found him sir. He didn't go far and the drone has picked him up in a small valley to the south west of here." Director Smith smiled a grim smile.

"Yes!" he said with satisfaction. "Okay, everybody mount up. We go back to the original plan." The soldiers all started to run back to the helicopters, as did the Director. I just managed to grab my walking stick back off the soldier next to me before he too ran off to his helicopter.

"What about us?" I asked. "Where do we go?"

"Stay here," the Director said over his shoulder. "We'll come back and get you after it's over."

"No!" I yelled. "We can help. You don't understand what you are going up against!" The helicopters, however, had already taken off, leaving Myfanwy and me alone in the snowy field.

"Myfanwy," I said. "Do you have enough energy to teleport us up there?" I pointed to the top of the highest nearby hill. She looked carefully.

"Just barely," she said and then we were there. From the top of this hill we could see the helicopters away in the distance, flying in formation and staying close to the tops of the trees. For a while they just flew in a straight line, then the two attack helicopters peeled off left and right. They moved ahead of the others and launched a converging attack: firing their rockets. However, instead of exploding into the ground, the rockets curved up into the sky and came back directly at the helicopters that had fired them. These exploded in flames. Then the two outermost of the five troop helicopters seemed to develop control problems and swerved into the ones next to them and all four crashed into the forest below. The final helicopter tried to swerve away but its engine must have failed because it rotated into the ground.

Myfanwy and I were quiet from a long time, watching the fires burn where the helicopters had crashed. Eventually Myfanwy said,

"The medic who checked me out, the soldier who carried me; they are both dead along with all the others." I nodded, too upset to speak. Myfanwy then knelt in the snow and made the sign of the cross. I hurriedly knelt down beside her. She pointed at the rocks that were scattered around the top of the hill and they flew together to form an upright cross. Briefly, they glowed red hot and then they were welded together, making a permanent monument.

"For all those who have died this morning," Myfanwy whispered. "May God keep them and may they rest in peace."

CHAPTER 27
Hot Chocolate and Battle

I stood up and surveyed our situation. It was cold and I knew we had to get off the top of this hill and into shelter. It was also clear that DIAP would not be coming back to get us and that Myfanwy was exhausted. There was a road at the foot of the hill and not far along it a small, stone building that looked like some sort of barn or animal shelter. I bent down and picked Myfanwy up in my arms, just as the soldier had done.

"Hey! Put me down!" she yelled as I started to walk down the hill. "What do you think you're doing?"

"I'm carrying you to shelter," I answered. "You're exhausted and anyway, if some random soldier can carry you, so can I." I could feel her relax in my arms.

"Yes," she said in an innocent voice. "But the soldier was big and strong. How far do you think you can carry me surfer boy?"

"Far enough," I answered. Actually, even carrying someone as small and light as Myfanwy through the snow was really, really hard work, especially as I hadn't managed a lot of sleep the night before. Still, she laid her head on my shoulder and was asleep before we reached the bottom of the hill so I wasn't going to disturb her. I just gritted my teeth and pushed on. Fortunately the building was not far down the road.

The building turned out to be a sort of summer barn where hay was stored for the livestock who, apart from unnatural summer snow storms, would be in the fields. It was full of hay and warm. Myafnwy stirred briefly as I kicked open the door but she quickly went to sleep again as she lay down in the hay, wrapped in her thick cloak. I also lay in the hay and rested but I couldn't get to sleep. There was too much going on in my head. I wondered if any of the soldiers had survived the crashes. Certainly not in the two attack helicopters but maybe in the others some had survived? I hoped so. What would have happened if we had gone with them? Would we have been able to help or would we just now also be dead? The image of the helicopters crashing kept playing over and over in my head. I just couldn't get rid of it. I prayed for sleep but no sleep came.

About midday, just as I was starting to get hungry, I heard the jingling of small bells outside the door. I went out to see what it was. On the road in front of the barn was an old fashioned gypsy caravan that I had seen before. In the traces was a small, white horse and seated on the driver's bench, an old army coat over an atrocious floral dress and a knitted wool cap pulled down tight over her ears, was Nain. I don't think I have ever been so happy to see a familiar face.

"Nain," I said. "As always, I am very pleased to see you." She climbed down from the caravan.

"Yes, well," she said. "My pony and cart are not as fast or as showy as Declan's great horse but we do get there in the end. Now, what have you done with my god-daughter?" As if on call, Myfanwy came running out of the barn and threw her arms around Nain, sobbing into her shoulder.

"Oh Nain!" she said. "Oh Nain, they all died. He killed them all." Nain patted her on the back.

"Yes dear, I know." She said. "Helicopters are such delicate machines and the men who fly them can be so arrogantly sure of themselves. It would have been all too easy for him." Eventually Myfanwy let go and wiped the tears from her eyes. Nain grinned.

"Now, it seems to me that you will both need a bit of hot comfort food," she said. "I know of a place in Crozet that serves warm chocolate croissants and large cups of hot chocolate. The croissants are good but the hot chocolate is the best in France. How about we go and have some lunch?"

We went down the road to Crozet with the pony pulling the caravan at normal sort of horse walking pace. Myfanwy sat silently on the front bench of the caravan for a long while.

Then she said, "Nain, why aren't I dead?" Nain looked at her in surprise and Myfanwy went on to explain how Apophis had attacked her and how he had broken through her guard but somehow not killed her. Nain was silent for a while, then she asked me,

"How did you feel when this happened?"

"I felt as if the life had been sucked out of me," I said. "I actually fell down with the shock of it." Nain nodded thoughtfully.

"The bond between you two is growing strong," she said. "If you have not decided for each other you will have to be very careful indeed or time and familiarity will make the decision for you." I looked at her puzzled. "Friends share a part of their being with each other: the closer the friendship, the greater this sharing. You have each become a significant part of the other," she explained. "That part of you which is bonded to Myfanwy couldn't be killed by Apophis and because of that, Myfanwy was protected. This would only happen under extreme stress. Strangely though, this makes you more vulnerable Thomas. If at that moment he had also managed to attack you, I think you may have died." I shrugged. An outside chance of vulnerability for me in exchange for a last resort, blanket protection for Myfanwy: it sounded like a good deal to me.

The little café that Nain knew was down a small paved walkway off the main street of Crozet. It had mullioned bay windows and wood paneling about half way up the walls. The croissants and the hot chocolate were both very good and we took our time telling Nain what had happened that morning.

As soon as he learned how fluent she was in French, the proprietor of the café came over and started chatting amiably to Myfanwy. My knowledge of French was nowhere near good enough to follow their conversation but I did notice when the mood changed and phrases like "Cést terrible" or "Cést catastrophe" appeared and I guessed they were talking about the helicopter crashes. Finally he leaned over the table and whispered in heavily accented English,

"NATO, Special Ops. training." He tapped the side of his nose knowingly and went off to serve other customers. Surprisingly, Myfanwy looked relieved.

"Not all of them died," she said. "In fact, on one helicopter most of the men survived, although only a handful of those on board the helicopters that collided did. Still, it's better than I feared. Everybody thinks it was a NATO training exercise gone horribly wrong." It didn't make me feel much better. Men had still died and at six o'clock this evening Apophis would try again.

As we walked out of the café and onto the main street, I noticed a familiar figure sitting at a table on the terrace of a hotel. It was director Smith and he seemed to be unharmed. Indeed, he was reading a newspaper. I rushed across the street and ran up the steps onto the terrace.

"Director Smith," I said. "You don't know how pleased I am to see you again." He looked at me over the top of his newspaper with a puzzled expression on his face.

"Do I know you young man?" he asked. I looked at him dumfounded. "And besides, aren't you a little young to be in need of our services?" he continued. By this time Myfanwy had come across and was standing beside me. "Look, go and live your life first. Enjoy your holiday with your young lady friend. Worry about retirement later." Now I was really confused.

"I'm sorry Sir," I said. "I don't understand."

"Oh very well," he said. "Here's my card. Contact the office and they will be able to help you with your queries. I really do not understand the younger generation's need for financial security." I looked at the card. It indicated that Mr. Smith was the director of DIAP: the Division of Insurance, Annuities and Pensions. I felt the blood drain from my face. This was something I had never imagined.

"He really believes it," Myfanwy whispered in my ear. "It's not an act." I mumbled some thanks and then we left and crossed over to the caravan. As we settled down on the front bench, next to Nain, Myfanwy said, "Apophis must have gotten to him." I shook my head.

"I don't think so," I said. "For all his power, Apophis is a fairly simple soul. His methods are more direct. If it had been Apophis, the director would simply be dead. No, this is subtle and cruel. To take the director of a top secret security agency and turn him into some sort of pen pushing insurance salesman – that's a grim joke indeed." Nain flicked the reins and the caravan started to move off, down the main street.

"It's Cadell," she said. "That's typical of him – both the subtlety and the cruelty. They are both here."

As we drove out of town, I looked at the people going about their normal lives not knowing how fragile it all was. All of it could be taken away: the traffic, the croissants, the hot chocolate, the amiable café owner. All of this was so fragile and tonight two psychopaths with magical powers were going to try and bring it all to an end. I knew we were going to try and stop them but I also knew that we needed help, help that wouldn't come from DIAP.

It was already mid-afternoon when we left the village and traveled at pony walk pace back down the road. Myfanwy was still recovering from the heavy use she had made of magic early in the day, so she went and lay down in the bunk in the back of the caravan. I was dozing off too, lulled to sleep by the rocking motion of the caravan, when a figure emerged from the field to our right. He was wearing a similar sort of camouflage uniform to that which the DIAP soldiers had been wearing and he was also carrying a very efficient looking automatic assault rifle.

"Vale Mater Semper Bene," he called. "Quo vadis Verendus Matris?"

"Pierre, stop trying to show off," Nain said crossly as she pulled the wagon to a stop. "We both know that your Latin is atrocious. Now, cut out that Reverend Mother business and get up here." He jumped up onto the caravan with an easy grace and sat down on the other side of Nain to me. Nain introduced us as she flicked the reins to get the pony to move once again.

"Pierre, this is Thomas O'Malley: a young Australian who is utterly immune to magic. Thomas, this Captain Pierre Gauthier of the Swiss Guard's special operations unit." He leaned over to shake my hand and I noticed the Vatican flag on his arm.

"I didn't know you guys had a special operations unit," I said. "I thought you were just a sort of ceremonial guard."

Pierre smiled broadly. "Excellent!" he said. "That is precisely what we would like people to think." He then turned to Nain and asked, "When you say he is immune to magic, do you mean he can resist, just a little bit, like us." Nain shook her head.

"No," she answered. "He is completely immune and without even trying. He has no need of your long hours of meditation and training. It is just a part of who he is." Pierre was silent for a while then he gave a crooked grin and said,

"Sometimes I think that maybe life is not fair." Soon after that we arrived at a point on the road nearest to where the fight with Apophis had taken place that morning. Nain pulled the caravan to a stop.

"This is where he was this morning; this is where they will come back to. They are too proud and too arrogant to do anything else," she said. "We must prepare. We don't have that much time. Pierre, call your men." Pierre pulled out a metal whistle and gave three sharp blasts. A few minutes later about fifteen men appeared silently and unexpectedly from the surrounding fields. I hadn't seen any sign of them coming. Pierre grinned.

"Not magic but still pretty good, eh?" he said. I could only agree. The whistle blasts had woken Myfanwy, who now came around from the back of the caravan. When he saw her, Pierre notably drew himself to attention.

"Captain Pierre Gauthier, this is my god-daughter, Myfanwy," Nain said.

"Reverend Mother, you did not tell me you had such a beautiful god-daughter," Pierre said as he took Myfanwy's hand and lightly kissed her fingers.

"Bonsoir, Monsieur Gauthier," Myfanwy said. "Have you been introduced to my close friend Thomas?"

"Her very close friend," I said for emphasis. Pierre looked at me and gave a shrug of his shoulders.

"The magical talent and the beautiful girl," he said. "Now I truly know that life is not fair."

"Enough of this nonsense," Nain said. "There is a battle coming and we must get organized." She then outlined her plan. Pierre and his men would apply what pressure they could from the east. Apparently, Captain Pierre's unit had a long history of opposing magical opponents and had developed mental techniques which made them more resistant to magic. They would not be as easy to kill as the DIAP agents. Even so, as well as adding their own attack, Nain and Myfanwy would try to protect them from the top of the hill where Apophis had last attacked Myfanwy. All of this, however, was essentially a diversion. I was to approach from the forest in the west and to cancel the magic of the one trying to interfere with the experiment in any way that I could. We only had to delay them ten minutes and it would be months before the experiment was run again and they had another chance. We all agreed. This was a plan that took the threat of magic seriously and it might just work.

Just as I was about to leave to take up my position in the forest, Myfanwy came over to me and said, "Tom, please leave your staff with me." She meant Declan's walking stick. I looked at her doubtfully.

"Myfanwy," I said. "This is a very useful stick."

"I know it is," she said. "I saw it in action this morning. That stick will give you the ability to kill whoever comes against you." She hesitated, and then she said softly, "Look, Apophis and Cadell may well deserve to die and they may well need killing, but I don't want you to be the one to do it. If you kill another person, no matter how justified the death may be, it damages your soul. Tom, I don't want your soul damaged in that way. I don't want you to be a killer." She looked at me with tears in her bright green eyes and I handed her the staff. Had she asked for my right arm I would have given it to her. She reached up and kissed me on the cheek. Then she hugged me.

"That was because I like you very much Thomas O'Malley," she said. "You be careful. I don't want to lose you." I kissed the top of her forehead.

"Myfanwy Ferchwyn," I said. "It will take more than a couple of psychopaths with weird powers to keep me away from you. A mountain would need to fall on me and even then I would be there for you. Myfanwy I…" I almost said what was in my heart but I looked up and saw Nain's eyes watching us intently, her expression unreadable. Instead of what I was going to say I said, "I'll see you when it's all over," and started to jog off to take up my position in the forest.

Cadell and Apophis both appeared just before six, exactly where Apophis had been that morning. Cadell was in a wheel chair and immediately spread his arms and swung his chair in a circle. Nain attacked first and a giant bubble like sphere appeared around Cadell and Apophis. Cadell spread his arms violently sideways and the sphere burst. Apophis spotted Nain and Myfanwy and yelled to Cadell. Cadell pointed both his arms and a wave of snow raced up the hill towards them. Nain and Myfanwy both held up their arms and the wave broke before it reached them. Then Pierre and his men started their attack. Unlike DIAP, they didn't issue a challenge. They just opened fire. Their tactics were also different from those of the DIAP agents. Instead of a frontal attack, each of their soldiers would only fire for a second and then take cover and change position while another soldier took up the attack. The total stream of bullets was almost continuous but it kept coming from different directions. I could see how it was a more effective attack. None of their bullets, however, were getting anywhere near Apophis and Cadell. They were all falling drastically short.

By this time I was running from my forest position towards the two psychopathic magic users. They hadn't noticed me, partly because I was difficult to see against the dark backdrop of the forest but mostly because they were distracted by the attacks of the others. I only had to run a few hundred meters but the snow lying on the ground was slowing me down. It was also dangerous, since I was running directly into the line of fire of Pierre's men.

Cadell was retaliating against them. He would throw a spell whenever he could catch one exposed. The guardsmen were resistant, however. Several times I saw one being hit and stumble but then get up and go on. Sometimes Nain would intervene and a soap bubble like shield would appear to protect a guardsman who have been in the clear too long. These tactics didn't always work. I saw three guardsmen fall face down in the snow and lay still. Even worse, one burst into flames and exploded. Occasionally Cadell would throw an attack at Nain and Myfanwy on the top of the hill but together they would easily ward it off. Apophis, meanwhile, was concentrating on the ground with his arms stretched downwards, just as he had been this morning.

I realized why the bullets were all falling short. Cadell's special gift was the ability to interfere with the fundamental constants of the universe. He had changed the gravitational constant in a ring around himself and Apophis. This ring a super high gravity was pulling all the bullets into the ground. I ran straight through where the ring would be and felt the momentary buzzing in my head and the faint 'pop' that I had felt when I walked through the defences Cadell had put around his home on Annwyn. I guessed that the super gravity protection ring was now destroyed.

Things then happened very quickly. The next burst of bullets came very close to Cadell and he was forced into full defensive mode as Pierre's men were encouraged to intensify their attack. I rugby tackled Apophis and brought him to the ground with one thought in my mind – no magic. We struggled very briefly but without magic he was no match for me and I soon had him held in an arm and wrist lock. When Cadell saw this, he gestured with both arms and sent a wave of snow towards the guardsmen. This crashed over the top of them, just like surf on a beach, and took them out of the contest for a while. He then pointed both his arms straight down in the same gesture as that used by Apophis.

"There are two of us boy, you can't stop both of us," he said. Unfortunately, he was right. There was a moment when his face was a picture of deep concentration but this quickly changed to anger and frustration. He looked up towards the top of the hill and there was Myfanwy, protected by one of Nain's bubbles, also concentrating on the ground with her arms extended.

What followed takes time to write but it only took a couple of seconds to happen. Cadell gave a growl of anger and then made a violent double arm gesture to the forest and the Jura Mountains just behind us. There was a loud roaring noise, like a hundred railway engines, behind us and Apophis called out something in Welsh. Cadell looked at him with a look of utter contempt and teleported away. However, one of the guardsmen had been quick to dig himself out of the snow and Cadell was hit by a burst of automatic fire as he teleported. I looked around to see what the sound was and only had time to think the word 'avalanche' before I was hit by a mountain of fast moving snow.

CHAPTER 28
The Monastery of St. Martin

When I woke, I was obviously in a hospital bed and in a hospital room. There were starched sheets, stainless steel fittings and the faint smell of antiseptic. Grey curtains were drawn across the large window that occupied the right hand wall. The only other person in the room, however, was dressed in the black habit of a Benedictine monk. He noticed when I stirred and said something in French. I shook my head to show I didn't understand.

"Pardon me," he said. "I am Brother Pius, the infirmarer here. I am glad that you have woken. I will inform the captain." He then bowed and left. A few minutes later Captain Pierre came in dressed in the uniform of the Pontifical Swiss Guard, not the colourful, ceremonial uniform but a more sober utility version of solid blue with a simple brown belt, a flat white collar and a black beret. He still looked as if he had just stepped out of the renaissance.

"I am glad to see that you are awake Thomas O'Malley." he said. "I was afraid you were going to sleep through our victory parade."

"Your men?" I asked. "I saw some of them go down." A shadow passed across his face.

"Four of them," he said. "Four of them are dead and one has had his mind affected so that he will need care for the rest of his life. Nevertheless, it was a victory: a great victory." He smiled. "Together we saved the world Thomas. Not that the world will ever know this, it will be our secret."

"Apophis?" I asked. "Did he get away?" Pierre shook his head.

"We found him dead under the snow," he said. "I don't think he ever regained consciousness after the avalanche hit. You would have been the same if it had not been for your young lady friend. Somehow she had got hold of one of those long poles they use to probe the snow for bodies and she knew just where you were." He smiled. "She kept yelling "He is here! He is here!" We had to dig you out just to make her keep quiet. She has also been sitting by your bed watching for over a day. Eventually the brother infirmarer found her asleep in the chair and her god-mother took her back to her quarters. Such devotion, you are a lucky man young Thomas." I nodded.

"I know," I said and I meant it. "Where am I by the way?" Pierre walked across to the window and pulled back the heavy curtain and I found myself looking over a castle wall to rocky, snow covered peaks.

"You are in the Monastery of St. Martin, high in the Italian alps," he said. "Officially it doesn't exist but it is our ancient headquarters and training base. Our unit has trained here ever since St. Parsifal returned from the disaster in Britain 1400 years ago." I frowned.

"The Swiss Guard isn't that old," I objected. Pierre smiled.

"No, but our unit is," he said. "It is only since 1882 that we have been formed as a detachment of the Pontifical Guard. Just don't tell the commandant that we exist."

At that moment Myfanwy appeared in the room. She ran up to my bed and then just stopped, looking at me.

"Hi," I said.

"Hi," she replied. "Are you okay?" I eased myself up into a sitting position and discovered how much my body hurt.

"Don't take this the wrong way," I said, "but every time I go anywhere with you I end up badly bruised. I hope this isn't going to become a habit." She gave me a crooked, little half smile.

"I was so worried," she said. "A mountain did fall on you, you silly boy, and you were there for me alright, but you were there under five feet of snow. I thought I'd lost you." I looked at her. She was still wearing her school uniform but she had obviously got dressed in a hurry because things were a bit askew. Her hair was a mass of untidy curls that cascaded down her shoulders and her pale skin was slightly flushed. I was struck again by how beautiful she was.

"By the way, you can have this back," she said as she handed me Declan's walking stick. "You're right. It is a very useful stick."

"Thank you, for everything." I said.

"You're very welcome," she replied. She took my hand and smiled and her normally solemn face became a thing of radiant joy. I thought how much I liked to see her smile. Just then both Nain and Professor Rhys appeared in the room.

"I wish you people would stop doing that!" Pierre exclaimed. "We have built all these doors and passageways and stairs for a purpose. They are not just decorations. They are to be used." Professor Rhys bowed to him and said,

"My apologies Herr Hauptmann but I felt that this was urgent. The boy was hurt after becoming involved in our affairs and our people have treated him badly. Thomas, I wanted to tell you as soon as possible that we are close on the trail of Cadell. We did something we have not done for five hundred years: we released the hunt onto mainland Europe." At this I noticed Pierre's hand go instinctively to the hilt of the dress sword he wore but the Professor continued. "Oh, don't worry captain. They have very specific instructions. Still, I think Iolo relishes the task he's been given. They found traces of him in a disused shepherds hut not far from Crozet. There was quiet a lot of his blood. He's bleeding badly from the wounds caused by the good Hauptmann's men. So, it will soon be over. He can't get far."

"At that point I will take my leave," Pierre said. "I have a parade to organize." He bowed deeply to Nain. "Reverend Mother," he said and left.

"I wish he would stop it with that 'reverend mother' business," Nain said crossly.

"It is a title of honour, Nain," I said.

"I know what it is boy," she said even more crossly. "It's just that it reminds me of things that happened a long time ago. That's the trouble with these people: they never forget." There was a story there but I decided to put it aside for the moment. I had a more important observation to make.

"Professor," I said. "I think you are being overly optimistic. Apophis is dead and Iolo may well catch his father but the people who helped them will still be at large." The Professor looked sharply at me.

"What people?" he asked. "How do you know anyone helped them?"

"When Myfanwy told me that she couldn't teleport to somewhere she hadn't been, I knew that Apophis must have had help. He teleported to the control room of a nuclear submarine, which means that he had been there before. Do you know how secure such a place would be? How did he get in? How did he even know where to go? The same is true of the power station. The same is true of the LHC. I don't believe that he was a student of Quantum Physics, so how did he know about the Large Hadron Collider and the potential of the experiments being done there. Someone was helping him, giving him information, someone with a lot of power and connections."

"But that would be crazy!" Myfanwy said. "He was trying to destroy the world." I shrugged. It didn't make sense to me either. The professor looked doubtful.

"Interesting," he said. "I very much hope you're wrong. Anyway, I have spoken to the doctor here and he has said that you should be able to travel by tomorrow. So I've booked the plane tickets and we'll have you back in London soon." A thought suddenly occurred to me.

"What day is it? How long have I been out?" I asked. "My mother will be frantic."

"It's Friday morning," Nain said. "You've been out of it for well over a day and Helen is currently in London explaining everything to your mother. We thought it better that she should know the truth." She looked at me thoughtfully. "We have been very worried about your concussion. How well do you remember what happened?"

"I remember it all," I said. "But I don't understand all of it. Why did Cadell just teleport out like that? He still had time, the experiment would still have been running. Why did he just give up?" Myfanwy laughed.

"That was me," she said. "I realized that you couldn't nullify both of them and that Cadell might still succeed, so I broke it." I looked at her puzzled. "The big ring of magnets, I broke it. I spilled all the stuff they use to keep it cold. They couldn't run the experiment anymore and without the experiment it was just Cadell standing in a field."

"That's brilliant!" I said laughing. "Simple and brilliant!" Myfanwy looked very pleased with herself. "Why didn't we just do that at the start and save all this trouble?"

"Because then Cadell and Apophis would still be around and waiting to cause trouble." Professor Rhys said. "Next time it might have been a missile silo or even just another experiment at the LHC. They had to be confronted."

"There's another thing I don't really understand," I said. "Just before Cadell teleported off, Apophis yelled something to him in Welsh. Whatever it was, it provoked a look of complete contempt from Cadell."

"Can you remember what it sounded like?" Myfanwy asked.

"Kind of," I said. "It sounded something like 'Da bless o cough north 'em' but that doesn't make sense."

Myfanwy sat quiet for a while thinking and then her face changed to a look akin to horror.

"Thomas, was it 'Da, blesio chyfnertha 'm'" she asked.

"Yes," I said. "That's it. What does it mean?" When Myfanwy replied it was in a very soft and sad voice.

"It means 'daddy, please help me'. Oh Thomas, he asked for help and the last thing he ever saw was the look of contempt on his father's face. It's just too sad." I nodded. Against all reasonable expectation, I suddenly felt sorry for Apophis. With Cadell as a father, what chance did he have? Myfanwy was right. The whole situation was just too sad.

The next day we were getting ready to leave. The night before the guardsmen, in their full ceremonial uniform with armour, had said the office for the dead and kept watch over their fallen comrades. Today the bodies were being sent back to their families. We were leaving at the same time to catch our plane back to London. I was out of bed and had nearly finished getting dressed very carefully, just about everything still hurt, when Myfanwy appeared in my room. I frowned at her.

"You really should knock before you do that," I said. "You might catch me in a state of undress." Her only reply was one of her mischievous grins but when I continued to frown she said,

"Okay, surfer boy, I'll be nice and I promise I'll protect your dignity. Here, I'll even help you on with your blazer." In that, I was grateful for the help. However, as she picked up my school blazer, a piece of paper fell from the pocket. I knew straight away what it was. It was the poem I had written for Mrs. Brown's romantic poetry exercise. I think I must have panicked because I immediately said,

"Don't look at that. That's just a thing. It's not important." This, of course was the worst thing I could have said to Myfanwy, who immediately opened up the piece of paper and read it.

> My Lady Myfanwy
>
> The birds no longer sing
> Now that you are gone.
> The sun no longer silvers
> The cloud and falling rain
>
> My Lady Myfanwy
>
> Of the night dark hair
> Of green, meadow soft eyes.
> A curl I held once then
> And softly I kissed
>
> My dearest Myfanwy.

"It was an exercise we had to write for Mrs. Brown," I explained. "We had to write a romantic poem but I didn't read it out in class or anything. Look, I know it's not very good. It doesn't even scan properly but…" I stopped talking. Myfanwy had finished reading the poem and, however much I tried to talk it down, I desperately wanted her to like it. She looked up at me with a frown on her face.

"Thomas, you silly, silly boy," she said. "Why would you want to kiss my hair when you could kiss me?" With that, she kissed me. She kissed me and instantly, all was right with the world.

It was a while later that she said, "You got a B." I looked at her puzzled. "For your poem," she explained. "Mrs. Brown gave you a B. I would have given you an A."

EPILOGUE

It was bizarre to go from a world of magic and secret military units to the world of exam preparation and study but that is what I had to do. Mum adjusted with surprising ease to the idea that there were people who could do magic abroad in the community. Her memories of the holiday on Annwn were now clear and she claimed to have always known that there was something special about Myfanwy. The gate to Aelred Abbey near our house was re-established and each weekend Myfanwy and I would be together: either in London going to art galleries and museums or in Norfolk walking along the beach. Week nights were strictly given over to study. Very strictly, Nain was in charge of policing our time together and she had very old fashioned standards.

In order to explain the week when I was missing, the story was put around the school that I had been in a climbing accident and that I had suffered bad bruising. Knowing this, Horace and his mates took great care to 'accidentally' bump into me whenever we passed in the corridors. They didn't do anymore, however. I guess the pressure of exams affected them too. Just as well, if they had decided to get physical, I was far too sore to do much about it. Eventually all the exams and assessment tasks were behind us. I knew that I had made a few mistakes but generally they were not as hard as I had feared they might be. Wilson was disgusted that they were so easy.

It was about a week after we got back that a Corporal Cooper of the 5th Lancashire Lancers was buried with full military honours. He and his team member, a staff sergeant Fisher, were both given high awards for bravery, although no one was told why. The press assumed it was for some hush-hush operation in Afghanistan. They would have been shocked to know that the combat had occurred in France.

I was still banished from Annwn and the council was still forbidding Myfanwy to have any contact with me. However, both Myfanwy and her family had simply decided to ignore the council. The one problem I had was that Mum and I were going back to Australia to spend the school holidays with Dad. I wanted to see Dad again of course but the idea of being separated from Myfanwy for weeks didn't please me. I told her about our travel plans while we were eating rapidly melting ice creams in Hyde Park.

"Oh good," Myfanwy said. "I've always wanted to visit Australia." I looked at her surprised. "That's if I'm invited, of course," she continued. "Of course Nain will have to come too, she's my chaperone, and I know that mum would love to go out there and paint some of your coastline. That means that Carwyn and Gwyneth will have to come as well…"

I laughed. "Of course you're invited. All of you, why not?" I said. "Angle Creek will love you."

When I had first come to London it had seemed to me limited, small and colourless: a small, colourless world full of small, colourless people. Now it seemed vibrant, exciting and full of life.

WHERE MERLIN RESTS
The second book of the Myfanwy's People Series

The dragons within the Earth are stirring and there are great earthquakes and volcanic eruptions all across the world. As the Earth faces the catastrophic possibility of an eruption of its super-volcanoes, a criminal gang is hunting Myfanwy and a monster stalks Tom. Together they must find Merlin, who alone can quieten the earth, and they must get to him before those trying to kill him. They also need to sort out their relationship.

THE THRONE OF ANNWN
The third book of the Myfanwy's People Series

The Council of Nobles is openly trying to kill Tom and civil war is threatened in Annwn if Myfanwy will not agree to marry Alwyn apBryn. Torn between her love of Tom and her love for her people, she accompanies Tom into the high Himalayas, to confront a group of rogue monks who are steering an asteroid towards the Earth.

www.ingramcontent.com/pod-product-compliance
Lightning Source LLC
Chambersburg PA
CBHW051439050726
47593CB00005B/1844